The Fortress

Jonathan R Walton

ISBN-13: 978-0-9898057-9-7

ACKNOWLEDGMENTS

I would like to thank all my editors for the hard work you poured into this book. Thanks to my friends who allowed me to bounce ideas around with you and for being an inspiration for certain parts of this story.

Thanks to Carl Howard, the first person to encourage me to write, particularly in the fiction genre. This book is the result of a dream we discussed many years ago.

Thanks to all those who have encouraged me, believed in me, and worked with me through the process of writing. May you be thoroughly entertained and completely inspired by this book to change your world.

Prologue

The man sat on the bulky leather couch, sank into its pliable back, unsurely glanced toward the ceiling, and curled his toes through the Berber carpet covering the living room floor. Leaning slightly forward, he reached for the bottle on the coffee table.

Fire in a bottle.

Instant fury or immediate comedic relief, depending on the drinker.

For him, it did neither. It seemed to anesthetize the pain some. However, after the initial numbness, it did nothing but bring on a more severe state of depression. He was finding it easier and easier to slip into this place.

He reached onto the table again and picked up the large blue pen nestled next to the bland notebook. The counselor had suggested that he write his feelings down. It was supposed to be therapeutic and cause him to discover truths about his emotional breakdown.

Another pointless ploy by psycho-analyzers who

thought they understood the workings of the world. He didn't know what made him feel worse; concentrating on his feelings enough to write them or drinking his way into oblivion.

Tonight was going to be different. He'd made up his mind. He was ending the madness.

His descent had been tragic. It had occurred quickly. It was always alarming how swiftly life could turn. One day he'd been on top of the world. A man of morals, raising a family with strong Christian virtues. The next day an empty shell of who he'd formally been. He didn't recognize himself anymore when he looked in the mirror.

He opened the journal and slowly began to write.

Journal Entry: July 4, 2012

Life is empty. Purposeless. Meaningless.

They've given up on finding him. So have I. Justice will never be issued. The guilty will continue to live freely.

There is no God. He can't be real.

The alternative is worse. He's real but gets a cosmic laugh at the twisted affairs of men. He finds pleasure in exerting His will over feeble humanity.

How could he be real and loving, when He lets so many traumatic events transpire in the lives of those who follow Him.

Shouldn't a believer be able to find comfort in his decision? Shouldn't the All-knowing be able to predict when calamity is about to strike? Doesn't He possess the power to make a difference?

If so… as I used to believe… then why doesn't He?

Why does He sit on His pious throne and watch as His people are pummeled with the rest of the world? Why does He allow innocence to be lost? Perfection marred? Those who have been faithful and true to be abused and forsaken?

Where is He? Why has He forgotten me? Why'd he allow it to happen? How could He ever expect me to love Him when all I can feel is betrayal and hate? They were my world. He took them. Or allowed them to be taken. And I'm supposed to love Him for it. In what sort of sick theology does that make sense?

I'm supposed to believe it's for my ultimate good. I'm supposed to blindly follow His lead into the barren wasteland of my own expectations.

I can't. He can have His frivolous worldview. I am done. He failed to protect what I valued most. I can no longer find it within my heart to love Him. I simply find it impossible to believe. It wasn't their fault. It was more mine. How is this fair to them? How is it fair to me?

I think I have found the truth. I think I am on to them. Why must it be this big? It seems there is nothing I can do. With nothing left to live for, I'm ready to leave this world. It holds nothing, means nothing, and has nothing for me anymore. If I must, I will leave this world like I came into it. I have left no indelible marks in this life. Only stains that I pray can be forgotten.

If He is *indeed real, I only ask to find forgiveness in possibly my final act of free will on this earth. If He isn't, it doesn't matter anyway. It really never has.*

Chapter One

The sirens wailed, uncharacteristically filling the modest neighborhood with a dreadful aura. Neighbors stood outside the safety of their homes watching the commotion with curious fascination.

Why were police cars surrounding their neighbor's home and putting yellow crime scene tape around the perimeter? Had he been murdered or finally snapped and murdered someone?

He used to be such a nice man. They used to be the perfect neighbors. A few months ago everything had changed in one vicious evening. Fate had altered this reality in the cruelest of ways.

A simple tan Toyota Corolla rolled onto the scene. The driver's door opened and a well-dressed detective stepped from the car. He was eagerly met by one of the first responders.

"Good to see you, Torben. This one's messy."

"Murder? Robbery?"

"Suicide."

"Why am I here? I'm homicide."

"Kent's on another case. You're all that was left."

"That busy huh? Another night in the big city."

"Besides, the rookie always gets the messed up cases. You've only been here a week."

The detective laughed as he stepped through the front door and into the dimly lit living room area. Blood was smeared against the back wall. A half empty bottle of Everclear had spilled on the oak coffee table. An open journal was overturned on the floor; small droplets of blood had fallen on its cover.

"Spatter," the detective pointed out. He inquisitively looked toward the other man. "Where's the body? How can I examine a scene without a body?"

"Oh," the man chuckled. "I see your confusion. The body is on its way to the hospital. Apparently, your suicide victim didn't finish the job. He's hanging on by a thread."

The detective slipped his hands into the latex free gloves he'd carried in. He stooped down and picked up the journal from the floor. Flipping through the pages, he was surprised to see that it was almost full.

"What's the victim's name?"

"Hayden."

"Hayden?"

"Yep. Hayden Smith. Thirty-five. Lives alone now. We've had dealings with him before. A lot actually. His story is tragic. His fall from grace took him from being an up and coming politician with connections to a public drunk."

"Politician huh? Sounds like an intelligent guy."

"He was. Graduated top of his class with some Ivy League law degree. Minored in theology. Immediately won a couple of high profile cases on the east coast. Tried politics because of his family connections. Would have been great at it from what I hear."

"That's quite an impressive resume for someone in his mid-thirties."

"That's not all either… That's just for starters. Before law school, Mr. Smith also served in the Marine Corp. Was one of the top recruits out of high school… Moved up quickly, the hard way. Refused to throw his family name around to earn his stripes. Have a brother who served with the man… Says he won the respect of everyone in class rather swiftly… Natural born leader… Some men have it, ya know… Anyway, he came home with some brass on his chest, though I don't know for what exactly."

"How'd he make the leap from the charmed life to attempted suicide?"

"How does anyone? World goes bad. Hope is lost. Nothing to live for, I guess…"

"What happened to him?"

"Lost his wife and three kids in an accident. Drunk driver on Highway Nine. About a year ago. Suspect was never apprehended."

"How's that possible?"

"The driver fled the scene but left enough evidence behind to make it clear he'd been drinkin'. Empty beer bottles were all over the road."

"So you didn't recover the vehicle or the driver?"

"Unfortunately, no. Neither was ever recovered."

Torben scowled, "That's strange. What's the status of the case now?"

"Officially cold. Closed actually. Too many bigger issues."

The detective nodded. "What type of dealings have we had with Mr. Smith?"

"He comes into our office every first Monday of the month asking if we've turned up any new leads. It eats at him. We know he wants nothing more than to bring justice to the man who caused the accident, but it's like he's the one who feels guilty.

"Why?"

"I guess for being the only survivor… and unfortunately,

I had the displeasure of informing him that the case had been closed."

"When?"

"This Monday. He took the news hard. He staggered around like he'd been shot. I'm afraid that's most likely the trigger for his suicide attempt… Gotta love this job."

The detective dropped the journal in a plastic bag and handed it to the other man.

"Make sure this gets processed."

He paused, as he moved back through the door, "And make sure you get me all the files that concern this man and his family. I'm gonna see what I can dig up."

Chapter Two

Two hours later Detective Torben Mayes stepped into his captain's office. After being directed to sit down, he chose a chair closest to where the captain was leaning against the front of his oversized desk. The two men were only a couple of feet apart.

"You asked to speak with me?"

"Yes… Yes, son, I did," he answered in a rugged tone. "Rumor has it that you've been asking for the files on the deaths of Laura Smith and her children… Why?"

"Mr. Smith attempted suicide tonight. I thought-"

"You thought what detective? You thought opening the case again would bring him back to the land of the living? You thought the good karma you create by reopening the case might transfer to him and cause him to stay alive? He's not going to make it, son. Just talked to the hospital. He has no chance of pulling through. Zero. They'd be calling in the family, if any were listed."

"Sorry, sir. I just feel there's something I can do. I don't believe in burying someone until they're dead. Where God's involved, there's always a chance, regardless how bleak the prognosis."

"How many times must I tell you to stop spreading your religious nonsense in my precinct? One more direct disobeying of my orders, and you're gonna be sent back where you came from. You got me?"

"Yes, sir. What I meant is that we can't just give up on him, and that file is just sitting there waiting on someone to pick it up. Surely it wouldn't hurt anything if I just took a look at it. A fresh set of eyes-"

"Detective, I want you to stay away from that file. That's an order. We've got more important things to worry about. I'll not have you wasting this department's time… Did you see that preliminary toxicology reports indicate that he was high on heroin? He's an addict son, shot himself full, and then tried to kill himself."

"If it would be okay, I'll just look into it on my days off? That way I'm not wasting the city's time."

"Listen very carefully, kid. There's nothing in those files that you need to see. They're sealed for a reason. Let it go. I'm trying to do you a favor here. Just let it go."

"But, sir. What is it about this case that has you so

defensive?"

The captain's face flushed a fiery red. "The suicide victim isn't exactly innocent. He's dangerous. And the driver… never mind kid… just leave this case alone."

The captain touched the detective on the shoulder as he stood. "This isn't a case you want to touch. Believe me. It's poison. Walk away."

Chapter Three

Detective Mayes sat in the waiting room at the hospital. An attractive nurse approached him in the silence of the early morning lobby. He'd been the only person sitting there for the last three hours.

He studied her as she moved closer. Her hair hung halfway down her navy blue scrub top. Her tennis shoes were old and worn. Her smile was warm and friendly, not in a flirtatious way, but in a way that suggested she loved her job and cared about people. Perhaps she wasn't much different than him. He'd started his career because he'd honestly valued the ability to help people. It's something people don't usually consider about law enforcement personnel. They view people on some of the worst days of their lives. Some people respond positively and want the help. Others respond emotionally or irrationally.

People always wonder why police officers seem hardened

and insensitive. He knew the truth. It wasn't always fair, but it was reality. Over time you just grow calloused. Dealing with violence, destruction, divorce, domestic disturbances, sexual misconduct, and other atrocities on a routine basis has a high cost, as does working twelve-hour shifts for unreasonably low pay. You serve people who are most often inconsiderate and rude, while wanting you to be a model of congeniality. You never know what type of situation you're walking in to and quite frankly, it's easier to go in hard and take the tone down, than to be forced into aggression later. There's much less trouble when one doesn't appear weak or sensitive. Most criminals don't push those who give off an aggressive vibe. Give potential perpetrators a sense of power, and that's where trouble starts. Cops learn not to take anything for granted. They learn the hard way what society can't understand. Violence stops violence.

Anyone could be the next troublemaker. Anyone can be dangerous. Appearances are costly. That's why many cops approach everyone with the same rough outlook. The common person gets angry, because they're innocent and being treated like a criminal, but the officer has the misfortune of knowing that there's a very thin line between the guilty and innocent, a line that's surprisingly easy to cross. There's truly something to be said about the depravity of human nature. Work in law enforcement long enough, and you'll see it rear its ugly head too many times. How can one walk among those exhibiting the basest of human behavior and others expect him to not be affected negatively? It doesn't make sense, and it's certainly not fair.

She sat down in the chair beside him and smiled.

"It's been a long night, detective. Why don't you go home?"

"How's he doing?"

"I don't know yet. He has a fifty-fifty chance of pulling through now. That's definitely more than we could have said a couple hours ago."

"If he makes it, what's the long term prognosis?"

"Don't know that either. He's just come through six hours of surgery. Doctors aren't sure how long before, or even if, he'll wake up."

She paused, "Is it true he's got no family?"

The detective nodded. "That's why I'm here. No man should be alone when he's fighting for his life."

She reassuringly placed her hand on his arm. His eyes were drawn to hers. He could feel their warmth, the compassion that seemed to be ebbing from her soul.

"He's in good hands detective. I'll make sure he's taken care of. I have to work a double. I'm not off until noon tomorrow. Go get some sleep. I'll keep him in the fight 'til then."

He studied her. "Can I ask you a personal question? If you don't want to answer, just ignore me."

"Sure," she smiled again.

"Are you a believer?"

"I believe in a lot of things. I believe you're a good person who cares more about others than himself. I believe you have a big heart, detective. I believe you should get some rest while you can."

"But, are you a believer in God?"

She removed her hand from his arm. "Follow me."

He inquisitively moved behind her, tailing her down the long hallway toward the intensive care unit. Moving through their halls, she stopped in front of door 0704 and pushed her way inside.

Two nurses were checking his vitals, as he lay strapped to various machines mechanically keeping him alive. She stood a few feet from his bedside. Torben moved close beside her, unsure if he were even supposed to be in the room. So far the two nurses had their backs turned and were unaware of their presence. She moved backwards a couple of steps, physically bumping into him as she did. She motioned for him to be quiet, before leaning close and whispering in his ear.

"I believe that God is the only thing that will get him through this night. What the best surgeons and technology can't do, I believe God can… Are you a believer, detective?"

"Of course. There's nothing else worth believing in but Him."

She nodded. "Let's pray for him then. He needs all the help he can get."

She took his hand and began to pray. He immediately joined her. After a few seconds, she let her hand fall from his and leaned close again.

"There's a reason they don't want you to investigate this case. You have to. The truth needs to come out. Lives are at stake."

"But I can't. I've been ordered off the case. I've been told that I can't access the files. My supervisor doesn't want me looking into… How'd you know about that anyway?"

"I know more than I should. I also know that you must find the truth."

One of the nurses taking the man's vitals turned toward the back of the room. A startled expression crossed her face.

"Sir, you can't be in here. You have to leave. Visiting hours are over and we have strict policies about that. I'm afraid you must leave now," she screamed, as she rushed toward him.

Torben turned to escort his companion out, but she'd vanished. The pretty blond who'd led him into the room was gone.

Chapter four

Hayden nervously searched the unfamiliar room. To admit confusion was an understatement. He'd awakened from a deep sleep less than twelve hours ago and couldn't remember how he'd gotten here. What he thought he remembered didn't make sense. This wasn't the world he knew.

He searched the room and found a blank scroll in one of the drawers. He found a writing tool lying on the counter top. Its point was dull, but it would do in a pinch. Somehow, he remembered that writing gave him comfort. He started to scribble across the page.

Journal Entry: Unsure

I don't know what's wrong with me. I'm afraid for my life. I woke up today and the world has drastically changed while I slept. I don't know what happened to me, but I must have been out for a long time.

I fear the worst has happened. Nuclear holocaust. That's the only answer. I attempted to venture outside today, but the whole world has gone mad. Nothing is as it was. I went to sleep in one of the country's largest industrial cities. Now, I'm not even sure our great country exists.

I'm terrified. It doesn't seem like we're at war. There are no soldiers marching the streets. No tanks causing the earth to tremble. No roar of jet engines flying overhead. The wreckage of nuclear devastation is curiously absent. The terror of living under such pressure appears my own. Having just awakened, this is all new to me. I went to sleep living a horrific dream and have awakened into a nightmare.

God is more dead to me now than He ever was. Why didn't He just let me die? Are His plans for me that vile? Was life not miserable enough? Although the agony seems from another world, I remember why I feel this way toward Him. I can't forget. It lingers in the recesses of my soul. My hate burns eternal. Nothing is as it was. The whole world has gone mad, and my heart beats with the rancid fury of its corrupt obscurity.

Hayden threw the pencil across the room and softly swore. He got up and walked to the window, peering through its vague contents at the rainy world outside. The weather had settled enough that he could venture out again. He scanned the tiny room for anything he could use as a weapon. Unfortunately, there was nothing that appeared threatening enough.

He opened the door and the warmth immediately pelted

him. Where were the bright lights and big city? Where was the hustle and bustle of traffic he'd come to dread? Where was the subway brimming with business? Instinctively, he felt this was the same place he'd called home for so many years, but it was markedly different. It was as if he'd entered a time warp and was standing now in the same place but a different century.

He stood alone on a dirt road surrounded by a maze of blended forestry. The once proud skyscrapers that had reached into the clouds were no longer there. They hadn't been reduced to rubble by a massive explosion. There was merely no sign they'd ever existed. The miles of dull concrete highways had been replaced by a mere two-foot-wide dirt path. The distinct sounds of industrial labor were deafeningly absent. Even the normally polluted air felt surprisingly clean. The sky was perfectly clear, void of the faintest hint of smog.

He wanted to make a call, to find out what had happened. He didn't really have anyone close enough to check on, but at least he'd know what had become of the world while he was sleeping. The problem was his phone was missing, and there hadn't been any inside the one room shack he'd awakened in. For the first time, He searched the area around him. He looked overhead and into the distance.

No cell phone towers.

No telephone lines.

No power lines.

This couldn't be happening. Where was he?

He ran back into the building, moving through it with urgent precision. He couldn't stay here. He had to move. Something gnawed at him, screaming for him to get away from this place. If he stayed too long, there would be trouble. He just had no idea where it was coming from, or what it might be.

That makes the decision most difficult. Where do you go when you have no idea where you are? Where do you turn when you have no clue what's waiting around the next corner? Where can you run when you feel danger but have no idea which direction represents safety?

He found a container to hold water. However, he was disappointed to find there was no plumbing. There was nothing that even resembled a sink, pipes, or faucet. To further his dilemma, there was nothing in the house that could be used as food. He was in trouble. He had to leave but had no food and limited water.

As he exited the house, he noticed the old well by the trees. The bucket was hanging by a rope over the empty hole. He eagerly ran toward it, muttering a half-hearted prayer. He primed it a few times, and then laughed when water flowed from the seemingly ancient metallic pipes. He splashed the cool liquid over his face and hair. He thirstily drank, not realizing how parched he'd been until the water's moistness permeated his cracked lips. After he'd swallowed all he could, he held the container under the well's sporadic flow. Once it was full, he clamped the lid and started his journey down the dusty road.

.　　.　　.

He'd traveled for hours with no sight of civilization. The water container was almost empty. He'd been trying to drink only what was needed, but the day had been incredibly hot and the road vengefully long. He stumbled from fatigue, and then quickly steadied himself when something rustled through the brush ahead and to his right. He charged to the opposite side of the road and dove for cover behind a large tree just as they emerged from the thick foliage.

There were three of them. Two males and a female. Each had a backpack strapped on their backs. They looked harmless enough. Tired, stressed, a bit traveled, but uncharacteristically happy.

The man in the middle laughed and tossed an apple to the man on his left. Hayden was afraid to reveal himself to them? They could be dangerous. Then again, they could be perfectly harmless, and they had food and probably water. Maybe they had transportation as well, or knew where he could find some. Regardless, they should be able to provide him with answers.

They grew awkwardly quiet when he emerged in front of them. The older man in the middle pushed the other two behind him and removed a thin blade from a leather scabbard.

"Who are you stranger? Where are you traveling from?"

"My name is Hayden Smith. I'm a United States citizen. I don't know where I am or how I got here."

"The United States? Where's that?"

Hayden scoffed. "You can't be serious. The wealthiest and most technologically advanced nation on earth. Military prowess. Ruler of the western hemisphere. Founders and keepers of democracy. Ring a bell?"

"Mr. Smith, sir, we don't want trouble. We'll just be on our way now."

"Wait. None of you have heard of the United States of America? George Washington? Abraham Lincoln? The American Revolution? Christopher Columbus? The Vietnam War? The Cold War? Seriously?"

The three people standing in front of him looked alarmed. The man in the middle held his dagger out a little further.

"Look sir, I don't know what you're trying to pull, but just let us be. We just need to be on our way."

Hayden backed away and held his hands up non-threateningly. "Wait! Answer one more question. Please! What year is this?"

"Year?" The man frowned. "Most of us stopped keeping time centuries ago. The Timekeeper is the only one who knows that, and he's not easy to find."

"Timekeeper?"

The young woman looked apprehensive. "Dad, we need to go. Something isn't right. He could be a Tweener."

The older man studied him carefully, sensing Hayden's genuine confusion and recognizing his garments was unlike any he'd ever seen. A spy would be much more likely to fit in.

"No. He's not a spy, M'ya. He's genuinely lost."

The sound of dogs barking penetrated the previous stillness of their conversation. Loud voices could be heard shouting in the background. Hayden ran to the side of the road and peered through the thick foliage. Someone yelled.

"Quick. Over here. The dogs are leading us toward the dirt road. That's gonna be far too easy."

"They probably crossed the border and didn't think we'd have the guts to follow them. If we hurry, we can catch them before they get in too deep. We can only risk going another mile or two."

The young woman turned to her father. "Please. Where can we go? They're gonna catch us."

"Wait," Hayden called. "Maybe I can help. Have you done anything wrong?"

The elderly man stepped toward him. "Son, we stole some fruit and vegetables from a Babylonian plantation. There are not much higher crimes we could have committed. If you don't want them to think you were with us, you better disappear too."

The man and his two companions started to run, heading for the trees on the opposite side of the road. After a brief hesitation, Hayden followed. He'd just bolted into the tree line when the first dog emerged from the opposite side. The dog's owner let the leash fall, sending the dog on the attack with a war-like shout.

The menacing dog bypassed Hayden without a second glance. He lunged at the first person past Hayden and pulled him to the ground. The young man fell headlong into a fallen tree and struggled against the dog's weight to stand up again. The canine snarled, as he pulled hard against the man's leg. The girl turned around and ran to his aid. She didn't have the strength to pull him away from the dog's vice-like bite. Hayden stopped alongside her and tugged with all his strength. The dog's grasp was momentarily broken, but he snapped and reconnected with the boy's shoe, knocking him off balance again.

The old man yelled for the girl, "M'ya, we must go. Now! M'ya!"

She turned to run, leaving the younger man lying in the road, still struggling against the slobbering beast. Hayden grabbed a fallen branch from the tree and clubbed the dog across the nose to no avail. He turned when he heard the quickly approaching footsteps. He spun around a moment too late. Something slammed into his side and knocked him to the ground. His body convulsed.

He rolled to his side, almost blinded by the searing pain. He could just make out the features of the girl and her father still running away. Suddenly, they were both enveloped by what appeared to be a large net. They struggled against its entangling grasp, but were more entwined the harder they resisted. Several men surrounded them and lifted them to their feet. Each were placed in chains and carried back to the small group that had gathered around Hayden and the other man the dog had caught.

Hayden's senses slowly cleared. He nervously studied his captors. They shoved the two others down beside him and the injured boy. Hayden looked at him more closely, realizing for the first time that he was no older than fifteen. His head was bleeding profusely from a deep wound where he'd fallen against the log. His leg was openly gushing blood from the damage the large dog had inflicted. Hayden leaned over to apply pressure to the wound.

The obvious leader of their attackers stepped forward. "Don't touch him. Just let him bleed out."

Hayden ignored him and pushed hard against the wound. He was rewarded with a hard blow to the head from one of the others. He whirled around to find a large stick pointed in his direction. It was a weapon he'd never seen before, but the others' reaction left little doubt that it was deadly. He reluctantly stayed away from the fallen boy while eyeing the man holding the weapon. The leader motioned for the man to stand down.

"We followed three people from The Rose Plantation. Now we have four. Which of you wasn't involved?"

None of them spoke.

"Let me make it easy for you," he prodded. "One of you will get to walk away from here today. Three of you are going to die... Again, which of you wasn't involved in the crimes against civilization?"

One of the men moved closer. "Sir. It's rather obvious,

this one wasn't involved."

He pointed toward Hayden. "He's the only one not carrying the evidence of thievery strapped to his back."

The man nodded. "That settles it."

He stepped forward toward Hayden and extended his hand. "I'm Captain of the King's Guard, Abaddon Dearth."

Hayden cautiously held his hand outward. Right before their hands touched, the captain spat in Hayden's face. He pulled his hand away and followed the spit with a hard slap. Hayden started to lunge forward but was stopped by the unknown weapons pointing in his direction.

"I don't touch a common fool. Who do you think you are to approach me? I should kill you just for your contemptuous stare. But, they're right. It appears you're guilty of no other crime than ignorance. The punishment for such apparent transgressions can easily be mete another day. You've got about as long a head start as it takes us to finish with these three, then if we aren't tired we're coming after you. Run!"

"Wait! What happens to them?"

"They pay the price for stealing. Everyone knows the penalty."

"C'mon! It's only a little fruit and vegetables. Only three smalls bags. They couldn't have caused that much damage from the stock of an entire plantation."

The leader spat hard into the dirt. "I don't make the rules stranger. I just enforce them."

"How much is the penalty. I'll help them pay."

The man laughed. "You'd do that?"

"Yes! I would."

"The penalty for stealing from a Babylonian plantation is death."

"What? That's preposterous. You can't be serious."

"If you know what's good for you, you'll run along now. And fast."

The leader motioned for his men to grab the other three and bring them closer.

Hayden moved nearer to him instead. "Wait. Please."

One of the first men threw a rope over a large tree branch. The noose on the other end made his intentions perfectly clear. Another of the men picked up the injured boy and carried him toward the rope. He kicked hard against them, trying his best to break loose.

His father screamed at him, "Die with dignity. Stop the wailing. Don't let them take your dignity, boy."

The teenager either didn't hear, or he was unable to cope with the realty of impending death. His struggle continued against the man carrying him. A second man joined the scrap, and they both positioned him under the rope hanging securely overhead. He finally quit crying out as the loop tightened around his neck.

The female captive whimpered in the grasp of her

captors. The one holding her shoved her to the ground. "Shhh. You're next if you don't stop that."

Hayden watched the scene unfold. It was too surreal a moment for a response. Surely they were just toying with the lad. They'd pull the noose tight and then let him go with no harm. He would've learned his lesson. His sister and father would be afraid to steal again. With such a near death experience, their criminal careers would be over. Anyone could see they weren't hardened felons in need of stiff punishment. They'd done no large-scale damage. The punitive results needed to match the crime.

Hayden gasped as the leader motioned and two of the men holding the other end of the rope tugged hard and lifted the boy into the air. The cinch tightened hard around his neck, as he was lifted two feet off the ground. His airway was immediately shut off.

This was brutal. It was inhumane. They weren't even ending it quickly. It was calculated to be a slow death. No snapping of the neck. They wanted his agony to last. They were enjoying the sport of watching him die. They were getting pleasure from the pain they were inflicting on his family.

The father hung his head. The girl tried to stifle tears.

Finally the father pleaded. "Please. I offer her life for his."

The leader motioned for the man holding the rope to drop it. The boy crashed to the ground. He squirmed to pull the noose away from his neck, opening his airway again. As he struggled to find air, the leader approached them.

"Now there's an idea."

The girl fearfully eyed her father. "Dad. Please? You know what they'll do to me."

He coldly returned her stare, and then his eyes fell again. "Her life for his. She's a beautiful girl. Do as you will with her. Only spare her life. She'll serve you forever."

Hayden felt sick. "Please. This is uncivilized. This is a sin against humanity. You can't do this."

The leader angrily stared toward him. "Uncivilized? You want to talk about sins against humanity. The law says *thou shalt not steal.* Everyone knows the penalty. It's inhumane to take what isn't yours."

"And you'd take her then? She doesn't belong to you. She's another man's daughter."

"Not anymore. He just gave her to me."

"No man has the power to give one life for another. It's her life. Her choice… Stop! Don't they at least deserve the fairness of a trial?"

The man appeared agitated. "They just had one. I've made my choice."

"Who made you God?"

"God?" The man mocked. "You talk to me about God? To which god do you refer? The pagan gods are too preoccupied to care about this. The Hebrew God hasn't been concerned in the affairs of man for thousands of years. Man is his own god, and right now, I'm in control."

"You don't have the power of life and death."

The man slammed his fist into Hayden's stomach. "Watch me."

He motioned for the men to pick the young boy back up from the ground. He kicked and struggled again, as he dangled two feet in the air. Hayden helplessly watched as the boy's life drained from his face. The boy's agony was apparent. His pants were stained with the emptying of his bladder into the fabric. Hayden tried to move toward him but was hammered again from behind. The leader allowed the boy to hang there until he was certain the boy was dead.

He looked into the eyes of the boy's father. "You may go. She stays with me. She'll serve me until I'm tired of her, and then she'll serve in a Babylonian synagogue. You know what kind of life that'll be for her."

She loudly cried. "Please. You killed him. Please let me go."

The men pulled her to her feet.

"Please," her father begged. "You can't take both of my children. Please."

"Go back to your people. Tell them what happens when you steal from a Babylonian plantation… Go now, before I change my mind."

The father took off through the trees. They watched him

go until he disappeared into the thick growth. Hayden winced from the sharp blow he'd received. The leader approached him.

"And you. You'll serve in our city as well."

They placed heavy cuffs around his wrists, locking his hands in place behind his back.

"And what's my crime?" Hayden demanded.

The leader smiled. "Code 417… A commoner isn't to speak out of turn or disrespect an Elite or Babylonian. I'm both."

With that, they shoved Hayden next to the terrified girl and escorted them both back toward the street.

Chapter Five

Journal Entry: Date Unknown

I don't know where I am. This place is beyond my understanding. The normal rules of society aren't followed here. The people have no conscience.

I've been granted only one request. They are amused that their prisoner asked for writing utensils and parchment. It appears most of them can't read. The captain can, but he's left me alone to my own care.

It's been three days since they murdered the boy in cold blood for stealing a few pieces of fruit, including tomatoes. As we were carried away from his still hanging body, the men left the bags of fruit where they had fallen. Their distress hadn't been the fruit at all. They were more concerned with some sort of vigilante justice.

M'ya hasn't spoken since. She's a pretty girl. Younger. Probably twenty-five. She's terrified. I've asked a few questions and discovered what happens to girls who must serve in the synagogues. It doesn't sound any different than a brothel. The only distinction is that she'd be required to do her duty in the name of religion.

These people serve some of the ancient gods. Like Greeks and Romans, their gods appear to be fictitious. The gods you cry to for years, only to ultimately realize your cries have fallen on deaf ears. They don't have the benefit of knowing their prayers have been discerned by an omniscient being with a higher purpose. They've had no miracles. They've witnessed no answers. They've seen no higher calling other than what they've intentionally created in the name of their religions.

It's no wonder they are so calloused and cold. They have no north star. No guiding light. Nothing to set their course other than their own flawed concepts and failed ingenuities. They drown in their own arrogance and ignorance, setting themselves up as demigods. They act as gods without mercy. There's nothing more tragic I've experienced.

What can I say? My god also failed me, and for that I cannot find it in my heart to forgive. However, I get the sense He's real. For there's no feeling I've ever known as dead as this place.

We've passed three plantations the past few days. They were all large, with a variable crop. Most consisted of fruits, vegetables, rice, and cotton. One was an extremely large cattle ranch.

I must admit that I was taken back by the work force. Hispanic and African American men and women were working tirelessly in the fields. It was obvious their effort wasn't being rewarded. This wasn't a job. It was slave labor. One elderly man was being beaten for not carrying his load. I tried to help him, but was immediately threatened with the unknown weapon.

The looks on these people's faces were heartbreaking. Emptiness.

Hopelessness. Loneliness. The greatest nightmare for a man is one without freedom. It appears they have none.

We entered the first big city last night. It was a stark contrast to the destitution on the outskirts. The plantations were nice and well kept, but the city is one of only modest industrial advancements.

The people here are different. They are all dressed in similar fashion. Tunics are the cultural norm. Many of the women are scantily clad, and many of the men appear almost barbaric in nature, behind their civilized outer appeal.

There are several skyscrapers shaped like large towers. It reminds me of a variation of New York or Chicago, but with a much harsher tone. The structures are something you'd imagine from the construction of ancient Egyptian towers. I'm reminded of the Tower of Babel.

The city streets are busy with commerce. The mode of transportation is different. There's a fast train that runs the perimeter of the city, stopping in various districts. Only the elite are allowed access to the mysterious train. The other people have no other means of transportation but to walk.

I'm lost in this horrible dream, praying only to awaken and find myself in a better place.

The tent flap opened with a snap of the fabric. Hayden calmly sat the pencil down and turned to view his intruder. He'd been surprised when they'd removed his restraints a couple of days before. They hadn't viewed him as a threat.

There were only ten of them. Truth be told, he could

have easily taken them out one by one in the middle of the night if he'd chosen to. However, his better judgment precluded him from that task. He didn't know what he was facing, and it's better to withhold decisions of huge consequence until one is certain of the facts.

Two guards approached him.

"You must come with us," one of them bellowed.

Hayden stood and followed them from the room. Two more guards stood outside and fell in behind them as he walked past. They walked for several minutes, until they came to a set of steps that ascended in spiral fashion upward to a large platform forty feet in the air. Beside the platform was a set of the train tracks he'd seen running around the city. The guards pushed him forward, until he'd climbed the staircase. He heard the smooth hum of the train's almost silent engine and felt the soft vibrations of it on the tracks. He was amazed at how quiet it ran. As the train approached, he noticed that it wasn't touching the track. It was suspended in the air about eight inches above the metallic surface. The train pulled to a stop next to the small group. An airtight door slid open, and the guards rushed him forward. One of the guards laughed at his reluctance to enter.

"Never rode the airTram have you? It's always frightening the first time."

"What's keeping it on line? It's not connected to anything."

"Magic!" The guard laughed, as the door slid shut with a muffled clank.

Twenty minutes later the airTram stopped in the center of a highly occupied city. A few miles ago, he'd passed the outskirts of the city. From that point he'd seen skyscrapers and large buildings that dwarfed most other structures he'd seen all day.

"Where are we?"

"You don't know? You're about to get your trial."

The guard flashed an ominous smile. "Don't worry. The sentence is usually carried out within minutes after a verdict. I'm afraid you won't be with us much longer."

As the door slid open again, he was forced onto a similar platform to the other one. The only difference was that this one stood eighty feet in the air and overlooked a large body of water. The view was breathtaking. The train sped away, and Hayden was left alone with the four guards, suspended high above the earth on the lonely platform. He looked to his right and there was an ocean as far as his eyes perceived. Behind him was a city more mystifyingly ancient than any he could remember. This place was astounding, an architectural masterpiece, a city on the sea.

He heard a faint sliding sound overhead and looked above to see what was coming. A large object was slowly moving toward the middle of the platform from overhead. The guards moved him to the perimeter of the deck until the descending object rested firmly on the floor.

It was made of glass on all sides, even the floor and ceiling. It was a five by five box that resembled an elevator. The panel of glass facing him abruptly opened.

"Hurry, get in. It only stays open for ten seconds."

Hayden stepped in, and two of the guards followed him. He followed their example and moved against the back panel of glass. Within a few seconds, he felt an invisible force pull him forward, as the wall re-appeared in front of him, creating a suction as it did. He regained his balance and uncomfortably stood as the clear box lifted from the ground and started moving toward the sky.

Hayden looked above but could not see through the denseness of the clouds overheard. Whatever was up there, he couldn't tell. They rose for what felt like minutes. The sites below had gone from small to microscopic. He searched above him again and still saw nothing but the clouds.

A few seconds later, the haziness enveloped them. It only lasted for moments, and then it was clear again. What he observed on the other side was like nothing he'd ever witnessed. It was obviously the pinnacles of several large towers, but they'd been linked together to form a solid foundation. Several smaller buildings had been constructed on this new floor.

This place was like a watchtower, a city above the city. It wasn't large enough to hold hundreds of people, but it was definitely a small-scale community. A walkway of wooden bridges linked one building to the next. In the center of the entire design was a tower that rose another hundred feet above the rest. This place was the center point of the entire city below.

The guards led him through a maze of bridges. He was

surprised how cold it was, and how hard it was to breathe. The air was razor thin. The wind ripped at him so hard at times that he felt he'd be lifted from the small bridge's surface.

They finally stopped at the tall tower in the center of the elevated city. Suddenly, a bottom portion of the wall opened, and the guards led him through the gap. They stepped onto another platform. The platform lifted upward, passing several floors, until it made it to the top and finally came to a rest. The platform had carried him into a large room. It was empty, except for the round pattern of tables. They formed a circle with an approximate twenty-five foot circumference. The tables had been strategically placed where one person could sit at each one.

Hayden quickly assessed the room. There were fifteen filled positions. Two of the chairs were empty. There was also an empty chair positioned in the middle of the circle of desks. The chair was sitting over a large glass funnel that extended ten feet downward below the floor, and then opened over the white fluff below.

The design was obvious. Whoever was sitting in the chair had to be ready for a painful death. The floor would open and the chair would swing forward, dumping its occupant into the funnel. With nothing to grasp, the chair's occupant would frantically struggle for something to stop them, until they spiraled completely through the tube and began a freefall toward the earth below. At this height, Hayden wasn't sure if lack of oxygen, low temperatures, or the impact at the bottom would kill the victim first.

The guards pushed him through the row of tables and motioned for him to sit in the dreadful seat in the center. He suspiciously eyed the men and women around the tables before sitting. There were twelve men and three women. Ten of the men appeared to be over sixty and two in their late forties to early fifties. The three women appeared much younger, probably mid to late thirties.

All fifteen of them were dressed similarly in silk white robes. A golden sash hung across from the left shoulder to the right hip. Each donned a carefully placed ring on their second finger. It was pure gold and carried a symbol that Hayden had never seen before.

Someone's voice finally broke the silence. Hayden looked forward and located the source, the most elderly looking man in the room. His eyes held a hard stare toward Hayden. He detected something in them. Wisdom? Guilt? Arrogance? Hayden wasn't sure, but he didn't like the feeling.

"What's your name, thief?"

Hayden considered not speaking, but there'd be nothing to gain by acting disrespectfully. Sitting in the chair of death made him strongly reconsider a dangerous response.

"My name is Hayden."

"Hayden, odd name. Never heard it before. Where are you from?"

"I honestly don't know."

The man's face twitched.

Hayden attempted to head off the man's anger. "I sincerely apologize, sir. I meant no disrespect. The truth is that I was recently in an accident. There's something wrong with my memory."

"You carry yourself well. You must be from good origin. You're definitely not from the Dregs."

Hayden shook his head. He wasn't sure what the man meant, but he didn't want to incite further anger.

"No, sir. I'm not from the Dregs. I don't remember much, but I have a feeling that would ring a bell."

"Nothing there but misfits, rascals, thieves, murderers, and harlots. You don't fit in with that crowd. Or do you, you were caught running with those who committed a capitol offense. That's why you're here today."

The man thoughtfully paused. "Are you fully aware of the serious nature of the allegations against you. As a non-citizen, you had no right to even be on Babylonian soil, much less be in possession of Babylonian goods. If you are found guilty, the penalty is death."

Hayden started to speak, but the man interrupted with an uplifted hand.

"Silence. You will speak only when the high court has asked for you to. Is that understood?"

Hayden nodded.

"We have spoken with the plantation owners who had supplies missing. There were seven pounds of apples, three pounds of bananas, and ten pounds of potatoes missing. There are also seven sacks of seeds unaccounted for. Ten pounds of dried meat finalizes the list against you. Your little posse had all of that in their possession when they were found."

Hayden started to speak but caught himself before going too far. He knew that was a lie. The three small sacks the people had been carrying on their backs hadn't been large enough but for four or five pounds each. At most fifteen pounds of goods could have been stolen. His outcome wasn't looking good.

The man continued, "Let me explain how this works. Your accusers have already spoken against you. Your arresting officer will present his case. You have been assigned legal representation. One of our officers-in-training has been given the details of your case. Should he or she choose to speak for you, you will be thus defended. If he or she feels that your case is weak, they may decline to defend you. In such case, you are considered guilty by default and the court will decide your penalty. I must tell you, Mr. Hayden, your life hangs in the balance, with only a young officer standing between you and judgment. Honestly, given the heinous allegations against you, you are staring eye to eye with the death penalty. This board doesn't tolerate aggression against the realm."

The door opened again, and Hayden watched as the captain of the guard marched toward them. He sat in one of the empty seats. Moments later another door opened and a young man wearing a linen robe and wire rimmed glasses stumbled into the room. The robe was quite filled out, as the young man was largely overweight. Mixed laughter and noises of disgust came from the panel surrounding him. The young man nervously sat down in the chair next to the captain of the host.

"Captain Abaddon Dearth, Defender of the Realm, Captain of the King's Guard, what do you say against this man? What do you recommend as the result of his selfish actions against mankind?"

Hayden bit his tongue, as the captain eyed him with a wicked smile. "I say that this villain should be punished by death. He assaulted me on the road in defense of his friends."

Hayden tried to stand from his chair to defend the false allegations, but was shocked to find he couldn't move. The chair had some sort of invisible restraints. He was locked into position, powerless to free himself if needed. He was completely at the mercy of this group of self-righteous bigots.

The older man angrily turned toward Hayden. "Assault, I wasn't aware of those allegations. The quick death may be too lenient for you. It may be better if he's forced into the arenas."

The captain smiled. "He would do fantastic there. I'm sure they could whip him into shape in no time. At least he could die with a little dignity."

The door opened again, and M'ya was pushed through and forced to stand on the outskirts of the tables.

Hayden locked eyes with her before looking at the

nerdish kid in the glasses. The kid was scouring some papers laid out in front of him. The older man followed Hayden's gaze.

"I wouldn't worry about her, boy. She's too pretty to die outright, and too young to waste that way. She'll do wonderful serving at our temples. Might even make me attend more, I'd say."

The counsel all laughed.

The man gave them a moment's humor before snapping them to attention again. "And I wouldn't put my hopes in him, boy. If an officer-in-training decides to try a case and loses it, the penalty for them is harsh. They lose their one chance to sit on the counsel, and their family is disgraced forever. It's not something they are ever willing to risk."

"Then why go through the farce of creating a fair trial?" Hayden demanded.

"You disgrace this court with your contemptuous tone. I dare you. Who do you think you are?"

"I don't think I'm anyone, sir. I don't know who I am. However, I know what's happening here isn't right. This is lunacy. The overwhelming arrogance of these proceedings is preposterous."

The old man whipped his head toward the young officer. "Do you wish to represent this fool? You've heard the allegations. Are you going to defend his satanic misgivings, or shall the court decide his fate now?"

The young man appeared stunned. He stammered, "I… I… I nnneed more time. I… I… don't think… I… I've got all the facts yet."

"Are you really going to risk your career and your family's integrity by going against the Captain of the King's Guard. Our guest has obviously insulted the Congressional panel, sinned against the realm, and maliciously attacked one of our most decorated leaders. Are you going to risk everything to defend him? How foolish for you to even consider such a notion."

The man looked at Hayden. He appeared in deep thought.

"Please," Hayden begged. "I'm innocent. I didn't steal anything. I didn't assault anyone. I did insult this panel, because their methods are mad. The travesty of this legal proceeding is that it's meant to seriously defend the people of this empire, but in its seriousness, it's become a joke."

The elder's anger was apparent by his flushed countenance and the bulging veins in his neck.

"I'll see you are murdered for this. You will not insult the sacredness of our proceedings and live. You don't know the sacrifice our ancestors went through to hand us these laws. They created them to protect our civilization. I won't have their memories shamed or their ideals mocked by the objections of a fool."

"I'm sure their intentions weren't created under such vile pretenses. Are you sure you haven't already corrupted their memories yourself by turning their pure laws into vindictive regulations of corruption that do nothing but promote hate and spread a self-righteous propaganda."

"So now you are an expert on our history. How, pray tell, do you know so much about what our ancestor's intended?"

"All I've witnessed since I've arrived with your people has been the baseness of human interaction. Mercy, compassion, or any other attribute of basic humanitarianism is remarkably lacking. That couldn't have been the intentions of your ancestors, or this civilization wouldn't have risen to the precipice of power on which it sits today. If your ancestors have always believed, felt, and acted with such hostility as you have, there'd be nothing left. This empire would have already been destroyed by the violence of its own corruption."

The elder was incensed. "You accuse us of living and upholding the law out of obligation. That's an outrage. We live this way because we choose to."

"I don't argue that point, sir. I'm saying that you have dishonored the memory of your founding fathers by the attitude with which you obey their decrees. Obedience to the law is of no effect if you essentially murder the spirit of the law by the way in which you obey it. If by carrying out the law you forget the heartbeat of the law in the first place, you have only sullied the names of those who sacrificed to establish it."

"Sacrilege. You should be burned for this."

"Your rage ruins the spirit of the law you so desperately attempt to defend. Do what you must, but the truth shall remain, and everyone here knows it. These proceedings do this people a grave injustice, and somewhere the voices of the dead cry out for you to re-examine your motives for contemplating justice… You know nothing about me. Where I'm from. What my past is. The high goals I've accomplished. My ideals and moral codes. You know nothing, yet you're willing to waste my life on an accusation before even allowing me the privilege of being heard. Where's the justice of your forefathers in that? Has the law hardened your hearts to the point that you've become nothing more than judgmental naval-gazers? You condemn others for their little faults, while blindly ignoring the fact that your intolerance and indifference has birthed a far greater sin inside of you. That's the epitome of pride."

"You speak well stranger, but your words have no meaning. You wag your tongue like a snake, but we aren't to be intoxicated by your lies. Death shall be your sentence."

The elder looked around the tables surrounding Hayden. "What does the panel say? Shall this stranger be excommunicated and left to survive on his own."

"Excommunicated? That's what you call throwing me from a thousand feet in the air? Survive on my own. Like I even have a chance… Unfortunately for you, I'm a man with nothing to lose. I don't fear death."

"That's what life is like outside of our laws, no survival. That's what happens to all who violate our codes."

"There's nothing wrong with your codes, sir. The problem is you. You violate your own law by the arrogance with which you live it."

"Death. Death. Death."

The panel erupted in the chant with him. "Death. Death. Death. Death."

The over-weight young man with the glasses stood. The room fell silent as he yelled against their incessant screaming.

"I… I… wasn't given my say. I'll re… re… represent him."

"What? Are you insane? You would defy us after we have given you a chance?"

"Hhhh… he's… right, and hhhhhhe speaks like one of us. He can't be an outsider. He has our blood in his veins."

The elder stepped forward and moved toward Hayden. "If you are right, he will bear the mark. If he doesn't, you shall not only be disbarred for this, you shall share in his fate."

"Bbbb… But…"

"But nothing. You should have held your tongue."

The elder stood over Hayden and ripped his shirt open. The crowd gasped. On Hayden's left breast, over his heart, was a small tattoo that resembled a birthmark. It was the same design the counsel members had on their rings.

One of them gasped. "He's a citizen of the realm."

The elder turned and frantically looked toward Abaddon Dearth. The two men exchanged fearful glances. Hayden studied them thoughtfully. He wasn't sure why they'd appeared so shaken.

The young officer-in-training interrupted his thoughts as he started speaking.

"Operating under our strict codes, if anyone falsely accuses a citizen of the realm, they are to be punished by the same penalty that was demanded of the accused."

The elder stepped backward, having obviously lost his fire. "But I didn't know he was a member of the realm."

The young man lost his nervous stammer. "It doesn't matter. The law makes it clear that a man is to be judged the way he judges others. If he was ready to pass a harsh judgment on a citizen, he too shall be judged harshly… The law is extremely detailed. It doesn't matter if it was an innocent mistake or not… That's why the law states that an accuser is to have all the facts before making an accusation."

He turned his attention to Abaddon. "It also states that the rules apply regardless of social position or military service… The allegations you both brought against my client are punishable by death. I demand that my client be released at once, and those responsible for this humiliating act of treason against him be punished immediately."

Hayden felt the invisible force against him lift. He quickly stood before whoever had released him changed their mind. Guards entered the room and seized the elder, pushing him toward the chair. Abaddon Dearth started to calmly walk from the room, when the guards surrounded him and pointed him toward the center as well. The elder seemed on the verge of a panic attack. The Captain of the Guard seemed calmly resigned to his fate.

Hayden loudly spoke. "Please. Wait. If I may speak? I don't believe these men should have to die. I understand the law, but I can offer another solution that may be favorable to everyone involved."

A new leader from the board stepped forward. "And what exactly is your proposal, sir?"

"One life for two. I propose that instead of passing judgment on this girl for her crimes, you grant her and her family citizenship. Give them a chance to start fresh. I'll be responsible for them."

The young, overweight man spoke. "This is provided for in the law of substitutions. His request is not unreasonable should the board approve it. All involved could live."

The new leader considered it. After a few seconds he replied. "You said one life for two. I will grant that request only. She will be released to your custody, not as a free Babylonian, but as your servant. She will have servant privileges only. Her family will remain as they are. If she is caught contacting or aiding them again, her opportunity is revoked."

He looked to the elder. "You may live, but you will live the rest of your days among the others below. You're days in the tower are over."

Tears filled the elder's eyes. "But I've given everything for this. This is my life."

"Not anymore," the new leader callously replied before turning his gaze to Abaddon.

"Mr. Dearth, you will resume your post as Captain of the Guard, but one other incident of this nature and you'll be stripped of all rank and privileges. You are to forget Mr. Hayden exists. Any attempts at revenge by you or others under your authority will be considered a violation, and you'll be immediately removed from duty. You and your entire family will be put to death."

He turned to the counsel. "Does the counsel second the verdict?"

Each member nodded an approval. M'ya was immediately released and shoved toward Hayden. Hayden smiled in the young man's direction.

"Thank you," he mouthed, before he and M'ya were escorted from back out of the building and placed on the elevator to endure the long ride back toward the ground. It wasn't an exciting ride, but it beat the alternative.

Chapter Six

Hayden and M'ya stood in awkward silence at the bottom of both platforms. He moved toward her, and she jerked backward, raising her hands in a defensive position. He lightly chuckled.

"You've nothing to be afraid of girl. I'm not gonna hurt you."

She didn't lower her defenses, defiantly staring into his eyes. "I'm no one's slave. My father moved to the Dregs to escape that horrific possibility. I'd rather die than serve a man's sadistic pleasure."

He shook his head. "M'ya, I get it. I do. This world, it's not kind. It's made you hard, and I understand why. But you have to understand something. You can stay with me as long as you want. I won't let anything happen to you. However, you can leave anytime you want to. If you make that choice,

I'm not responsible for you. Do you understand?"

"You mean, I can leave?"

"Yes."

"Anytime?"

"Yes, M'ya. You control your own destiny."

She relaxed. He smiled at her and turned to move away. After a few seconds he heard her soft footsteps behind him. She walked in his shadow for a few moments before calling out to him.

"Where are we going from here?"

"We?"

She looked embarrassed. "Yes. I think my destiny lies with you."

He nodded. "I don't rightly know."

They heard the glass door open again behind them and turned. The overweight young lad shuffled heavily toward them. By the time he covered the thirty feet, he was sorely out of breath. He stopped in front of them.

"Please, ride with me. My carriage awaits."

"Where to?" Hayden inquired.

"Does it matter? You're in the center of the Babylonian heartland; surely you aren't planning on walking through by yourself. Not with her."

"Why not?"

"You bear the mark of Babylonian society. Surely you understand."

The young man saw the confusion on Hayden's face. "You really don't know, do you?"

Hayden shrugged. "Sorry. I'm lost here."

"How long has it been since you've come around?"

"Long enough," Hayden replied, hoping the young man couldn't read his obvious attempts at lying.

"Well, a lot has obviously changed. Babylon is a dangerous place."

M'ya spoke for the first time. "It's a bed of corruption, spreading the filthy disease across the known world. It's a den of whoremongers, the most evil place on the planet."

The younger man grew quickly agitated. "Hold your tongue woman. You have no right to speak. I could have your tongue removed."

He lifted his hand and struck her across the face. She fell to the ground but leapt to her feet quickly, facing him. Before she had her balance fully regained, she saw the large man rock backward. He landed with a thud a few feet away, the wind knocked out of him. Hayden stood over him.

"Hit her again, and next time I'll have your tongue."

The man struggled to get up. His obvious size made it more difficult than it should have been. Hayden helped him up by grasping his left shoulder and pulling firmly. The young man knocked Hayden's hand away as soon as he was steady.

"You'd defile a brother for a Dreggish slave? A brother who just risked his life to save yours nonetheless."

Hayden stepped toward him and spoke low. "No brother of mine would hit a young, defenseless woman. You dishonor me by proclaiming the same heritage while hiding behind titles and bloodlines. No brother of mine need hide behind the skirts of ancestry. We are men."

"You are right. We are men. She's a woman. She has no right to speak. I'm Babylonian. She certainly has no right to speak here. This isn't the wilderness."

"It isn't? Maybe the buildings and dress are different, but from what I've seen so far, this place is the epitome of incivility. How can it not be wild when the law of the wilderness beats in the heart of the people? There's no respect for fellowman nor respect for those who are different."

"Who are you? Where are you really from?"

"Doesn't matter. You've got a lot to learn about life."

"I'd say you're the one who needs to learn, sir. You cannot defy the laws of your heritage and expect to live. You'll be dead within three days."

"If your decrees make it possible for you to melt and stammer while standing before greater men, only to take your humiliation out on women and weaker vessels who can do nothing to defend themselves, they aren't worth following."

"Your words, they aren't Babylonian. You disgrace your own blood."

"Any man who would hit a woman is a coward. That may not be the Babylonian doctrine, but it should be. A Babylonian warrior isn't trained to fight the feeble. We aren't taught to take out aggression on those who can't defend themselves. The heart of the warrior is forged of tougher alloys. You prove your heart only melts when you abuse the less fortunate. You may be Babylonian in name, but you're not Babylonian in heart."

A sudden noise to their right startled both of them. They both turned to see the man who had taken the role of the leader upstairs. He extended his hand toward Hayden. Hayden took his hand to shake it. The man looked at him awkwardly. He removed his hand from the grasp and immediately clasped his hand along Hayden's forearm. Hayden tried to hide his grimace. He'd made another mistake. Obviously they preferred the greeting of the ancient Romans than the modern handshake.

The man spoke, "Very well spoken, sir. My name is Marcus Shamash, new leader of the Elect… You must tell me where you nurtured your philosophies. It's obvious you have higher learning."

"School of hard knocks," Hayden laughed.

The man placed his hand on his chin, obviously deep in thought. "Never heard of it. Whereby does it exist?"

The larger boy interrupted. "You've had formal schooling? I apologize for my disposition. I shouldn't have come against you."

"Don't apologize to me. Address your apology to the lady."

"Lady," he scoffed, "show me a lady and I'll..."

Hayden stepped toward him again. The younger man looked toward the girl as he stumbled backward.

"Sorry ma'am."

She contemptuously smiled. "It's okay, but next time I'll take care of you myself. I'll..."

Hayden put his hand over her lips. "Shh, let's not get carried away here."

The elder man stifled a smile. "Let's be off. I would like for you to come dine with me."

He looked from Hayden to M'ya. "You and the lady of course."

M'ya quickly spoke, "Thank you, sir, but we must be on our way. We've..."

Hayden interrupted, "We'd be delighted to. Thank you for your hospitality. Please, show us the way.

The man turned to leave, motioning for them to follow.

"Sir," Hayden called, "if it would be no additional bother, I'd like my new friend to attend as well. He stuck his neck out for me today. It's the least I could do."

"Certainly," the man called back without looking over his shoulder. "He's my grandson. He eats with me every night anyway."

The man led them to a small carriage drawn by two horses. It was a simple design, nothing that stood out. Another carriage in front was elaborate, almost appearing to be made from gold. Six horses stood before it, their harnesses made of the finest leather. He opened the door and motioned for the three of them to climb inside. The chubby one clambered in first. The girl followed him and sat on the seat facing him. Hayden entered and sat beside her. The man closed the door and made his way to the carriage in front.

The horses started moving forward with an unexpected jerk. The trio sat in silence. The only sound was the creaking of the leather harnesses, the clomping of the horse's hooves, and the rickety creak of the wagon's wheels across the brick road top.

Finally, Hayden broke the silence. "What's your name, boy?"

"My name is Amarsin."

"And you wear it so well," M'ya sneered.

"I don't understand," Hayden whispered to her.

She leaned close to him. "His name means the brightness of sin. It's common among them to name their children after their lustful and arrogant ways."

"Amarsin," Hayden addressed him. "Pleasure to officially meet you. Can we forget our prior differences and move forward with a new understanding?"

"Sure," he reluctantly agreed.

"M'ya?" Hayden asked.

She rolled her eyes upward, but shook her head. "Anything you ask," she mockingly offered.

Amarsin studied him. "Why are you so different? How have you strayed so far from your customs and heritage?"

Hayden looked at himself for the first time through their eyes. He was wearing blue jeans, brown sandals, and a Superman t-shirt. He was comically out of place in their world of tunics and gowns.

"The pursuit of truth."

"Truth? There is no truth but what we create. It's the Babylonian way to live in pursuit of happiness."

"There can be no happiness outside of truth, Amarsin; there's only the strange wandering toward emotional security. A man may feel better by his choices, but he can't make himself better through them. He is what he is. The nature of a man can't be changed through his own wisdom."

"Truth. To you it's one thing, to her another, and to me another still. How can there be truth, when it has so many variations."

"Because Amarsin, truth wasn't created by man;

therefore, it cannot be defined by man."

"Ah, the gods… You are a believer in the gods. They created the worlds. They control the climates. They make us what we are. They establish truth. You truly believe in them?"

"Him."

"Him? As in one?"

Hayden caught himself. He was instinctively telling them about Christ. The same Christ he'd been at odds with. The same Christ he didn't want to serve any more.

"Just forget about it, Amarsin. Just know that truth isn't relative. It isn't conditional. It's forever established and eternally significant. You can find it if you seek it with all your heart."

He shook his head. "You're a strange man, Hayden, and as I said earlier, you won't last long."

"Why not?"

"Because you stick out. Your clothes are horrific. Your manners are lacking. Your respect for Babylonian culture is wanting. You travel with a slave, and a beautiful one at that. She'd fetch a fair wage on the market, or make a good… uh… servant in the temples. Yes, your days are numbered."

"Help me then, Amarsin. Make us stand out less."

"I could do that I suppose, but then again, what's the fun in that. Besides, your days would still be numbered."

"And why is that?"

"Because you've offended Abaddon Dearth, and despite what my grandfather decrees, he won't leave you alone. Today you survived, but today you were also marked as a dead man."

Chapter Seven

The wagon stopped abruptly, causing Hayden and M'ya to slide forward in their seat. They'd been riding for over an hour. Along the way, the landscape had drastically changed. The almost surreal technology of the inner city had disappeared. Gotham City had been replaced by the dark ages.

The door opened and their host was waiting below. They each climbed from the carriage and made their way behind Marcus. His house was obviously one of the best in this part of the country. Armed guards moved about every few feet around the perimeter of the house. Others were stationed around the entrances to the house itself.

Hayden curiously asked, "Where's the technology of the city?"

Marcus laughed. "You're a strange Babylonian, Sir

Hayden Smith… You should be aware that the rest of the world is far behind the beauty of Babylon's celestial city. We have advancements they aren't privy too, for if we revealed them, they could never comprehend."

Hayden nodded as if he agreed and continued looking around. The house was mortar based. It was interesting, reminiscent of Orient design from centuries ago. Upon entering the room, several men with basins of water approached them. An elderly black man rushed toward Hayden.

"Ya foot, suh."

Hayden watched his host and followed his example. He held his right foot up, allowing the slave to pull his sandal loose. The man then positioned a second, empty basin under Hayden's upheld foot. He poured the warm water over Hayden's foot with one hand and washed it with the other. He repeated the process for the opposite leg. When he was finished, he moved away from Hayden further inside the house.

"Over heh, suh," he said. As Hayden followed him, the vat of water the slave carried slipped from his fingers and crashed to the floor. The water splashed on Hayden's pants leg.

"Imbecile," Amarsin groaned. "You must be punished."

The sick emotion in the slave's eyes struck Hayden. Marcus motioned for one of the guards to carry the slave away. The guard reached him, harshly shoving him toward the doorway.

"Flogging will suffice," Marcus said. "Ten strikes. That should teach him not to humiliate my guests again."

"Wait," Hayden interjected. "It's my fault. I moved too quickly and knocked the water from his hand. He's been nothing but a gracious host thus far. He's brought nothing but honor to your house. To flog him without cause would bring a worse shame."

The man looked sadly into Hayden's eyes. "Thank ya, suh, but I shouldna dropped tha pitcha. I wet you. I must be punished."

Hayden extended his hand toward the man, causing him to recoil quickly, moving away from Hayden, terrified.

"Suh, you mustn't defile yourself by touching me. I'm not worthy to be touched."

Marcus motioned for the guard. "Take him away, and send his daughter to clean up this mess."

He turned his attention toward Hayden. "I understand that you must have been away for a while, but I'd ask you to remember that you're in my home. My home, my rules. Don't usurp my authority again, sir."

Hayden winced. "Sorry, I meant no disrespect."

Marcus stared at him for a moment, then waved his hand in the air, as if swatting off a fly. Then he motioned them all further into his home. There were three rooms inside, each divided by an animal skin flap. The large room had no furniture, other than a small table in the center. The table had been freshly set. In the middle was a large stew pot. Several vegetables had been slowly simmered with succulent meat. Marcus motioned for them to sit around the small table.

He removed a small piece of bread from a pan and tore a chunk of it from the center with his fingers. He then took the bread and dipped it into the stew, allowing it to soak the juices. He dug through the pot with his other hand until he found the best piece of meat. He tore it from the rest and dropped it into the center of the bread.

"To my honored guest. My home is your home while you are here. May no man get to you behind my walls, as I have pledged my place as your safe haven for as long as you remain."

Hayden was about to respond, when Marcus took the bread and meat and moved it toward Hayden's mouth. He instinctively opened, and Marcus pushed the food inside, allowing him to savor the moist bread and soft meat. Hayden curiously looked at the others. They were following the host's example and making a spoon from the bread they'd been provided. They each dipped their hands into the bowl, taking turns removing food. Hayden wasn't sure how to respond. This wasn't what he was accustomed to. He longed for spoons, forks, and knives. This experience was way too primitive. He smiled as he watched M'ya eat. She dipped into the meat like this was her best meal in years. Chances were, it probably was.

. . .

The meal was suddenly interrupted by the agonizing

screams of the elderly black man being beaten. Hayden could hear the whip strike the man's flesh. The hard blow was followed by a loud wail that pierced the evening air. After a few seconds, the wail turned to a whimper, only to be followed by another blow and painful cry. Hayden visibly recoiled as the merciless flogging continued. Each strike caused his jaw line to tighten and his eyes to narrow. Observing the others at the table further sickened him.

To them, this behavior was commonplace. They ate like nothing unordinary was occurring. A man was being brutally assaulted within earshot, and they were able to ignore his anguish. He'd witnessed some rough crimes in his time, but nothing this vile. He'd never heard a man beaten within an inch of his life for the simple mistake of spilling water.

Was the value of human life so insignificant? Was compassion not a necessary virtue? Did affection for fellowman, regardless of race, education, or social status not matter in this world? Where was the decency of human kindness? Where was God in all of this? Where was love?

Finally, the beating stopped. The affliction was over. Hayden was certain the slave had it worse, but having to listen had been torturous enough.

Amarsin crookedly smirked, "I'll bet he won't drop the water again. Stupid nigger."

Hayden cringed. His body shook. He shoved himself away from the small table. It had been a long time since he'd witnessed the sheer ignorance of racial injustice in such an intolerable manner. It was true that racism was still rampant in the world as he'd known it, but it wasn't what it had been.

People like Dr. Martin Luther King Jr., Thurgood Marshall, and Rosa Parks had valiantly fought to bridge the gap of equality for all people. History told the stories of Sojourner Truth, John Brown, Prudence Crandall, Frederick Douglas, Harriet Tubman, Harriet Beecher Stowe, and many others who had brazenly stood against the intimidating issue of inequality.

A man should never be judged by the color of his skin. For that matter, a man shouldn't even be judged for his bloodline. Family is important, but each man must make his own way. Each man makes his own choices and thus pens his own story on the parchment of eternity.

It hadn't been perfect by any means. He wasn't blind to that fact. Just a few weeks ago, his world had been reeling under the scrutiny of the high profile case against George Zimmerman for the murder of Trayvon Martin. He'd been appalled how quickly people had chosen sides. The truth hadn't been given time to reveal itself. Yet, many promoted their version of the truth based on no other logic than racial motivation. The world was full of such cases. Even outside of America, the Jews and Arab Nations were still at war. African villages were still being pummeled from enemies who want to destroy them for no other reason than they've learned to hate. It's become a lifestyle.

No, it wasn't a perfect world, but it wasn't like this.

He'd stood hand in hand with Christian brothers and sisters from many races and prayed for a truthful outcome.

He'd broken bread and fellowshipped with many African-American pastors and their families in days gone by. He'd loved them, and they'd loved him. There'd been no pretenses, no judgment, no hidden agendas. There was something pure about God's love that had penetrated each person's heart to the core. His love had permeated the very essence of their being and transformed them into His likeness.

Racial hatred is learned. It's learned because ignorant people teach it to their children by the way they live and the words they say. The negative stares, the judgmental names, the hurtful connotations, the stereotypes. None of it came from God. He who sits high above the earth looks down on all men equally. Every man stands evenly finite in his infinite presence. Every man is brought low and humbled by the magnificence and grandeur of God. There is no black, white, yellow, red, or any other color in his presence. Man looks at the outward appearance, while God views the integrity of a man's heart. God's love saturates every fiber of one's being, until there's nothing left but the radiance of His presence.

Now, he couldn't imagine how the world had come to this. What had transpired while he'd been sleeping that had divided the people along racial lines greater than ever before? Every bit of the progress made over the last hundred and fifty years had totally vanished within a few days. He'd awakened to the nightmarish reality that the world had reverted back to the animalistic behavior of slavery, with all of its inhumane actions.

Amarsin interrupted his thoughts. "I see you have found displeasure in my grandfather's house yet again, sir. You dishonor him by your contempt."

Hayden looked toward them. Marcus was curiously waiting for his response. He was torn. His father had taught him a long time ago that evil prevails as long as the good fail to respond to its presence. He remembered sitting on his father's knee as a child and hearing him say: *"You have to stand for something in this world, son. If you can't fight for what you believe in, you might as well not be living. That's what sets us apart from the rest of God's creations. We get to believe in something, son, and when we do, we get to pursue it, defend it, and live it with everything we can. Never forget that, son. Evil thrives when we forget what we believe in, when we're too preoccupied to respond, or when we're just too lost to care."*

He wanted to let them know how he felt. He wanted to retaliate, to grab the whip and slam it across Amarsin's back a few times. However, he knew Christ wasn't in that either. He looked at M'ya. Her expression was empty. He was at a loss for words. There was nothing to say. He was trapped. He didn't agree with what was taking place. He couldn't find it in his heart to pretend he understood. To accept their erroneous beliefs would make him feel as though he'd empowered them to continue. He knew there was a difference between acceptance and agreement, but the two seemed only a fraction apart in his mind. This uncivilized hatred just couldn't survive in his heart.

"I don't want to fight with you, Amarsin. I will do nothing to bring dishonor to your family's name. Your house. Your rules."

Marcus smiled with glee. "Again, your wisdom astounds me. You have chosen well."

He paused a moment, thoughtfully contemplating his next move. Finally, he extended his hands toward the second outer room of his home.

"Hayden, and companion, I would like to offer you my home for your lodging place tonight. There are two empty spots here I'd be honored for you to fill. Please rest here with us."

Hayden reluctantly nodded. Keep your friends close and your enemies closer. Right?

"Yes. We'd be honored," he replied, much to M'ya's displeasure

. . .

An hour later they each lay in a row on small blankets across the floor. The others slept peacefully in the cool air of the room. Hayden lay peering at the stars through the open roof.

How had God allowed this to happen? How had he let the world get this bad? Perhaps he'd already come and gone. Maybe this was the only remnant of life left.

However, that conjecture didn't feel right. It didn't seem like the answer. Something else was in play. He wasn't sure what, but gazing into the heavens, he made up his mind; he was going to find out.

Chapter Eight

Hayden awakened with a start. He wasn't sure what had startled him, but something had brought him from a dead sleep. He listened intently into the stillness.

Someone was moving through the house. He carefully rolled over. M'ya was curled in a quilted blanket a few feet away. Amarsin and Marcus were spread out further down, both sleeping soundly. However, something wasn't right. He couldn't place it, but his senses were highly acute.

He gently nudged M'ya. She woke up more easily than he'd imagined. She didn't need prodding. This was a woman accustomed to the cruelty of life. She'd grown used to preparing for the worst. There was no moment too big for her. She was that sort of woman.

He listened intently, frightened to move. He wasn't sure what was lurking beyond the walls. Finally, his curiosity was too great to contain. He stealthily made his way to the outskirts of the room, crawling through the shadows like a snake.

Invisible.

Hidden.

Attentive.

Somewhat cautious.

He made his way from the enclosure and out into the open courtyard. He wasn't sure the hour, but the light of the morning had yet to chase the darkness away. He slinked his way through the dimness, inching toward the voices. He was close enough to hear them talking, but not near enough to understand their words.

He held his breath; nervous they'd perceive his light exhalation. However, the low murmur continued. They were completely unaware of his presence. He knelt beside the large tree in front and inched more closely toward them.

There were two men, both taking every precaution to not arouse the sleeping occupants of the house. He could finally comprehend their words.

"Ya sho my masta don't know whatcha plannin'? He be canny."

"Yes. He won't see it coming until it's too late. By the time he rallies the guards, his house will already be conquered. Trust me… Did you get the relic I requested?"

"Yes, suh. I gots it. But, I don' know what ta think. I feels bad. He always been fair wit' me. I wuz skeered. So, I hid it. I bring it to ya nex' time."

"Has he been fair? Or has he been generous? I'm offering charity beyond what you've ever dreamed."

"How I know you have what you say? What you offa… uh… it be charitable to say tha leas'. However, considerin' tha trouble that culd happ'n, I thank my price should be doubled."

"I'm just a representative. I don't renegotiate contracts. Whatever you agreed on; that's your price. Mr. Dearth doesn't appreciate exploitation or blackmail."

The intimidation in the other man's voice was immediately obvious. "Fraid you misundastood. I not trying ta ex… explo… exploit nobody, suh. Not at all. And nobody tole me I wuz wurkin' fo Mr. Dearth."

The second man interrupted, "I'll be glad to pass along your sincere apology, although I'm sure if you'd carry out your arrangement for half the price, he'd be much more appreciative and less likely to retaliate against your original threat."

"But… I didn't threaten-"

"Of course, if you'd just like me to approach him with the renewed negotiation you offered, I'll be more than happy to do so."

"No. Please. It be on discount. And I get him what he

want. I get it fast… Please. You gotta let em know. I meant no disrespect to Mr. Dearth."

"He'll be glad to hear of your new arrangement. You can expect half payment in two days. The other half will be paid two days after the job is done."

"What 'xactly you doin'?"

"Let's just say it's dangerous for a man's family when he goes against the wishes of Abaddon Dearth. Marcus will be sorry he jockeyed for political power at Mr. Dearth's expense. Then, he has the audacity to host Mr. Dearth's newest enemy. This stranger has topped our most wanted list. We'll have his head before the week is out, and the Shamash clan will be quietly eradicated for pampering him instead of just delivering him to us…

No survivors…

No sons…

No heirs…

Someone of Dearth blood will hold the open position on the high court again. The purity of the gods will once more rest on those sanctioned to lead the realm. Our heritage will again be preserved by those with the right to rule. The infidel's fleeting hold on the Parliament is about to be revoked. The weak will be destroyed. Only the uncorrupted of heart shall be able to lead the Babylonian thrust. We are the past. We are the present. We are the future… After this week, no one will ever question the Dearth name again. Our lineage is preserved."

"And my lineage?"

"A slave has no lineage other than that granted by his master. You serve the Dearth house now. You're with us. You alone may live. All others must die."

"But suh, I got a wife. A child. I can't leave dem ta suffa tha fate of tha Shamash."

"We have room for only one. Your decision."

The man sat in silence. Hayden couldn't believe what he was hearing. How could a man consider abandoning his family in a murderous scandal? The most feared man in Babylon or not, there's no way he'd ever leave someone behind.

Finally the man spoke, "Can't ya make room for my wife an' baby? Please!"

"She can help in the temples-"

"Please… not dat… let her be wit' me. Ya keep yo money. Let tha price for my help be dere ticket ta serve in the sanctuary of your family's blessings."

There was no compassion in his tone. "As I said, she can pay her penance in the temples. There's never a shortage of need for beautiful, young women there. Your son will serve as cupbearer to Xartes Dearth. It has been settled."

"But he's… he's a…"

"A what? You dare blaspheme our name?"

"Sorry. It's only that… he… he-"

"He's a pedophile. Is that what you mean? Wake up slave. So is half of Babylon. It's his penance. Take it or leave it."

"Please reconsider? I'm beggin' ya."

"You have no position from which to beg. You're nothing. Dog's dung on my shoe. You have no voice."

The man's emotions broke, his voice choked on harsh tears. "Please."

"One more word infidel, and the offer will be rescinded. We are taking the Shamash clan with or without you. You can have them marked, and they will live. Mark them not, and they will be trampled into the dust with all those associated with Shamash bloodlines."

Someone stirred inside the house. Both voices grew silent.

"Please, suh. Ya must go. They mustn't find you here."

"If they have our mark, we'll spare them and keep the said arrangements. If we do, they must pay the said price. It's your decision, slave. Three mornings from now. Be ready."

Hayden listened, as the man ran into the darkness. The slave turned and sulked back toward the house. The torchlight illuminated his face as he passed Hayden's hiding spot. Hayden didn't recognize him, but as soon as the sun's rays made it possible to see, he planned on looking. Abaddon Dearth would soon discover that he didn't plan on dying so easily, and there's nothing more frightening than fighting a man who feels he's got nothing to lose.

Chapter Nine

The sun beat brightly down on the tent flaps, heating the inside of the building fifteen degrees within an hour. Every one was awake now, each person embracing the newness of the morning in his or her own way.

Hayden sat alone in the courtyard. He intently studied each slave that walked past. He attentively listened to every voice, hoping to recognize the one from that morning's secret meeting. M'ya walked up and handed him a cup of cool water.

"I drew it fresh from the well."

"Thanks M'ya. I appreciate it."

She looked into his concerned eyes. "Your wardrobe is more proper today. The fat man set you up?"

Hayden tried to conceal his grin. "Yes, he did… You

don't look half bad either. That Babylonian robe is becoming… Much better than the grimy farmer's clothes."

She ignored his compliment. "You figure out who it is yet?"

"Not yet. Been watching since daylight. Two hours and nothing to show for it."

"You gonna talk to Marcus?"

"I don't have a choice. I can't allow his house to be destroyed because of me."

"You trust him?"

"No."

"Then what makes you think he won't take you immediately to Abaddon as a peace offering?"

"I guess there's always that possibility."

He shrugged his shoulders tightly. "I don't know M'ya. I can't just let an entire family be murdered without cause. What kind of man would I be if I allowed that?"

"A smart one… A living one… Don't think for a second that he wouldn't do it to you if the roles were reversed. He'd sell you out in a heartbeat."

Hayden seriously contemplated her words before answering. Finally, he nodded a silent agreement.

"He still might. However, I can't make decisions based on what others might say. I must make choices based on who

I am. My character defines me, not anyone else's."

He sullenly frowned before continuing, "It's as good a reason to die as any I suppose… Or, perhaps you should have more faith in people."

"Faith in people? When these merciless savages have murdered half your family… When you've been offered as a sex slave on some perverted stone altar… When your own father is willing to sacrifice you to save your injured brother… When you have to steal to eat… Then talk to me about where I should place my faith."

He recoiled, "I'm sorry M'ya. I didn't mean to bring back so many painful memories. I just meant-"

"I don't care what you meant. Their word is no good. They are Babylonians. They serve only themselves."

"And me? What of me?"

"I dunno what you are, Hayden, but you're no Babylonian. You may carry the mark. You may share their blood, but you're not of their kind."

They stopped talking because of the heavy footsteps marching toward them. It was obvious that a large group was approaching from around the corner. Hayden readied himself. There were at least six people in the approaching party, and probably as many as ten. Their steps were weighty. The group mainly consisted of men, and they were in a hurry.

Marcus Shamash was the first man around the corner. He immediately pointed toward Hayden.

"Place him under house arrest."

Two guards moved toward him, each grabbing an arm. Two more drew back their bows, pointing them in his direction. If he tried anything, he'd be staring down the pointy end of an arrow.

"Mr. Shamash. You've been a congenial host thus far. What have I done so vile that I'm now to be incarcerated?"

Marcus looked red-faced. "Are you really going to pretend you aren't aware of my reasons?"

"I'm afraid I honestly don't know, sir."

Mr. Shamash's blood raged. He scowled. "One of my slaves saw you snooping around before daylight, and it just so happens that a priceless family heirloom is missing."

"I don't know anything about your missing property. I'd never steal from you."

"My guards are searching your things as we speak. If they find anything on you, I'll-"

"Choose your words carefully, Marcus, for if they don't find your heirloom among my things, I shall make you eat them."

"How dare you speak to me like-"

"What's missing? Perhaps I can help find it."

"A sword. The sword of Tiber."

M'ya groaned. She tugged on his shirt. "We're in trouble

if you took it. Its value is world renowned."

"If? You honestly think I would have stolen it?"

"I trust no one Hayden. The sooner you learn that, the better off we'll be. Anyone is capable of the unthinkable. Therefore, all are capable of far less. It's the way of the world."

Hayden shook his head. "It doesn't have to be."

A guard ran to Mr. Shamash. "Your Honor. We done like ya said. It's not wit' his stuff. He prolly hid it somewheres."

Hayden recognized the voice. His eyes suspiciously narrowed on the slave. He abruptly turned to Marcus.

"Mr. Shamash, I know where you can find your heirloom, but before I give it up, I need some guarantees."

"Babylonian policy is that we don't negotiate with criminals. Ever!"

"Then say goodbye to your artifact, and to your family while you're at it."

"Are you threatening me? You arrogant fool. I should have you tortured. You'll talk."

"Violence. It's always a means to an end with you isn't it? But do I look like a man who'd waver so easily?"

"You're right. You wouldn't. I'd have better luck pulling milk from the teat of a boar… However, I know what will make you talk."

He motioned for two more of his men. "Bring her to the red tent. Have the Tormentors cut out her tongue."

The men seized her.

Hayden interrupted, "Wait, Marcus. Enough of the games. I'll tell you what you need to know, but you must agree to allow us to go free afterward."

"I'll guarantee her safe passage, but if you've stolen from me, I'll have you strung up by the neck until you're dead."

"Tell him what you know," M'ya pleaded, trying to resist them.

"Okay. Okay," he muttered. "I'll tell you."

He looked at the slave who had searched through his things. "Mr. Shamash, if you'll have your guards examine his living quarters, I'm certain you'll find what you're looking for."

Marcus suspiciously sent the two guards away. He didn't expect them to find anything, but he'd learned years ago to investigate thoroughly before making assumptions.

"You better hope you're telling the truth. If you aren't, you and the lady are in serious trouble," he agitatedly said.

The guards came back five minutes later holding a golden case. "It was there, sir. Just like he said."

The slave was afraid. "He... He musta put it dere. I don' know how it-"

Hayden interrupted. "It's not his fault, sir. May I please

have a word in private?"

Marcus motioned for the guards to allow Hayden to step toward him. He walked toward the garden and signaled for Hayden to follow. He turned back to the guards.

"If he tries anything, anything at all, kill him."

"I won't Marcus. If I really wanted to, I would have tried already."

Marcus reluctantly nodded. "How'd you know he had it? He's been one of my most loyal slaves."

"Loyalty isn't given out of fear. It's earned through mutual respect and forged through affliction."

Marcus challenged him, "So you think my slaves would sell me out to the highest bidder?"

"No, but I think whoever they fear most will ultimately control them. If a man pledges his life only because he's afraid you'll take it from him, how is that true allegiance? Give a man a choice, and if he chooses to die serving you instead of betray you for more dangerous men, that's the most honorable fidelity."

Marcus nodded his approval, "You speak well, Hayden, but you still haven't answered my question. How did you know?"

"I was out this morning. Whoever said they saw me was telling the truth. However, my intentions were honorable. I heard someone stealthily walking around the perimeter. I snuck through the courtyard and stood close enough to hear them."

"And what of it? What did you learn?"

"I learned that someone would have your head, sir. You've offended a ruthless man. I also learned that your man is extremely terrified of him."

"Abaddon Dearth," he muttered, more a statement than a question. "I'm aware of Mr. Dearth's recent stance against me. I'm also aware that he's been trying to steal the sword for weeks now. Tell me something I don't know."

"Mr. Dearth also has a price on my head."

Marcus laughed. "Then I should turn you in myself and collect a hero's reward."

"Don't think that didn't cross my mind. I've debated telling you this all morning."

"So, why are you?"

"Because behind your hardened Babylonian exterior, you're an honorable man. It's why the people on the Council immediately looked to you when it was time to choose a new leader. You don't realize it, but your integrity speaks volumes."

Marcus groaned, "Don't tell anyone. I'm afraid my reputation need not be thus known."

"But why? What's wrong with being a virtuous man in the midst of the decline and chaos? Why can't you stand for truth in the midst of violence and hypocrisy?"

"You don't understand. It's not that easy."

"The truth is never easy, Marcus. If it were easy, anybody could live it. It takes someone special to go against the grain of culture and fight the overwhelming tide of human indecency."

"In Babylon, that could get a man killed."

"It could also get a man noticed. I know you have political aspirations. Don't you think people are tired of the mundane? Aren't they sick of following selfish bigots? Wouldn't they rather follow a man who passionately pursues truth and reason? A rebel who has their best interests at heart?"

"Perhaps one day we shall see, but for now, I'm afraid I must remain quiet. I must live to fight another day. Sometimes the only mode of attack is to retreat."

"You don't really believe that do you? Is that one of the Babylonian combat codes, or are you just afraid of facing a man as powerful as Abaddon Dearth?"

"Enough! I'll not be humiliated in my own home."

Hayden hung his head. "I apologize again, sir. I'm afraid I overstepped my boundaries."

Marcus shrugged. "You only speak your heart. In a way, I respect that about you. You've stated your feelings about my integrity. I'm afraid I've misjudged you… That's why I must ask you to do something for me."

"What can I possibly do for you?" He asked, sounding

rather shocked he was being asked.

"I'm aware of Mr. Dearth's plans to destroy my family. I was also aware of your spy charade this morning."

Hayden barely changed expressions, but Marcus chuckled anyway. "I didn't survive this long and rise in the Parliament by being weak and unperceptive. My political ties are far reaching. My pockets are deep. In Babylon, as you know, money and alliances are everything, and I've got both. I've already contacted the king. He's assured me that the Captain of his Host will not move on me personally, nor shall he invade my immediate family. However, if Mr. Dearth were to have a private quarrel with a close family member, for uh… personal reasons… There's nothing the king would do… His men's honor must be defended."

"So you're protected? Your immediate family is safe? But, others close to you are in danger, if they could be somehow accused of offending the Captain?"

"Exactly! Abaddon has been made aware of this by now. He knows he can't touch me. However, he also knows that he would pierce my heart if he harmed my grandson. I'm afraid that Amarsin's actions to save you yesterday could have landed him in quite a predicament… You know he will also be coming after you and the girl."

"So, what would you have me do?"

"I want you to flee for your life. Escape to the Fortress."

"The Fortress?"

Marcus was astounded. "You aren't aware of the Fortress? You're a strange man indeed Mr. Hayden. The Fortress is the substance of legend."

"What is it?"

Marcus removed a large scroll from a hollow cylinder and placed it on a stand. He knocked gardening tools from the top to make more room. He unrolled the scroll. It was a map. He pointed to a spot on the western side.

"We are here!"

Hayden looked closely. It was roughly drawn, but reminded him of the maps he was accustomed to. However, the names were eerily unfamiliar. The earth looked exactly as he remembered, but it was divided into seven sections. Each section was expertly labeled by a slight change in color pattern. Each section was also labeled as a Kingdom or Empire. The names of the continents and separate countries he remembered were absent. There were few distinct cities.

Each kingdom was divided into seven smaller districts, regardless of the enormity of the ground it covered. There was no discernible method to the madness. The kingdoms weren't equally divided. They weren't separated by major landmasses or bodies of water. They varied in size and shape.

Hayden was amazed. He was viewing the world for the first time. His heart beat solidly in his tightening chest. He found it difficult to breath.

There was no United States. Babylon was located where he knew New York City to be. The tower he'd been thrust into for his trial was situated near what he remembered as the Hudson River. The large body of water he'd viewed on his ascent up the stairs had no doubt been the Atlantic Ocean. The tower, although much different than the New York City skyline, stood extremely close to the site of the Empire State Building.

"Marcus, at the risk of sounding uneducated, may I ask a few simple questions concerning what you're showing me?"

"Certainly. Anything. Just make it quick. You must needs be on your journey."

"How have these kingdoms been divided? There appears to be no method."

"There once was. They were divided according to land maps. The ancients divided the land evenly according to the Treaty of Babel. It was divided according to major bodies of water and mountain ranges. However, the peace of that treaty only lasted a few years. Since that time, the kingdoms have been divided according to how well a kingdom can hold its land. The boundaries are continually being redrawn as the kingdoms are constantly at war. The Treaty of Babel had its positives, but creating world peace wasn't one of them. Some argue that it only led to the destruction of what little peace the world was moving toward."

Hayden was afraid, but curious. "What exactly did this treaty do?"

"It unified the nations. The great Babylonian tower was constructed many generations ago. History teaches that the Hebrew God of the earth destroyed the tower because people were getting too close to the heavens. He then confused the world by creating various languages for people to speak. The breakdown in communication led to chaos, and the world was cast into abysmal failure. The purpose of the Treaty of Babel was to reverse that calamity and once again unify the nations."

"So you're telling me that all the people were given one language again? They agreed to that?"

"Yes, all but one of them. The Jews were the only people who resisted the change. They felt it violated the will of their Jehovah. They felt it would lead to worse judgment than the first time. For five generations they were proven wrong. The peace lasted, and each kingdom taught the new language to their children. Today, the world is still unified in discourse, but it's never been more divided in policy."

"That seems absurd. How could the entire world, billions of people be taught one language?"

Marcus scoffed, "Billions? I'm afraid you're mistaken. The world has never housed billions. The population is much much smaller I'm afraid."

Hayden left it alone. He could only ask so many questions without it being obvious that he had no clue what was happening. He looked at the map again. It was straight forward but confusing. The Babylonian Empire wasn't that sizeable. It extended from the east coast and made a section roughly the size of Texas, Louisiana, and Arkansas combined. The rest of what should have been the United States was labeled as the Forsaken Land.

Mexico was labeled as The Dregs. All of Central and South America carried that label as well. The African continent was marked as the Egyptian Empire. Most of Europe was branded as the Roman Empire. The parts of the Soviet Union not under Roman authority were labeled as the Kingdom of the Entitled. Asia was branded simply as the Orient. Australia and Antarctica didn't exist.

Hayden studied the map for a few moments longer. Finally, Marcus interrupted his thoughts.

"Sorry to end to this basic geography lesson, but you've got some ground to cover. You must get a head start. We can't have Abaddon catching you before you get out of the kingdom."

"Where is this fortress of which you speak?"

Marcus moved his finger down a lengthy body of water. Hayden recognized it as the Mississippi River. His finger came to rest on a discolored portion labeled the Fortress. It was around the mouth of the river, near what would have been the port of New Orleans.

"Why should I head there?"

"Because the Fortress is the only safe place you can live. It's the only remaining city of refuge. Once you enter it, he can't touch you. No one can. There's no crime. No violence. It's another of the legacies from the Treaty of Babel. Every kingdom still honors the code. It's a home to vagabonds and rejects. It's a place of second chances."

"So in the city, their past is forgotten?"

"Their past is left at the gates. As long as they're inside the walls, they're free from the damnation of their former lives. Leave the city, and one must embrace the memory of his or her former self. You're only as free as the life you live under the protection of the Fortress."

"And why are you so concerned about my safety?"

"To be quite candid sir, I'm not. As I mentioned before, I'm concerned about my grandson. I want you to take him with you. Once you get him there, you may do as you wish."

"I have no weapons. No protection. I need another man to travel with us."

"I'm afraid I don't have anyone to spare. I need to keep my soldiers here just in case Abaddon Dearth goes completely mad. The more people you have, the slower you'll move."

"I don't want soldiers."

"Whom would you then ask for?"

"What will become of the one who took the sword?"

Marcus was straightforward and stern. "He will be executed. It's the law."

"Spare his life, as a means to help protect your grandson. Make him pledge an oath as Amarsin's protector. You lose nothing. You would only have him killed anyway. Give him a chance to regain what little honor can be earned by a slave."

Marcus seemed in conflict. Reluctantly he agreed. "You

can have your man. Anything else?"

"Yes. The old servant in your house. The one who spoiled my clothes. I would have him as a guide."

"What makes you think he could help you? He's never been more than a mile off the plantation."

"Call it a hunch. Again, he's old… feeble… you lose nothing."

"Done… Those two and no more." He impatiently replied.

"Agreed, under one condition."

"What is that my friend?"

"If they travel with me but their minds are back home, it could be dangerous-"

"No. I'll not release their families to travel with you. They will surely run the first chance they get."

"Not what I'm asking. Assure them that their families will be well cared for in their absence. Reward them for their sacrificial oaths. Give them a reason to fight for you and a cause worth coming back to."

"You're wise beyond your years, Mr. Hayden. It shall be done."

"I still have no weapons," he stated, a hint of sarcasm and suggestion in his tone.

"But you do. I'll give you the Sword of Tiber."

Hayden could tell that he should be impressed, though he wasn't sure why.

"And what's so important about that sword, Mr. Shamash?"

"It was forged in the fires of the gods and carried by none other than Tiber the Conqueror. He was so mighty that he's known as half man and half deity and still worshiped in the shrines of Tiberia only miles from here. He who wields this sword is said to carry the favor of the gods."

Hayden's bitterness was apparent. "There's only one god's favor I need, and He walked out on me a long time ago."

Marcus shrugged, "Still, carry it with honor, and it will save you. You can trust its strength... It's been in my family for centuries. Its value is priceless... Get my grandson to the Fortress, Mr. Hayden, and the Sword of Tiber is yours forever.

Hayden committed the map to memory and turned to face Marcus. "I assure you, I will carry it no different than I would any other, and if needed, I shall not hesitate to use it."

Chapter Ten

Detective Mayes walked to the nurses' station and stood at the first open counter. Two nurses were standing a few feet back, going over notes in a chart. He could barely read the name on the tab. Hayden Smith.

He struggled hard to hear what they were saying, but the words were mostly unintelligible garble. He leaned a little forward, hoping to gain an advantage. However, the extra foot he moved closer did nothing to aid his understanding of their hushed tones.

Finally one of the nurses looked up and noticed him leaning toward them.

"Can I help you, sir? Is there something you need?"

He nervously flashed his badge in their direction. "Detective Torben Mayes. I'm investigating the case concerning Mr. Hayden Smith. Anything you can tell me about his condition?"

The two nurses looked at each other. He cleared his throat, reminding them that he was there, just in case they'd forgotten.

The stronger of the two spoke first. "Dr. Poole will be here in a couple hours. I'd suggest waiting until then for your questions. We aren't allowed to tell anyone anything."

"Nothing? Not even he's in ICU, probably not gonna make it. He's in surgery right now officer, his chances are fifty/fifty. He died an hour ago, sir… You mean seriously, you can't tell me anything?"

She shook her head. "Unless you've got a warrant, we can't release private information. It's against the law. HIPAA violations. You should know that, shouldn't you?"

He fought back the urge to say something he'd regret later. It wasn't worth ruining the rest of his already messed up evening to tell her something that someone should have a long time ago. He smiled and shook his head.

"Has the doc at least decided if he thinks its to be ruled a suicide attempt? Can you at least tell me that? I could use a general direction here."

The elevator across the hall dinged. An elderly gentleman stepped from the elevator and moved rather quickly toward them with an extended hand, approaching just in time to hear the last of the conversation.

"Pardon us; we aren't trying to be complicated. It's been a tough couple of months around here. We're in the midst of an administration change, and the new leadership is taking the red tape and legal ramifications of this hospital to a completely different level… However, I understand that the nature of your work is time sensitive. So, we'll move as quickly as possible."

"Thank you, sir. You are?"

"Oh… sorry. I'm Doctor Harrison Poole. I was the one with Mr. Smith through his surgeries a few hours ago. I'm afraid the prognosis is rather bleak. I honestly don't know if he's going to make it through. We've done all we can. The rest is up to him and his maker."

"So… you're a Christian then?"

"Of course. I wouldn't even have a job if it weren't for the goodness of God. None of us here at St. Francis would."

"What do you mean?" Torben asked, obviously intrigued.

"Well, if God wouldn't have sent his only Son to take away the sins of the world, we wouldn't even have hospitals today. I'm afraid the value of human life was rather low in the Old Testament. There were no medical centers established as places for practicing medicine. Then Christ came, and his message changed the world."

"You mean his message advocating the value of every life?"

"Precisely. His message about loving your fellowman

shook the foundations of an inhumane world. Suddenly, Christians were united in efforts to help the less fortunate and needy. Places of refuge and healing were established."

"The world's first hospitals?"

"Yes, sir. The world's very first hospitals."

"You really believe they wouldn't have been established anyway? I'm a devout Christian myself, Doctor Poole, but don't others criticize your opinion for being too narrow?"

"Narrow? It takes more faith to believe they would have been established. First of all, there was no reason to establish hospitals before Christ. There was little value placed on human life. For example, take the parable of the Good Samaritan. We view that story through modern understanding and are appalled that a priest and Levite could walk past an injured man without helping him. However, in Jesus' day, that would have been common practice."

"I see. Because life meant little, so for the most part, people ignored the suffering of others."

"Pretty much. So when Jesus taught this parable, he was going against the cultural norm. His teaching was pretty revolutionary... The second reason I don't believe we'd have hospitals without Christ is because for thousands of years we didn't. Then Christ came and within decades Christians became unified in efforts to provide both short-term and long-term care to those who needed it. From this, the concept of the modern hospital was birthed."

"I see. It makes sense. It's still just so hard to fathom."

"Not really. Not when you consider that every early hospital around the world began as a direct result of Christian mercy. The buildings were established to care for various degrees of the sick according to Christ's commands to do those very things. They were considered ministry opportunities."

"It makes sense," Torben smiled, "every day I find a new reason to acknowledge God's power and authority in this earth."

"Agreed, detective… Now how can I help you on your case?"

"Would you agree that this was a suicide attempt? Or do you suspect foul play?"

"Everything I've seen suggests this was an apparent suicide attempt. However, I'm no forensic specialist, you can't quote me on that."

"Of course not. Is there anything else you can tell me about the man? Other ailments? Observations?"

"Not really… But again, I'm just a medical doctor. I've no training in forensics. I wouldn't even begin to know what sort of things to look for… Why is the police department so interested in this case? When everything appears to be open and shut."

"Honestly, I don't know. I was given this case by a fluke in the system, but for some reason I can't shake the feeling that it wasn't an accident. I get the feeling there's more to this story than meets the eye."

The doctor eyed him cautiously, as if trying to decide if he should continue with his next statement or not. Finally, he made up his mind.

"That's funny you mention that, detective. I wouldn't normally say this, but I have a feeling you're going to understand. Earlier, in the surgery center, I had that same feeling. Something bigger than me was happening. I wasn't there by accident. This man is important somehow to the overall tapestry of life. I knew it was no accident that I was helping him."

Torben felt the chills run up the small of his back and onto the hairs on his neck. "Honest assessment, doc… Is he gonna pull through?"

"I don't know, detective. I wish I did. All I know is that right now he's in a coma. He's not responding. He's not breathing on his own. There's not much brain activity. Only a fraction enough to justify keeping him alive. I'm afraid if he doesn't get a miracle soon, he's not going to make it."

"I'll keep him in my prayers, as I know you have been. I guess he's truly in the hands of God now."

Chapter Eleven

The horses forced their way through the partially opened gate like a battering ram. The guard hadn't been given enough time to swing the heavy, wooden blockade all the way against the side. He was knocked sprawling to the hard packed ground. He barely cleared the path before he was trampled beneath sixty pounding hooves.

The people looked on from their random locations around the plantation. The warhorses clomped their way to the main house, pulling up in a furious whirl of dust. Three men marched from the interior of the clay home and stood before the horses. One of the men on horseback opened a large scroll and began to read.

"By order of King Sharrukin, ruler of Babylon, and servant of the mighty Baal, I henceforth decree that Amarsin Shamash is an outlaw against the people of Babylon and must be brought before the Parliament immediately. It has also been decreed that Marcus Shamash, newly appointed leader of the Parliament shall be placed under house arrest until the proceedings be completed. His influence at the Parliamentary hearing would be disadvantageous to the fairness of the trial. Now, Amarsin Shamash, show yourself."

He stopped reading and looked up from the scroll. He found who he was looking for.

"Parliamentarian Shamash, have you anything to say concerning your king's decrees?"

Marcus stepped closer to the man with the scroll. As he did, several armed men appeared from around the house. Slaves walked from the fields and stood behind the group of armed cavalrymen. They held axes, sickles, hoes, and other farming tools. The horses naturally shuffled closer together. They were directed into two back-to-back columns, each seven horses deep. The lone man on the end was the one carrying the parchment. He rolled it and clutched it tightly under his left arm. He uncomfortably shifted his gaze from Marcus Shamash to the large faction slowly encircling them.

"Parliamentarian Shamash, you'd dare usurp your kings authority by confronting his men with armed guards?" His words were fiery by design, but his voice didn't convey the same passion. He was obviously rattled.

"May I see your papers, sir? I didn't see the king's seal. I almost believe you're here under another's orders. I wish to confirm your intentions before I disarm my guards."

"I should have you disbarred and crucified for insurrection."

"I've recently spoken with the good King Zarek. He assured my safety. So, unless this decree was written within the past two hours, I can't accept its words. May I please see the written declaration?"

The man appeared more nervous. "I shall not be forced to demonstrate my authority. I shall return with more men, and I shall have your head."

"I really hope it doesn't come to that. Although I'm quite stricken in years, I'm afraid I've grown rather fond of it."

"You would make a mockery of your king's men? You'd scorn his prescribed treatment. I dare you be so brazen."

"On the contrary, sir, I would do no such thing. However, I question the legitimacy of this being the king's command. I saw half these men just yesterday riding under the flag of Abaddon Dearth. I will indeed make sure to speak with my king at first chance I'm granted audience. You can be certain that my grievances against you shall be heard. You can also be assured that I will bear witness concerning your false decree in his name. Whose head do you suppose will be endangered then."

"The Captain of the Host is a powerful man, Parliamentarian Shamash. You'd do well to attempt to move toward his good side."

"I'd do well to remember that my first allegiance is to the sacred oath I swore concerning service to King Zarek. As would you, sir. Long live the King."

"To serve the captain's purpose is to serve the purpose of

the king. You should be so wise as to see the symmetry."

"And you should be so wise as to note the difference. Only one wears the crown. All others only give orders by the sole authority that he has granted them. Don't make the grave mistake of aligning yourself with a weaker man because his pride bloats him to the point of overshadowing the throne. By over-serving a crook, you dishonor the crown."

A horse barged from the center of the half formed lines. A soldier removed his helmet and spat to the earth. There was an audible gasp from the crowd. Marcus uncontrollably widened his eyes.

"Abaddon Dearth. What a surprise!"

"You will address me with respect. I am your captain."

"You must be mistaken, sir. I retired from the military years ago. I'm afraid I'm far too old to be under your command. I'd be no use to you, unless you have an advisory position. I'm sure I could accommodate in that capacity."

Abaddon cursed under his breath. He dismounted his steed and charged toward Marcus in a rage. The loud rustling of the Shamash men stopped him. He glared at them.

"You cannot serve two masters. You'd die for a Shamash dog. The king shall hear of this…"

He turned to Marcus and inched closer toward him. "And you and I shall meet again."

"I truly hope not, Sir Dearth. The pleasure has been all yours, I assure you."

Abaddon grunted and returned to his horse. He climbed into the saddle and swung close to Marcus. Marcus didn't step backward; allowing the horse to almost hit him in the chest. A few more inches, and he would have been knocked to the ground. Abaddon stopped right past him and turned his head.

"I'm gonna save you until the end. But know this, your grandson's head will rot on the end of a spear. I'll have him crucified, along with the Babylonian imposter and nomadic harlot he's traveling with."

Marcus immediately looked to the northwest, before composing himself. "Good luck on your journeys, Captain Dearth. I hope you don't find what you're looking for."

Abaddon smashed his heels into the horse's side and held on tightly while it galloped away. The two lines fell in behind him. Abaddon stopped them over the first hilltop. The man with the parchment rode to the front to meet him. Abaddon circled his horse to approach the other rider side-by-side.

"Mr. Shamash accidentally revealed their path. Their heading to the northwest, probably gonna try to disappear into the forsaken lands. The gypsy girl will probably be able to help them disappear if we allow them to move too far in. I will advance on them at once. They couldn't have gone far since this morning. It's only a little after midday."

The message bearer explored the ground. There appeared to be no hoof prints heading away from the plantation. He looked up.

"If it pleases you, sir, I'll leave you at once, gather more men, and send you the Tracker. He will find them in no time, gypsy traveler or not."

"It pleases me. Find him. Tell him I'll pay him twice what he's worth, and double that when he finds them."

Abaddon watched as the lone horse galloped away. Soon he'd have the Tracker and more soldiers then he could control. They wouldn't make it very far. Somewhere to the northwest, two men and a woman were breathing their last breaths.

As the riders disappeared into the afternoon air, the barn stable was opened and five horses with riders slowly moved out. They stopped in front of Marcus. He extended his hand to the first rider. The rider shook his forearm.

He was wearing light armor, with a shield attached to his saddle. A large sword sat in an ancient leather scabbard. The hilt of the sword glistened like gold in the sweltering sun.

"Take care of him, Hayden. Get him there in one piece."

Hayden nodded, and then glanced toward the two black men behind him. "And what of their families, sir?"

Marcus motioned toward the house. The door opened and two women with several children ran from the room. They embraced their husbands, cried together, and said warm goodbyes. After a minute Hayden interrupted.

"Sorry gentlemen, but it's time to go."

The women cried, tears half of sorrow and half of joy. The wife of the man accused of stealing turned for one final word. "Make us proud... Please do us proud."

As the women were escorted away, Marcus addressed the men. "Your wives and families will be given the utmost respect while you are gone. They have all been moved into the master's slave quarters, where they will remain until your return. If you get my grandson safely to his destination, you will be rewarded greatly. If he fails to make it, you will have earned no respect and your preordained fates will still be carried out. This is your only opportunity to better your families. This comes once in a lifetime. Don't squander the opportunity before you."

The older man nodded a gracious thank you. The younger man held back tears. "We won' let ya down, suh. We won' let ya down."

Hayden nodded. "Thanks, Marcus. I saw what you did. Having them head northwest was brilliant. It will be a day or two before they realize they're chasing their tails to the north. Brilliant strategy glancing in that direction."

Marcus smiled. "Luck, Sir Hayden, and I'm afraid you'll need the good fortune of the gods to complete your journey. Peace be with you."

Hayden tapped his heel to the horse and moved away. After a few minutes he glanced back. The plantation was growing smaller in the distance. M'ya was behind him, riding her mare with grace. Amarsin filled the saddle with an awkward discomfort. The elder man was next in line. He looked born to ride. The younger man rode like a soldier. He had no idea what they were riding in to, but he felt better knowing M'ya and the two men he'd chosen were there, and they each had something to fight for.

Chapter Twelve

Amarsin angrily threw sticks into the fire. They'd decided to build one before the sun faded completely. Thirsty flames glaring through the night's darkness would be too much of a welcome sign to those they'd rather not host. They didn't know if Abaddon's crew had caught wind of their deception yet. They would be heavily pursued soon enough and needed to act like death was chasing them.

Amarsin huffed. "You should fetch my food, slave, if you knew what was good for you. I'm hungry."

The younger black man rolled his eyes in the direction of the elder one.

"You hearing anythang? I ain't heard nuttin'."

The elder casually turned away. He wasn't going to take chances on eliminating the opportunity that had presented itself. He planned on minding his manners, getting the obese brat to the Fortress, and then disappearing into the security of the city. He'd heard that even slaves were accepted there. It could be the new beginning he'd always needed. At sixty-five, he'd already lived a full life, and was well past the age most men made it to.

He wasn't sure why the gods had favored him. Many days he'd thought it was a cruel joke. When the majority of men only lived to be forty, how was it that he'd lived so long and still had such great health? The gods only wanted to spite him, forcing him to endure the humiliation and hardships of slavery a while longer.

He had questions, so many questions. Many slave owners believed the lower class didn't have souls. Because he was a slave, he was granted one temporary life. There was no moving on to the next world. He'd never really believed that were true. It didn't seem to fit. However, not being sure, he planned to hold on to his life as long as possible.

He muttered something under his breath to remind himself as such. Amarsin smugly prodded him.

"What did you say, old slave?"

The elder man turned to face him. "Nothing, suh. I wuz only speakin' to myself. Old habit. I sorry. I didn't mean fo ya ta hear. I be more careful."

The younger black man stepped forward abruptly. "Sorry. You sorry. What you sorry foe? Dat man ain't got no right to make you sorry. You can say what you like."

Amarsin indignantly rose to his feet. "I'll dare you talk to me like that. I'll have your family stoned before the sun goes down. You cannot disrespect the son of Bablonian royalty."

The young man stepped toward him in a fury. "Not if I kill you where you stand."

Hayden lunged between them. He hit the young slave and sent him sprawling into the dirt. He turned and shoved Amarsin, knocking him off balance, causing him to land awkwardly on his backside. He struggled to get up, but couldn't regain his balance.

M'ya laughed, "He kicks like a turtle flipped on its back. The boys too heavy to get up, yet thinks he's a man."

"Enough," Hayden irately yelled. "We have enough of a fight coming. We're going to need every one in this group to get to the Fortress. The battle is out there. Stop making trouble here."

He stared into the eyes of Amarsin. "You fool. These men have sworn an oath to protect you. While they are in this company, they are no longer slaves; they are your guardians. You will treat them as such."

Amarsin was smug. "I'll do no such thing. And you are out of line. You'll be punished severely for this. Before the day is out you'll be dangling from the looped end of a rope."

"Think of what you're saying. We're in the middle of a wasteland. We've got a small army of killers coming for us from behind. You've got little food or water. You're almost a full days ride from home and don't know your way because you've never ventured out this far. You're a spoiled brat who talks too much, and I'm your only chance at staying alive. I have your grandfather's blessings and was given his seal for safe passage in places of Babylonian authority. How do you suppose to get the message to whoever it is you think will do your bidding?"

"Others will hear of your gross negligence and be appalled by your conduct. It's unbecoming of a Babylonian citizen."

"And what is my charge, Amarsin?"

"Insurrection, sir. You are inciting riot. Everyone knows to empower a slave only provokes a passion within to be free. You have opened a door today that I'm afraid cannot be stifled again. To allow them to glimpse the luxury of choice that we enjoy only serves to make them lonesome for more of it. You have created a beast that devours all in its path and stops only when its destructive appetite is well fed."

"Freedom isn't a luxury that should only be allotted to a few, Amarsin. While these men are under my employ, they will be treated with the same respect you'd pay any other man who was willing to lay his life down to protect yours. Do you understand?"

The young slave interrupted. "Of coase he don't, suh. He slow in tha head. Shallow, suh."

Hayden stepped toward him, "And you, sir. You will not speak out of turn again. I will treat you with respect and decency, something you have never been afforded. However, respect isn't owed to you. It's an honor. You must earn it.

Work hard, defend well, prove yourself worthy of freedom's privilege, and I shall do all I can to make sure you keep it."

He stepped closer and placed his hand on the young man's shoulder. "However, if you cross me again, or disrespect Mr. Amarsin, I'll have you brought back to the plantation. You and your family can live the rest of your days as slaves. Only now you'll carry the painful memory of what could have been… I've taken a chance on you. I've risked my Babylonian name on the chance that I thought you would have enough sense to recognize a once in a lifetime opportunity when you were given it. Don't mess this up for you, or your family."

The man held his head low. A tear had formed in his right eye. He brushed it away, causing it to fall to the ground.

Hayden pulled him nearer. "There's no shame in tears. They are the essence of human emotion. Embrace them. They are the silent springs of joy, the melancholy showers of sorrow, and the bitter stings of shame. However, no matter the cause, they are signs of life. As long as you can cry, your soul lives. Don't forget."

Hayden turned his head and looked into his eyes. "What is your name?"

The young man looked surprised. No Babylonian had ever asked his name before. "My name is Darius. Son of Darion of Aksum."

Amarsin whipped his head around. "Aksum? The Kingdom?"

Darius spoke without looking up. "Even slaves have a story."

"All men do," Hayden agreed.

He slowly extended his hand. "Darius of Aksum. I, Hayden Smith of Babylonian heritage, do grant you temporary Babylonian reprieve."

"Reprieve?" Amarsin was incredulous. "That's preposterous. A slave has never been granted reprieve. That's for criminals of Babylonian blood."

"I couldn't sleep last night, Amarsin. I studied your grandfather's law books. You should know the edicts. Reprieve can be temporarily granted to visiting dignitaries. It entitles someone of lessor blood lines to enjoy the same benefits as a Babylonian while on a good will mission from their country."

"I'm well aware of the law, but you know it was never intended to violate Babylonian culture. He isn't on a good will mission. The law was never meant to be a loophole to embrace… uh-"

"Embrace what, Amarsin? People of a different skin color. His father is King of a large Ethiopian province. He has royal blood in his veins. How is he any different because his skin is a darker shade than yours? I fail to understand the difference. If a law isn't strong enough to withstand diversity, it's pretty shallow… weak."

"You'd so easily tread on Babylonian supremacy. There's a marked difference between their unlearned and uncivilized manner and the Babylonian way. The elders will not stand for this."

"They would, Amarsin, if young men like you would see the light. You weren't born with hate inside. You didn't inherit the arrogant cancer growing in your spirit. You learned it. You learned they were different. You learned they were inferior. You can just as easily unlearn it; if you'll choose to."

Amarsin was repulsed. "It's absurd to think we should embrace the Ethiopians as brothers. The only reason we set foot on their putrid ground is to ensnare more of them to bring back as slaves. That's the only value of the Ethiopian provinces. The gods don't even bless their kind."

Hayden cringed. Here was God again. His bitterness precluded him from eagerly defending God, yet his heart knew the truth hadn't changed. He faced Amarsin.

"The one God is no respecter of persons. Perhaps its time you learn His philosophy and leave the weaker gods in their places."

Amarsin was now confused. "One God? You are no Babylonian, Hayden. You spit in the face of our gods to discuss a myth. One day you're gonna reveal your true colors, and I only pray that I'm there to see the wrath of the Babylonian ancients rain down their fury on you. You can't disrespect them and not expect vengeance."

"Let them come. The wrath of your gods can't be more painful than this one's anger."

Darius interrupted. "I'm truly sorry. I'll not let you down, sir. I know you have taken a great risk for me. I pledge my life to you and your cause of getting this windbag to the Fortress. You have my word as an Aksumite."

Hayden smirked, recognizing Darius' sudden dialectical difference. "You speak well, for a slave."

He grinned. "I couldn't exactly demonstrate higher education. I would have been branded an outcast in both worlds. Only my family knows. And you now."

"More family Darius. Family isn't only blood. We're connected. God has made it so."

Amarsin sneered, "Family! A Babylonian rebel and an Aksumite slave! What's next? The older darkie is the son of Anu?"

The elder coldly stared at him. "Anu reigns from the third heaven. He speaks and it becomes reality. If he had chosen it, do you not think he could empower me to rule?"

Amarsin was stymied. To answer yes would go against Babylonian beliefs by acknowledging an outsider could rule in their governmental framework. To answer no would be a direct violation by proclaiming that Anu could not perform whatever directive he desired. There was no right answer.

M'ya had been eagerly listening and erupted with laughter. "Well spoken, slave."

She punched Amarsin in the shoulder. "It appears you were wrong. He isn't the son of Anu. He's the son of Ea."

"Ah," the elder replied. "The Lord of Wisdom."

"Sacrilege," Amarsin wailed. "You will all be devoured. How can you entertain such vile ideas? He has no such power. Our gods alone rule over Babylon. What's wrong with you?"

The elder's lips pursed defiantly. "I'd be ashamed ta serve gods dat was only entitled ta rule in one domain. Give me gods dat can rule the world."

"They can… They… They have that power…" He weakly defended.

"Den why they limited to your kinda peoples? Why can dey not choose me?"

"Because… because it would be unthinkable. You're not even human."

"Wouldn't that furtha prove dere divinity? Choosin' an inhuman being. Wouldn't that solidify your god's supremacy?"

"But… that's outrageous… the gods have nothing to prove. They've always been. They've ruled forever. They don't have to make their case to the likes of you."

"Yet, I'm not tha one doubtin' their divine authority. I say tha gods may chose who dey will. To empower slaves is no more difficult to the gods than to empower a magistrate. It makes no difference. They are omnipotent. Are they not?"

Amarsin was visibly shaken. He huffed away from the fire and sat down on a log at the outskirts of the makeshift camp. Hayden moved closer to Darius.

"Tell me your story, sir. I'd be glad to hear it."

"I'm afraid there's not much to it. Wouldn't be worth hearing."

"You're too modest. You're obviously some sort of prince who has been forced into slavery. You've never tried to escape and even started a family here. Those facts leave lots of questions."

"Not to a man who minds his business."

Hayden nodded. "You're right, Darius. I have over-spoken. Just know… if you ever need a man in whom to confide, time will reveal to you that I can be trusted."

"I'd never trust a pale man."

The elder stepped toward them from where he'd been pretending not to listen.

"You are a fool, Darius, Son of Darion of Aksum."

"And what do you know of foolishness old man?"

"I know that where I'm from a man is judged by his heart. We are all the same in that way. Remove a leopard's skin and underneath he is only muscle and bones."

Darius looked confused, so the old man took it further.

"Remove our superficial coloring, and we are all the same underneath. The gods have made us so. We weren't made for the temporal. We were made for the eternal. The skin fades away and sinks into oblivion. The soul lives forever. You must remove your eyes from the mess of the racist theology you've been taught and learn the truth."

"The truth? You want the truth. The truth is that I wasn't taught hatred. I learned it. The pale men came and took me away from my family. The wife I have today isn't my first. My first wife and my first child were taken from my arms. Their screams were ignored. They were shipped to another part of the world. They wouldn't even let us stay together. My mother was killed trying to defend me. Two of my brothers were murdered for sport, simply because they were not considered fit enough for travel. Instead of just allowing them to live, they executed them. Do I hate? You better believe I hate. It's what keeps me alive."

The elder hung his head. "I feel no pity for you Darius. I feel only sorrow. The world is a cruel place. It isn't fair. Never has been. But to hate all lions because one devours a cub is unfair. To judge entire races because of your few experiences with some isn't just. Some have treated you harshly, but one stands before you now who has done nothing but present opportunity for freedom. You bite the hand that feeds you because you're too filled with rage to recognize a friend when he stands before you."

"Friend?" Darius unbelievingly questioned, "He is Babylonian. Babylonians are incapable of friendship. You've been around them long enough. You've witnessed it first hand. There's no loyalty among them. They betray their own everyday. How much more do they look for opportunity to betray others?"

Hayden moved forward. "Your assessment of Babylonian culture is fair. I'll not argue. However, I will remind you that I have battled the Babylonian way of life on several points. I've been accused of heresy. I'm being hunted down for my beliefs. I've offered you a chance at redemption and been nothing but compassionate considering you were to be killed. I've asked for nothing in return, nor shall I, other than that you not group me in the mass of mad men who live only to belittle those who are not identical to them. There's nothing more dangerous than a man who claims freedom while yet imprisoned by the bigoted misgivings of his own heart."

"But you don't understand. You never could. You haven't lived on my side of the hatred. You've existed safely on your side of the divide. You've never known the bitterness of losing everything merely because your skin is dark. You've never been hunted like an animal because your father is of Ethiopian descent. You could never get it."

"No, Darius. You're right. I can't identify with that pain. However, the world must change. There's no greater time to alter those perceptions than now. The change must begin one dark man and one pale man at a time. Why not us, my friend?"

"The world will never change, sir. You must realize that. It's been this way forever. The misguided notions of the majority will always be against those who are different. It's the way of the white man."

"So, I judge you because you are dark, and I'm wrong for that. You judge me because I'm pale skinned, and you're vindicated because of the atrocities of the past? Darius, don't you understand that if this is true, we're both playing into the hands of those who created this structure? We're both manipulated by a system that neither of us believe in."

Darius considered the question. Hayden took it further. "And what of your children Darius. They've been treated fairly by Parliamentarian Shamash. You could have been living on any number of plantations where the masters would've molested your wife continually and your children sold from you at will. You've been blessed."

Darius was resistant. "Yet, I've still been ruled. I'm not free."

"But you have that chance now. Your sons can be free."

He shook his head. "And for that I'm grateful."

"However, Darius, you must understand my point. Please listen. If we continue down the road we are on, your children will grow up with the stings of your bigotry in their heart, after experiencing none of the atrocities that you have. Why should they develop under that unfairness?"

The elder placed his arm around Darius' shoulder. "He speak tha truth, Darius of Aksum. It be wrong foe him to teach his children hate, but it be just as wrong foe you ta do tha same. Tha world shall be changed as long as great men dream of it. Once doz dreams be acted on, once doz brave voices be heard, tha world will transform."

"I do dream of such a day, but I don't believe it will just magically occur. I think you two are only embracing a fantasy."

"You're correct, Darius, but it won't magically occur. Fantasy don' become reality wit'out blood, sweat, and tears. A few generations must pass befoe tha change can be recognized. But if both sides commit to raising they children a diff'rant way, den ova time tha world view will be altered."

Amarsin laughed from his corner. "My kind could never respect your kind old man. You're not worth the dung left behind by Babylonian cattle."

Hayden interrupted. "Yet, even that dung is used to start the fires 'round a hundred Babylonian campfires. Which is more than I can say for you, Amarsin. You've proven yourself worthless. I'll be glad to reach the Fortress if for nothing else than to be rid of your constant sniveling. How is it that you've become so miserable of a man?"

"My family isn't ignorantly racist. We never have been. It's just our culture. There's nothing wrong with embracing the beauty of one's own upbringing."

Hayden was furious. "There is when one's upbringing devalues another's life solely because of nationality or skin color. You aren't unlearned, Amarsin. You must know that just because prejudice is hidden, that doesn't mean it doesn't exist."

"What are you insinuating?"

"I'm insinuating nothing, Amarsin. I'm stating the facts. Just because someone hides their feelings, that doesn't negate the arrogant thoughts of his own heart. Racism thought and felt is no better than racism practiced. In any form, it doesn't demonstrate the calling of higher purpose.

Amarsin ignored him. Hayden turned back toward the two black men. He removed a knife from his belt and slit open his hand. Blood spilled to the thirsty earth below.

"Darius of Aksum, if you'll accept it, I pledge my brotherhood to you and your family from this day forward. We will become the change we wish to see."

Darius paused, looking back and forth from Hayden to the elder. Finally, he made a slit in his own hand with the blade and extended his arm forward. The two men embraced hands, their blood mingling together.

"My brother," Darius exclaimed. "My brother."

Chapter Thirteen

Abaddon swung his horse alongside the tracker. "It's been three days, why haven't we caught them yet?"

"For starters, sir, you headed the wrong way. They were one full day in the opposite direction before I caught up. That error put them two days ahead. Secondly, someone is very discreetly wiping their tracks. They have someone with them who is skilled in the art of concealing the paths they're taking. I've never encountered an adversary as thorough."

"How much ahead of us do you think they are?"

"Probably two days still. A little more. They're traveling light and fast. We're too many. Slows us down."

"I'll have half of this legion sent home. Will that speed you up some?"

"Should. Yes. We should overtake them in four to five

days. Although you should probably not worry. They're heading straight into the Forbidden City. They won't know they've reached it until its too late. It's not visible at all until the traveler is already standing within its gates. Once there, the traveler is surrounded and encouraged to stay the night. He is wined and dined with the city's elite."

"That doesn't sound too dangerous, tracker. Why should I be concerned this city will get the glory of my kills?"

"Because, things aren't as they appear in the Forbidden City. An ancient shaman rules there. He has encased it with the corruption of darkness. It's a place of lust and temptation. Evil spirits do his bidding. However, they cannot overthrow a vessel of pure heart. Beginning at darkness, every weakness a visitor has will be challenged. If the guest is not a man of honor, the darkness will ravage him until daybreak, when he'll be left as only the shell of the man he was when he entered."

Abaddon swore, "We can't go there. How can we endure such testing?"

"I'd avoid it, but you're in luck. I'm aware of its location, and we will take every precaution to move around its perimeter. However, that will put us behind another day. If they get through unharmed, they will have gained valuable time."

"There's no way they can make it through unscathed. Amarsin will tip the scale in our favor. The gods will have a field day wreaking havoc on his obese arrogance."

"I'm afraid the man behind the mask doesn't attack all

members of the party. He only goes after the leader. It's the law of the spirits. They can't attack the members that are under a solid leader's covering. If their leader is pure of heart, they'll be protected."

"How is it you know so much about this place?"

"I lost my father there. He wasn't pure. He gave in to the temptation of the city and was never heard from again."

"Well, may the city devour them all, and if not, may they find us waiting on the other side."

Chapter Fourteen

The animals nervously whinnied. The small group had
moved through the forest without incident for the past
several hours. However, the tree line had suddenly just
enclosed them. The horses panicked, snorting their
discomfort into the evening air. The atmosphere was charged
with feelings of impending dread.

Suddenly, a large gate appeared around them. It had been
expertly hidden in the velvety greenery of the high trees.
They moved toward the entrance, but it quickly closed. Walls
of vines and ivy rose twenty feet in the air. They were boxed
into an area forty yards long and twenty yards wide. The
small group drew in to each other and formed a semicircle,
each facing a portion of the newly discernible hedge.

M'ya pulled near Hayden, attempting to mask her fear.
"It's a trap. We're boxed in. What shall we do?"

"Hold tight," Hayden anxiously demanded. "Force them to show themselves."

They could hear movement in every direction, but could not perceive the threat.

"Show yourselves," Amarsin screamed into the twilight.

Finally, one section of the forest opened and several archers became visible. Their bows were drawn back, a fury of arrows ready to be unleashed upon command. Another section of the leafy partition fell, revealing fifty swordsmen waiting to advance. Hayden moved his hand to the hilt of the sword at his side. Even as he touched it, he knew there were too many of them.

After several seconds of awkward silence a shrill voice whined. They couldn't tell where it was coming from.

"Who is your leader?"

The voice was decrepit and dark. They were afraid to answer.

The voice shrieked again. "How about you, fat man? You ready to step into the darkness. Time for your true nature to be revealed. If you pass, you and your friends shall live. If you fail, you all fail. The cost is your lives."

Amarsin whimpered, "But… but… I'm not the leader.

"Of course you aren't," Darius groaned. "It takes a murderous voice to make you admit your lack of qualities."

"Well, you certainly talk enough, Darius," Amarsin

quipped. "Why don't you tell them who our leader is?"

Hayden ended the suspense. "I'm the leader," he replied, as he moved toward the swordsmen.

The voice echoed again, "The others will join us later. Tonight, you're our special guest. Welcome to our little city."

A few minutes later, Hayden was asked to dismount his horse and stand before a small group of men and women. As he dismounted, an elderly black gentleman stepped forward.

"Follow me," he sternly stated, as he moved down a long hallway lit by small torches every few feet.

Hayden silently followed. He wanted to ask questions, but his captors were in control. To disrespect them now could mean the lives of those who were depending on him. He had to pass whatever tests they were forcing him to undergo.

The black man stopped abruptly. Hayden stepped into a room and stood beside him. The man motioned for him to take a seat on a chair carved from stone. Hayden sat down. The man stood before him, with only three feet separating them. The man crookedly smiled.

"Do you consider yourself a virtuous man?"

"Maybe at one time. Not anymore. My heart has been blackened by lack of faith. I don't even know if God is real."

"Oh, but you do, Mr. Hayden. If you didn't, I would have destroyed you already."

"What?"

"Deep down, you know He's real. You know He's still in control. You know He still has all the power. If you didn't, I'd have possessed you immediately."

"No disrespect, but I'm afraid I'm confused, sir."

The black man's eyes slanted, his face contorted in an unnatural way. "I'm the ruler of this city."

The black man faded from sight and a pillar of smoke stood before Hayden. It furiously whirled for a few seconds before calming. In its wake it left a flurry of dust that Hayden struggled to see through. As the dust settled, a figure moved toward him through the haze. It was grotesque, unlike anything he'd ever seen. Its eyes glared like brazen coals. Its chest appeared like that of a man, but its legs were awkwardly bent backward at the knees. Hooves appeared where the feet should have been. The face was blank and expressionless, except for the melting eyes that stared back.

"I've come to possess your soul. If you have an opening, I'll find it. You will be mine."

"An opening?"

"You know I cannot just possess any vessel. However, I've conquered all that's not pure of heart. Not one has escaped the grasp of this city. You'll not be the first."

Hayden looked sick. "I'm just a simple man struggling to believe. How is it that you haven't beaten me yet?"

"Your faith is stronger than you want to admit, but I'll

find the chink in your armor. You'll not leave this city alive."

The demonic figure spun around and disappeared into the smoke again. The smoke whirled toward the top of the room with a screech. It almost sounded like an explosion as it blew through the ceiling. No sooner had it disappeared, when Hayden heard movement from his right. A door opened and a beautiful young handmaiden stood before him.

"Come with me, sir. They are waiting for you to start the feast."

Hayden followed her down another long hallway lit by similar torches, as the last one. It opened into a large dining hall. All the townspeople seemed fit into the confines of the building. There was music, laughing, dancing, and food fit for the gods. As Hayden entered the room, the gaiety stopped. A heavyset man moved toward him from the crowd.

"Sir Hayden, one of the greatest of Babylon. Respected, trusted, warrior who carries the sword of Tiber. He's loved by the maidens, respected by the soldiers, feared by the enemy, and afraid of nothing."

The crowd roared its approval. Several men patted him on the back or shook his hand as he made his way further into the room. The girl moved close to him.

"You're a hero, sir. The people have heard of you. They love you."

The heavyset man approached and extended his hand. "We love him indeed. You're a true man's man, and deserving of a champion's welcome. Take whatever you'd like from us tonight. We're at your service. If it's companionship you want, choose any woman here. She's yours. Food, wine, money. Just ask. I'll make sure you have it."

Hayden thoughtfully searched the interior. It was full of the most beautiful women he'd ever seen. The food on the tables looked more delectable than any banquet he'd ever beheld. Gold coins and precious jewels were randomly thrown about. He moved through the room. The crowd continued to throng him. The wine looked intoxicatingly smooth.

"Take what you want, sir. Just eat, drink, have your fill. All we have is yours."

Hayden picked up a cup of the most cool and clear water he'd ever known. He looked from the water and into the man's eyes. He saw the same deep void he'd recognized in the elder black man earlier. He smiled.

"Ah, you have found something you like. Just take it my friend. Rejoice with us, as we are overjoyed by bringing a true Babylonian hero such pleasure. There's no finer water to be swallowed in all the earth. Once it touches your pursed lips, you'll have taste for no other than from the wells of our city."

Hayden stared into his eyes again. He then took the glass and turned it upside down, spilling the water onto the floor.

"I'll not eat, drink, or celebrate in any manner, until my friends are also privileged to be a part of the celebration."

The music stopped, and every townsperson stared at him. It was as if he'd unknowingly offended their pretentious engagements toward him. The heavyset man was wroth.

"You'd dare disrespect the people of this city by wasting their precious water to soak into the soil at your feet."

"Not at all, sir. The soil of this city is more worthy of the water than am I. This is an honorable place, and I'm no honorable man. I'm undeserving of the best you have to offer… Furthermore, my friends are of better reputation than I. They deserve the pleasantries of this city more than I do."

The heavyset man's face began to distort. Hayden moved toward him.

"Who are you?"

"Lasciviousness. Selfishness. You've spoken and chosen well. You've beaten me by your willingness to put the welfare of others before your own needs and desires. But the night isn't over. You'll be devoured soon. I'm still coming for you."

After he'd spoken, the man turned to smoke and blew from the room. The beautiful girl approached Hayden again.

"Let's go, sir. I'm afraid the party is over now. Some of the people are upset with you. It's best we don't stay and take a chance that their anger is unleashed on you."

She moved into another hallway of lights. Hayden followed her to the end. It opened into a small room. Seven people sat at a table facing a small group of others. One man was in a makeshift stockade, unable to free himself. An executioner stood beside him, a double-edged sword in his hand.

The man in the center of the seven made a motion for Hayden and the girl to move further into the room. He was wearing a special robe. The three people to his right were women. The three to his left were men. His garment signified him as the distinguished leader of the group. He waved at them to stop when they were fully inside.

"It's so nice of you to join us here tonight. I'm aware that you've recently spent some time in the midst of a Babylonian courtroom. The death penalty was the verdict the prosecution was seeking, if I recall properly?"

"Yes, sir. They wanted me dead for crimes I didn't commit."

"Do you know how many times I've heard that one before? I truly don't think I've ever convicted a man who was guilty of his crime. Every one is innocent."

"I didn't say I was an innocent man, sir. I said I was innocent of what they charged me with. It was wrong place, wrong time. I don't deny that I can understand their confusion."

"Well, perhaps with your experience in such matters, you can shed some light into this case for us. This man seems to have been caught in the act of killing his neighbor's calf for food. He denies the allegations. The penalty for such transgression is death. If you produce a right ruling in this case, one of your friends will be spared. If you rule incorrectly, one of your friends will die. Choose wisely."

The man in the stockade whimpered. "I swear on my life, I didn't kill the calf. I found it dead. A lion had mauled it. I only butchered it to take the meat before it completely spoiled. This should be no transgression. A worse crime would've been to let the meat waste while my family starved."

"And to what of the witnesses who saw you take the calf while it still lived?"

"There can be no such witnesses-"

"They are credible, sir, and you appear to be a guilty man. You shouldn't live out the hour."

"But I swear to you, I didn't do this. I only wanted to save my starving family. I'll work for the meat I took. I'll repay my neighbor three times over. I'll-"

"The incoherent babblings of a transgressor."

The judge looked toward Hayden. "What do you say, sir? You've seen the panicked expression of the guilty firsthand. Does he not look culpable to you?"

Hayden studied the man, and then calmly looked toward the members of the court. "I find no reason to take a man's life in exchange for a young cow. The value of the one by far out weighs the value of the other."

"But... it is the law. That's something you Babylonians are supposed to fully understand-"

"As we do. I have no trouble understanding law. However, law was established to protect life, not devour it without cause."

"You refuse to judge this man?"

"I cannot judge this man. Nor can anyone here. There's no evidence. The court should have on its back the burden of proof. You can't state for certain that this man has committed the act for which he is in question. With such questions unanswered, I can't sentence a man to death-"

"Even knowing that one of your friends will die if you rule incorrectly, you still have difficulty pronouncing the sentence? It should be an easy decision. The people of our city want him to pay. Why not just give them what they want. The blood of a guilty man for the freedom of a friend."

"If I chose to do so, I would only defile myself. His blood would be on my hands-"

"And if your friends die, their blood shall be on your hands as well."

"No! If they die, their blood is on your hands. We didn't ask for this. You brought us here."

"So this is your final decision? You refuse to convict him, even with credible witnesses?"

"I have seen no such witnesses. I've only heard your statement of their existence-"

"And you'd doubt my integrity?"

"No offense, sir, but if I'm to take a man's life, I should examine the facts myself. I should look into the eyes of the witness, just as certainly as I must look into the face of the accused."

The judge leapt from the table and angrily moved toward him. "How dare you insult me in such an appalling way."

He stared deep into Hayden's eyes. Hayden coolly returned the gaze. Finally the man spun into a whirl of black haziness. He shrieked, as he disappeared from the room.

The man from the stockades looked up at him. "Judgmentalism. You defeated it."

The girl came for him again. "Hurry, they're coming. They aren't happy with you. We have to get out of here."

She ran from the room, urging him to follow. This time, they didn't enter a hallway. She bolted from the door, and they ran into the village. She rounded a corner with him a few steps behind. She pulled up suddenly and pointed to their right. Ten soldiers were moving toward the building they'd just exited. The soldier in the front stopped and turned to face his men.

"Kill them both. Kill him for his atrocities against our city. Kill the girl for helping him run. They both die. We've already murdered her family. Let's not stop there."

The girl immediately put her head down and began to cry.

"Shhh," Hayden held her close. "I'm sorry for your loss, but they're looking to kill us both. We need to get away from here."

She nodded a silent agreement and led him away from the soldiers. They moved stealthily through the city, passing several tent-like structures, until they finally reached one on the outskirts. The girl pulled back the tent flap and held it open as he stepped inside.

"They won't find us here?"

"No. No one knows this place is mine. It's not registered. The law being as such around here, it's advantageous for people to keep places that aren't on the books. You'd be surprised how often we have to hide."

"I'm sorry. It's really not fair to you."

"Sometimes life isn't fair. It hurts. I wish we could all just get what we truly wanted."

"As do I."

She stepped toward the center of the room and lit a single lantern. The firelight danced around the inside of the tent. He was amazed how beautiful she was. It wasn't as if he hadn't noticed before, but this was different. The incandescent firelight shimmered off her skin, causing her to glow with the radiance of an angel. Her skin was smooth and flawless. Her figure was pristine. It had been a long time since he had been with a woman.

He suddenly shook his head. Where were these thoughts coming from? He hardly knew her. She was going through one of the most difficult moments of her life. She didn't need his focus on her sexuality.

She moved close to him. Her hand touched his. Before he knew it, her head was on his chest.

"Please just hold me for a moment. I need to feel safe."

He cautiously and uncomfortably placed his arm around her small shoulders. "It's going to be okay. I won't let anything happen to you."

She pulled her face away from his chest and looked up. She smiled. He wasn't sure if it was meant to be seductive, but there was no denying it sparked something inside of him. She inched closer.

"Do you find me beautiful?"

"Yes. I can't lie. I do find you extremely attractive."

"As I do you. Is there a reason we should not be together tonight?"

He moved away from her. "I don't even know your name. Aren't you uncomfortable with that fact?"

"Not really. I don't have to know your name to enjoy the qualities you possess."

He thought for a moment, trying to clear his head. "It's not smart. Men are looking to murder us. We need to stay alert."

"But I assure you. We are safe here. We have this place completely to ourselves. You can survive the night here with me. Once the sun comes up in the morning, you'll have overcome the test, and you and your friends shall be released. Just enjoy the night. We've got a little time. Alone."

She moved toward him again, and embraced him, once

again burying her face in his chest. Finally, she looked up, staring longingly into his eyes. She pursed her lips and stepped upward on her toes to kiss him. He stumbled backward.

"No! I'm sorry. It isn't right."

"What's not right, Hayden? You're a man. I'm a woman. Why not? Am I not good enough for you? I don't appear so fair as the women of Babylon?"

"It's not you, believe me. You're more beautiful than any of the Babylonian women I've seen. But, I'm sorry."

"It's only one act Hayden. It doesn't mean anything. It's just two adults consoling each other. Two grown, independent people having a good time. What's wrong with that?"

"There's more to it than that. The act you're considering is sacred. It's intended to be more than just a lustful action to fulfill one's carnal desires."

She rubbed her hand across his chest. "So you are resisting me? Can I do nothing to persuade you? No one will find us. We are safe. No one would ever know. It could be our secret."

"I would know. I can't do it. I'm sorry."

He brushed her hand aside and moved away. His back was facing her. He heard a muffled gasp and quickly spun around. Her body was contorted like something had slammed into her from behind. Her head turned sideways, just as she released a terrible scream. As the scream escaped her lips, she spoke to him again. However, the voice wasn't hers. It was sharp and harsh. Its hollow reverberation resounded through the room.

"Your heart belongs to another. Is that true?"

"Yes."

"But wasn't she taken from you? Didn't she slip between your fingers? Isn't her sinful soul now floundering in eternity? How could god have allowed that to happen to you? Aren't you angry with him? This is your chance to get even. Follow your passions, not your heart. Forget his rules."

"What? I don't know-"

The girl groaned loudly. Her body contorted again into a black, filmy mist. As the smoke cleared, Hayden gasped. Someone familiar was standing before him. He couldn't place her, although he had the distinct feeling that he should have been able to.

"Hayden, you should just curse god, and let go. Just let go. You can join me soon. Just slip away from it all."

Tears filled his eyes.

"Hayden, you're still holding on to life. Let it go. Let your friends die here. Just have fun. Do what the girl wants. Then you'll be with me soon."

"I don't understand. Why should I give in to her desires?"

"You have to defy the rules of that world, Hayden. You

have to let them all die. Let them slip away. Quit caring about what happens there. You know it's not real. Let it go."

"I can't. You can't ask me to-"

"Hayden, if you love me, you will do as I ask."

"But God wouldn't want that-"

"God? The same god you're upset with. Are you referring to that god? The one who kills children in their innocence? I can't just forgive and forget. I'm surprised that you've moved on so easily."

"Easily? It's been anything but easy for me-"

"Then let go. Now, Hayden, just let it go."

He shook his head. "I can't. I'm struggling to believe. I'm angry, but I'm not ready to publicly denounce God."

He turned toward her. "I don't know who you are, but you're not who you pretend to be."

"I am. You can see me for yourself. You know I'm real."

"Your vision is as real as ever, but your words aren't. I'll not surrender my will."

The voice shrieked again. The image disappeared. He heard the sound of approaching footsteps outside. The tent flap opened and armed soldiers stepped in. The soldier in charge raised his sword.

"I'm sorry, sir, but my orders are to kill you on sight."

"Do what you must, but I'll not give in to this city's lustful temptations."

The man nodded perceptively. He moved forward and raised his sword into the air. Hayden knelt down in front of him and closed his eyes. This was it. He was going to be executed.

As he sat on his knees, he heard a loud hissing sound overhead. He opened his eyes and looked up. The sun had just started to rise and was warmly pouring into the tent. The hissing sound was the soldier with the sword evaporating in front of him. He was confused. He heard more footsteps, and suddenly Amarsin, M'ya, Darius, and the Elder stood before him. Another man he did not recognize stepped in behind them.

"Hayden of Babylon, you have been granted passage through the Forbidden City. You've been deemed an honorable man. Hatred, lust, pride, envy, greed, selfishness, and judgmentalism could not get you to turn away from your convictions. Because of your heart, you will cross. Your friends may pass as well."

The man exited the tent. No sooner had he moved from the tents barriers then the tent itself completely disappeared. The small group was standing among the tall wall of greenery again. There was no movement this time. Hayden looked forward to the gate that stood before them. An inscription was sealed across its frame. *Only the righteous may exit.*

He touched the door and it miraculously opened in front of them. They stepped through together and the walls of vinery fell away.

"How'd you do it?" Mya asked. "Is your heart so brazenly pure? Even when you doubt your god."

"Not at all… I believed in the purity of others. Their strength helped me across. Their belief and faith is what helped me find courage."

"I don't understand."

"We aren't in this journey alone, M'ya. No one gets out by the power of his or her own strength. The only way to travel through life successfully is with the love and support of others. Sometimes you need something to believe in, even when it's not yourself."

She winked at him. "You're a strange man, Mr. Hayden, but I'm glad to know you. I suspect if what you're saying is true, you're a good man to call a friend."

He put his arm on her shoulder. "And you're a great woman as well."

"Let's get out of here," he called, as he spurred his horse, urging him to gallop away from the invisible city.

Chapter Fifteen

Detective Torben Mayes made his way through the file room. He had already passed three rows of shelves stacked four layers high. He regretted sneaking into the cold case warehouse, but his curiosity wouldn't let him leave it alone. It wouldn't hurt to just browse the contents of the files for just a few moments. No one would ever have to know he'd been in the building. He painstakingly avoided the video cameras in the hallway, making sure to not look up when he was within their view. From above, he looked like most of the younger, slim and fit recruits.

The "warehouse." He internally laughed. It was actually nothing more than a climate controlled storage shed linked to three others just like it. It was an extension about ninety feet from the southeast corner of the police station. It was well protected from outsiders, but easy enough to gain entry for anyone with police access. It hadn't been difficult at all. It was three in the morning. No one was around but the remnants of the night shift. Not long ago, most of them had been called to a house fire on Second Street. For at least thirty minutes, he'd have the building to himself.

He held his flashlight at chest level and inched his way forward. He stopped at the row of boxes that began with the letter *S*. He moved until he found the right box. In big letters he read the names, *Hayden and Laura Smith*.

He grasped the box tightly and removed it from under the weight of the four boxes on top. He quickly carried it to a small table set up to the side of the room. He was surprised how light the box felt compared to the others he'd moved. He agitatedly slammed his fist onto the table as he opened the box and peered inside. The contents comprised of only two folders. Both of them appeared relatively thin.

He opened the first. It was a report concerning the death of the children involved in the accident. The second was the report concerning Laura Smith. She had died from massive internal injuries resulting from the collision.

And where were the other documents? The suspect's vehicle? The notes about the accident? The photos? The investigators' reports? Witnesses' statements? Follow-up details? The incident report of the stolen vehicle involved in the accident? How was the complete chain of evidence from this investigation missing?

If the wreck had left Lauren and the children dead on impact, surely whoever had been driving the other vehicle would have left his DNA at the scene. How had he just walked away? None of it made sense.

He resealed the files in the box and hurriedly placed them exactly as he'd found them in the shelves. He walked to the door and turned back into the room to look one last time. He nonchalantly turned off the lights. He was just about to open the door when he heard voices directly outside. His heart raced.

He lunged behind the first row of boxes just as the door slid open. He saw two shadows bouncing off the wall, as the intruders cautiously moved toward the isle he had just come from.

"Did you leave the door unlocked?"

"No sir. I'm pretty sure I locked up when I left. I've only been gone a few minutes."

"Then why was it open?"

"I don't know… I was in a rush… I must have left it open by mistake… I'm sorry, sir… It won't happen again.

"Well, did you at least get all the pertinent info removed?"

"Yes. I thought this was finished. No one suspected anything. Why'd he go and try to kill himself. If he woulda just lived out his days, we woulda gotten away with it."

"I know. I can't believe he would do a stupid thing like this."

"You destroyed them?"

"The files?"

"Of course… the files. What else could I be referring to? Did you wipe them away permanently?"

"Yes. They've been destroyed. Nothing left. No trace will ever be found."

The other voice was pleased. "Good, because if those files would have been found, it could have jeopardized the entire department."

"Only if the wrong people found out. I made sure that wouldn't happen."

The person speaking opened the box. "As you can see, the only thing left is the actual death certificates. Everything else is gone."

"Good. We don't want any loose ends."

The two figures walked to the door and closed it behind them. Torben heard the deadbolt clink from the other side. He pulled his cell from his pocket and looked at the signal. None.

He was alone in the warehouse having found nothing he'd come for. His inquisitive investigation had only led to more questions. Now, he was only more confused, and whoever had the answers had made sure they were permanently destroyed. This was no way to solve a case.

Chapter Sixteen

It had been six days since they'd left the Forbidden City. It had been three days since they'd found a water source. Hayden tipped his metal canteen into the air. A couple of trickles of hot water fell onto his parched tongue. M'ya pulled the plug from her leather container and offered him a swallow. He shook his head. He'd downed all of his; he wouldn't dare start on hers.

Amarsin groaned, "If we don't find water soon, we're all going to die out here. Is that what the old man wanted. I thought you were supposed to make sure I made it safely into the city. You should have just left me to fend for myself against Abaddon. I would stand a better chance of defeating him in battle than lasting another day in this miserable heat without water."

Darius shook his head and raised his arm as if to slap the chubby cheeks of the man he greatly disliked.

"Perhaps we shall still grant you that opportunity, pig boy. We aren't dead yet."

The elder black man scoured the land around them. "I been noticin' small tracks through tha brush foe tha past couple miles."

"That's just great," Amarsin wailed. "We need water, and the old slave wants to feed us."

Darius frowned. "Since when have you ever not groveled for food, pig boy? Don't pretend to be all high and mighty now. You'd eat your fill if given the chance."

Hayden raised his hand. "Stop it. Both of you. Where there are rodents, there's water. The two aren't likely separated by much."

He looked toward the elder black man. "Do the tracks point you in any general direction?"

"Yes, dey do. But dere's somethin' else, Suh Hayden. We being watched... and followed."

M'ya panicked. "Have they caught up to us then? We knew it was only a matter of time."

He shook his head. "Not yet. It ain't them. But since yestaday murnin' I had dat feeling. Dis murnin' I knew fa sho. Every now and den I think I see somethin' mirage-like in tha distance. Only it's not tha shimmerin' dance of utopia or the fadin' fallacy of water. It's discernibly real. Someone is out dere."

"Dangerous?" she asked. "Are we in trouble?"

"I don't rightly know, but we'll all be out of wata in tha next few hours. This is as good a place to stop as any. Whoever is out dere, we at dey mercy."

"Why?" Amarsin demanded. "There are five of us. We have proven ourselves worthy adversaries of whoever would come."

"Cuz Amarsin, dey don' have ta come. Dat tha point. Dey can merely wait us out, and allow us ta succumb to tha fear of our own delusions."

"Delusions? Who's delusional, old man?"

"We all gonna be if we don' get wata soon."

Hayden approached him. "Do you think our best chance of survival is to wait here and see what transpires? That seems pretty thin."

"What's tha alternative? I suggest we invite tha stranga in. Perhaps he knows where we can find wata. If not, we lost nothin'."

"Are you sure there's only one?"

"No, but one is all I being seen."

Hayden looked toward M'ya and Darius. "Let's gather a few sticks and build a fire. Hopefully the stranger will recognize what we're doing and move in to investigate. Perhaps he'll come close enough that we can call to him."

Something moved in the brush a few feet from where they were standing. Darius quickly removed a bow from his shoulders and laced an arrow, drawing it toward the sound. Hayden had the sword of Tiber half out of its scabbard.

"Or perhaps the stranger is already among you," a tiny voice called from below them.

The leaves from a heavy shrub moved a few feet away and a little man emerged. He was no taller than three-and-a-half feet and had extremely short legs.

"What's this?" Amarsin bellowed. "Has Shu-Alu unleashed one of its imps to imprison us and transport us to the other side?"

Hayden almost laughed at the trembling in his voice. "You think our friend here is a guest from the gathering place of the dead? Amarsin, this man is no more dead than you are."

"I am actually more alive, sir," the small man mocked. "I have not need of water. I have recently had my fill. And yet I know of the water's edge still."

M'ya dismounted her horse and stood before the small man. Even in her smaller stature, she was still easily two feet taller than he was.

"Sir, would you be so kind as to escort my friends and me to this water's edge of which you speak. We're desperately in need."

"I'd be happy too. However, I'm afraid that your kind are not allowed to go there."

Hayden dismounted as well. "Our kind? My friend, we

are all different kinds here. I'm afraid I'm an unsure what you mean."

The small man looked up. "Have you ever even seen someone of my stature?"

Amarsin laughed. "I have. You're a dwarf, a freak of nature. You don't belong among society. It's not decent."

"Yet, here I stand, all four feet of me, all that keeps you from death."

Amarsin dismounted and violently rushed toward him. "That's a tall feat for such a short man. I think I shall beat the answer out of you."

"I wouldn't."

His sharp answer made Amarsin warily pull up. Something wasn't right. The man should have been afraid. Amarsin outweighed him by at least three hundred pounds. The dwarf spoke way too confidently for a man in his position.

Amarsin struggled to speak and it came out barely more audible than a whisper.

"And why not?"

"Because I'm not the stranger here. You are. This area is crawling with my kind. If anything happens to me, finding water will be the least of your concerns."

Hayden stepped forward and shoved Amarsin back toward his horse.

"When are you going to learn that you aren't our spokesman? You have no authority and no right to even open your mouth. Get back on your horse."

"But-"

He kept his voice low, but the authority was undeniable. "Now, Amarsin, I'll not ask you again."

Amarsin reluctantly complied. The little man smiled as he passed.

"Poor horse, he must have a permanent sway in his spinal column."

Darius chuckled, unable to hide his emotion at the humor. Amarsin's face flushed fiery crimson.

"Go head. Mock me. Your day is coming. Imp."

The small man laughed, "But not today big man. Not today."

Hayden stood over him. He knelt down, getting on the man's level. He extended his hand.

"My name is Hayden Smith. I'm of partial Babylonian heritage. Whom do I have the pleasure addressing?"

"Pleasure? T'is no pleasure to speak to me. I do you no honor. However, the Gov'nah wishes to speak to you."

"Me? How does he know me?"

"In just a short time, Mr. Hayden, your legend has birthed. You're a wanted man."

Hayden smiled. "It's not a good thing to be wanted. I'd much prefer the quieter path."

"There's nothing wrong with being wanted, as long as you're okay with the one doing the wanting."

"I guess so. I'd still prefer the more subtle way."

"Subtlety, such a fruitless word. Nothing's ever gained by playing it safe. Risk, now there's the word which offers immense reward."

"Or sure defeat and bankruptcy."

"Ah, a truth. But you can't have the one without risking the other… That is unless of course you're born into it."

Hayden sniggered. "You're right little man. There is no easier path to blessing than by birthright."

"Yet, no more empty feeling than defending prosperity one didn't earn. There's a disease that accompanies inherited wealth. Complacency. Men have a hard time devoting themselves to causes they don't understand. And, they seldom understand causes they didn't create. The never ending cycle of the silver spoon."

"And what do you know of silver spoons?"

The man shook is head. "I know nothing of them. Of that you'd have to speak to my older brother."

"And where might I have this discussion? He lives with you?"

"Ha! Really? You mustn't know the unspoken laws of the

land. His kind, my kind, they don't mingle. He's the golden boy. I'm a disgrace."

"A disgrace? How could you believe such a thing? You're highly intelligent and well spoken."

"I'm an aberration, Mr. Smith. The world wasn't made to stand the likes of me."

"You're of little stature but great intellect. If you're an aberration, doesn't that say a lot toward this world's current state of disgrace?"

"It does. But it's the way of this world. My brother stands six feet tall, as does my father, and his father before him. I came from the womb a wee man."

"So what of it?"

"So now I'm an outcast, living in a land of outcast. I'm a nobody, staying among the nothings, a slight wave in the dreadful ocean of misfits."

Hayden nodded. "You continue to see yourself as such a little man, and that's exactly how you will remain to be perceived."

"And if I change my lowly views to lofty, men will suddenly respect my opinion and ask me to sit at the king's counsels?"

"I would if I were king."

Amarsin could hold it no longer. "All you'd be in my kingdom is the lonely jester. I'd laugh at you everyday, and mock at those stubby, knee-less legs."

The man ignored him. He looked hard into Hayden's eyes.

"Your world would never accept the mindless ramblings of a dwarf. You mock me by assuming I'd not know different."

"No, but they'd accept the wisdom of experience and the pure heart of honest intuition."

The man didn't smile. "If only your beliefs were true. The world would be a warmer place."

He looked to the others. "Make yourselves ready. We're gonna take you to the Gov'nah. He wishes to make your acquaintance."

"We?" M'ya asked, as she quickly looked around.

The woods soon came alive with the quick movements of many other men of the first one's stature. They carried weapons that they appeared more than capable of using.

"Great!" Amarsin started, "We've become prisoners of a platoon of pygmies. We shall forever be remembered in shame."

Two hours later, the small group stood outside a cave dwelling. They could hear the animated talking inside. It was apparent that some of the people who made up this motley band wanted them here, while others felt their presence was a threat. Finally, the small man emerged with a terse expression on his face.

"He wishes to speak to you, Mr. Hayden. Only you."

Hayden followed the man into the cave. He immediately felt the cool air wisp across his neck. It caused chills to spread across his body. He was surprised how quickly the climate changed.

He was led to stand in front of an average sized man sitting on a makeshift throne. The short man motioned to the man on the chair.

"Mr. Smith, this is the Gov'nah. Mr. Gov'nah, this is Mr. Smith, the one we've heard so much about."

The governor sat emotionless. His hollow eyes stared holes through Hayden's face. He seemed to peer into the furthest recesses of Hayden's being. Finally, he spoke.

"What are you afraid of, Mr. Smith? Your journey cannot end until you embrace the reality of who you are. You must resolve the veracity of your imperfections. You must live with the consequences of your most selfish choices."

Hayden staggered backward. "Wh... What do you mean?"

"You were selfish, but you don't have to stay that way. She wouldn't want you to fade into oblivion by egoistically ending your journey. She'd want you to honor her memory by making a mark. Leaving a legacy."

"I'm afraid I don't know what you speak of. I'm not ending my life."

"Not this one, Hayden. But in the other-"

A man came bursting into the room. "Gov'nah! Gov'nah! They're only an hour's journey from our village! There are thirty of them. Riding hard."

The governor blankly stared at Hayden again. "Abaddon Dearth. He's come for you. I'm afraid you bring high risk to my peaceful village. We've lived for years without controversy. Now, you invite trouble into our midst."

"Let us go, sir, and we will be on our way. I assure you, we mean no harm to come to you and your people. We'll leave no sign of our passing."

"It's too late for that, Sir Hayden. If I release you now, you will be swallowed by the dangers of the forest. You must move slowly through its many layers, or you risk being devoured. I can't risk you dying here."

"Why am I of such interest to you?"

"If you die here, you die there."

"What? I don't get it. You aren't making sense. Please. Help me understand."

"You mustn't die in this world, Hayden. If you do-"

The man who had previously entered spoke abruptly again. "Sir, they must leave immediately. The group is quickly closing in. We initially thought an hour. Scouts are telling us that their arrival is imminent."

Hayden looked to the man on the throne. "Please, governor, just let us go. We'll take our chances out there. We don't want to endanger your people."

"No!" The governor emphatically pounded his fist on the side of his chair.

Hayden resisted, "But we aren't safe here, and you aren't safe allowing us to stay."

"No! We'll not be bullied by Babylonian heretics."

The man standing with them appeared concerned. "Then, what shall we do, sir? He's right. If they are caught with us, we are all going to be punished, and they will be killed. No one wins."

The governor motioned, as he turned to walk away. "I have a plan. Quick, follow me."

.   .   .

Abaddon Dearth steadied his horse, and then gallantly trotted him into the center of the dirt path they'd been marching down.

"Hello! We know you are there. Come out. We're not here to harm you."

Nothing stirred.

Abaddon looked toward the tracker. "Are you certain we aren't alone?"

"There is no doubt."

"I'll spill your blood if you make me look like a fool."

"Sir, I'm certain they're out there; I'm not certain they will answer."

"Then find them, and I'll have their blood for not yielding to Babylonian authority."

The tracker dismounted his steed and stepped toward the brush. He knelt down and looked into the dirt.

"They were here. Someone covered their tracks well, but they were here at some point in the past couple of days."

Suddenly, the tracker jumped backward, almost tripping. The men around him drew their swords. The horses anxiously stamped their hooves into the ground. They all looked into the brush to discover what had startled the tracker. A small man walked into their midst.

"You're right. They were here, but now they're gone."

"And just what are you?" Abaddon insisted.

"I'm but a wee man. Only a small problem. A miniscule nuisance. A tiny glitch in human existence. I shall only speak when spoken to, answer your questions, and be on my way."

"Have you been following us?"

"I have indeed. A diminutive dilemma, I insist. My persistence in trailing you was only to ensure the safety of the people under my charge. I meant no disrespect. Pray that none was taken."

"Why did you not answer when I beckoned you?"

"An infinitesimal misunderstanding; perhaps brought on by the minute fear I possess of thee. I have no wish to stand before the great Abaddon Dearth, High Captain of Babylon, in such low regard."

"Next time I speak, you will immediately answer, or you will be feverishly punished."

"I'm truly sorry, Captain Dearth. I planned on being with you more… uh… shortly… I shall make a more concerted effort in the future."

Abaddon angrily shook his head. "Never mind. Where have they gone, wee man?"

"I'm afraid I have slight knowledge of their whereabouts. I only know they traveled somewhere between the four horizons."

Abaddon drew his dagger and lunged toward the man, who immediately threw up his hands.

"I'm sorry, sir. That's my way of saying that I have no idea of their whereabouts. Sorry, but I'm trying to impress you with my vocabulary in hopes you'll let me stay alive."

Abaddon stopped and replaced the knife in its leather pouch. "I'd never be impressed by the likes of an elf. Save the intelligence charade for those of lessor intellect… I demand to meet the one who calls himself your leader."

"Certainly. You may see him, but he shall not be seeing you."

"Enough of the cryptic speech, or I'll have your tongue removed by tongs and replaced with hot coals."

The small man loudly gulped. "I need my tongue, sir,

without it, I'd not have the inclination of enunciation. I shall do whatever I must to protect it."

"Then let's be on our way at once."

The short man motioned for the group to follow. Abaddon led the way. The tracker and ten soldiers followed closely. The others kept their distance, keeping to their prearranged orders in the case events like these transpired.

They passed through an ancient labyrinthine corridor that opened to an elegant outcropping of small buildings. In the center of the buildings was an old cistern. Raggedy buckets were scattered around the cistern's edge, obviously having not been used for a few days.

Abaddon pulled up. "What is that repugnant smell?"

The tracker neared him. "We must keep moving, sir. This place is marked with the stench of death."

"What is this place, wee man?"

"It's the first sector of our home. We call it the First Ward."

"The first ward?" The tracker stamped about uncomfortably. "I thought that was only a place of legend."

"Some legends are birthed in truth, sir. Surely you must know that, being of Babylonian heritage. Or are all Babylonian legacies fictitiously fabricated?"

The tracker replied before Abaddon could become angry. "No. I understand, but if the first ward is what I've heard, why are we here?"

"We're just passing through, sirs. The quicker we walk, the less chance we have of catching the sickness. I pass through all the time and have not been devoured yet."

"Keep walking then, wee man. The odds are greater for us. There are less of you to be caught."

The short man moved forward again. No sooner had he moved than the group heard moaning ahead.

"Unclean. Unclean. Unclean."

The wails unexpectedly erupted from the porch of the largest building. Abaddon turned to view the horrific clamoring. A large group of bandaged men and women were strewn across the building's terrace. It wasn't enough room to hold all of them, so many of the diseased were helplessly crying out from the front yard.

Most of the bandages were filled with the repulsive sight of blood. Many of the bodies behind the bandages were grossly disfigured. Missing fingers, toes, and even entire limbs were a commonality among these discomfited. Abaddon turned away disgustedly.

"The First Ward is a leper colony?"

The small man turned to face him again. "I'm afraid so, sir. We are a wee band of misfits here. Welcome to the home of the world's most rejected souls. Unaccepted by others, we've found solace in the embrace of those who have faced the cruelty that comes with being different."

Abaddon quickly pushed through the opening and entered the second winding hallway.

"You people aren't different! You're castaways. The banished. You're being punished for prior sins from another life."

"I'm sorry I don't have the mental height to share your opinion. One of the few advantages to being vertically challenged."

Abaddon ignored his comment. "I have politely asked to see your leader. Take me through another one of those hellish wards, and I'll have you stripped and wrapped in the spoiled garments of the lowest leper in the lot. You'll be eating their discarded extremities for supper tonight."

The man moved forward again, obviously not excited by the thoughts. After several minutes, Abaddon Dearth and his small group were ushered into a separate cavern. He looked toward the center of the room and found a man occupying a makeshift throne.

"Who are you?" Abaddon demanded.

"I'm Abi-Maras. Governor of this Province."

"Province? You have no province here. You're still under the Babylonian banner, and our great state doesn't recognize a league of the infirmed."

"Sorry you feel that way, Captain Dearth. Yet, here you stand in my cavern, a guest in my province."

"You should be more careful how you address me."

The man coldly stared back into Abaddon's eyes. Abaddon shuddered at the feeling he received, as this man appeared to inflict his very soul. After a few seconds he looked away, consciously breaking eye contact. The man unwaveringly addressed him.

"Why must you look away, sir?"

"I… I don't know."

"Or you do. You passed through the First Ward and it affected you, but do you comprehend why your mind is reeling to the oppression of what you've witnessed?"

"No… I don't know what-"

"It's because you have witnessed first hand the malignity of your own moral character. You too easily identify with the trapped beings in the diseased garments. You wear your arrogant assumptions like they wear their colored robs of identification. Your rancid nature screams at the moral fiber of humanity the way they cry into society. Therein lies the difference between you and them, Captain Dearth. They are sensitive to the wellbeing of others. You, on the other hand, proudly display a façade while willfully commanding others to do your darkest biddings."

Abaddon stumbled forward, but the man on the crude throne continued.

"The only reason you haven't butchered me thus far is because deep down inside, you know the truth hurts. I see more than the average man, Captain Dearth, and your soul has been blackened by deeds too dark to discuss."

"When I've found the traitors and crucified them in the streets, I'll have my men come back and cleanse this colony by burning out every diseased and scum filled edifice we find. Your wards will be reduced to rubble reminiscent of the value of your sickened soul."

The man on the throne shook violently in his chair. His back arched, thrusting his head upward. He appeared to be caught in a grimaced convulsion. Finally, the trembling stopped. His eyes snapped opened revealing nothing but white emptiness. His voice was shrill.

"You have your mother's eyes, Captain Dearth. Has anyone ever told you that?"

Abaddon was obviously shaken. "On… only once, but-"

"That's right, isn't it, Captain Dearth? Only one man dared tell you that, and then you killed him… Why?"

"How… how do you… I don't-"

"I do not have eyes, but I can clearly see. Those blue eyes still haunt you, the last memories of your loving mother, as you took her last breath to prove your loyalty to Baal."

"No. You can't know. You-"

"You can still see them, can't you? When you lay down to sleep, they're still there, haunting your dreams. She trusted you. She loved you. She would have given anything, including her life to protect you. And you took it from her anyway. You stole what she would have freely given."

Abaddon almost ran toward the exit. He stopped and

turned back to face the man on the throne.

"Your days are numbered. No one insults a captain of the hosts and lives out his days. No one."

The tracker stepped toward him. "Be careful, sir. He's a Seer. You shouldn't mess with-"

Abaddon's blade struck the tracker slightly beneath the chin. His head slowly disconnected from his neck and landed with a hard thump on the ground. The man on the throne intensely spoke.

"You should leave now, Captain Dearth. You have spilled blood on sacred ground. He wished only to serve you."

"He served me better with his silence."

"Captain Dearth!"

Abaddon stopped just inside the entry point. He wheeled around again. The Seer's voice was cold but concerned.

"Beware the bronzed warrior near the cobblestone path when the waters flow past the brim. The sands will not run through before you'll face eternity, in the light of a harvest moon."

Abaddon stormed from the room and didn't look back. His faithful entourage followed him. Yet, beneath his visible hardened exterior, for the first time in his life, Abaddon Dearth knew what it was like to be afraid.

Chapter Seventeen

A man in the watchtower excitedly motioned across the long field to a woman in another tower on the opposite side. She tossed a stone, causing it to land beside a man sleeping on the ground next to the ladder below her. He woke up with a start. She enthusiastically gestured, and he immediately picked up the small mirror from its perch at the base of the tower's southern most leg. The sun's reflection beamed off the mirror, sending an invisible ray toward the south.

The short man burst into the cavern. "Gov'nah, we received the signal. Abaddon and his men have crossed the plains. We're safe."

The governor nodded approvingly. "Good. I was most worried how that would play out. I've never seen such evil in all my life. If he does return to our village, he'll do as he says. None of us are safe as long as he lives."

"Then we shall pray to the gods he lives not much longer."

"Yes. But I'm afraid of what I saw… He carries in his soul the darkness of Ba'al."

"Are you certain?"

"I've never seen more clearly."

He motioned for the man to follow him. His guards followed, as he and the small man silently made their way to First Ward. The governor stood by the broken cistern. Five of his guards marched to the porch of the afflicted. Each one picked up a leper and carried him to the well. They were each gently placed before the governor.

"Remove their bandages. Let me look upon them."

The guards carefully worked to remove the bandages, making sure not to let the spoiled linens touch them. The largest man spoke first, as soon as the white cloth fell from his lips.

"Water… please… water… I almost suffocated in there. Do you think it were possible to have left me in those disgraceful robes any longer?"

The governor grimaced. "How gracious you are to extol such gratitude toward us for saving your miserable life."

"Please… just give me to drink. My lips are most parched. I can't stand another moment without the coolness of water touching them."

The governor nodded his head forward, and one of the guards held a bottle to the man's thirsty mouth. He savored its moistness, as he loudly gulped the water until there was none left in the vessel.

A few moments later, all five lepers were sitting before the governor free from their leprous clothing. Hayden turned toward the people he had just been sitting in close proximity to. They were a miserable lot.

However, the moaning had ceased. One of the men stumbled toward them. Hayden looked into his eyes.

"Thank you again, sir, for hiding us among your people. It was a measured risk for sure, but one you didn't have to take. I don't view your graciousness lightly, and we're forever indebted to you for your kindness."

The leper held his head high. "Good luck on your journey, sir. You owe us nothing. The respect you've shown our feeble lot has lifted my spirits. You're certainly a rarity, Sir Hayden Smith."

Hayden frowned. "I wish that were not so. Perhaps that shall change, one person at a time."

"I would that it would be so."

Hayden moved more closely to him. "You're a great leader. How is it that you have kept the spirits of the oppressed so high? Most of them appear on the verge of death. If not, they've certainly resigned themselves to living without the pleasantries of full human capabilities. Do their handicaps bother them?"

"Bother us, of course. We're no different than you. Any man's limitations worry him. However, I've taught them that physical imperfections don't preclude us from the enjoyment of emotional wellbeing. To be sick does not mean we cannot love, and where love exists, the spell of depression is broken. The world must learn to love again."

"Again?"

"Yes, again. This world and everything in it was created in acts of love. It's the essence of every tangible and intangible thing in existence. Every fiber of every being, every filament and thread of humanity; it all originates in the love of its creator."

He stopped talking and sadly looked toward the ground. After a few seconds he looked up again.

"That has changed, Sir Hayden. The world has been influenced by the vile spread of sin's filth. Its consequences have destroyed the very fiber of our existence. Hate, jealousy, envy, pride, selfishness, and the like have replaced the efficiency of love's embrace. The world is saddened and confused only because of love's forced disappearance."

"I think I understand… You're able to keep your people's spirits higher because they understand the power of love's emergence."

He nodded. "We know our time is short. However, we live more in our few years than most live in a lifetime. We are broken, but we aren't mentally anguished. We're poor in finances but not poor in spirit. We're in pain, but we're at peace. We live long, because we live in love."

Hayden smiled, "And may love continue to reign in your hearts and radiate through you into the darkness of the world. May your lights shine as beacons onto the shadowy shorelines of every people around the world."

The governor moved toward them. "I'm sorry, but, Mr. Smith, you should be going. They are moving away from you for now, but you will need every head start you can muster."

The leper nodded again toward Hayden. "Spread what you've seen. I only ask you to remember. Please remember. Love. It's your weapon against the tide of oncoming hate. Bitterness can't thrive in the heart that is drowned in love's incessant tide."

Hayden shook his head in understanding. "I shall never forget, sir. You and your humble lot have been a most surprising inspiration. Thank you."

After he had spoken, the governor led the group of five through many long corridors. Each ended in an opening that revealed separate wards like the first. The Second Ward was an institution for the blind. The governor had remarked how he had come from the second ward to lead the Province. They'd elected him only because he'd been blessed with the gift of vision beyond what the normal eye could see. His insight had helped the impoverished in times of their greatest needs.

The Third Ward was home to amputees of various degrees. Several had lost limbs or had been born without them. The Fourth Ward was a dwelling place for the deaf and mutes. A cruel twist of fate had landed these two groups together. However, Hayden had been astonished by their ingenuity in communication.

The Fifth Ward was the place of fallen heroes. Gladiators, soldiers, and other honorable men who had been maimed beyond repair dwelt there. Of all the Wards, it was the most heartbreaking. These men carried with them the memories of glorious days, but they'd eventually been defeated by someone younger, faster, or a little better trained. In one moment of weakness, they'd been bested, and that defeat had landed them among the dishonorable champions of yesterday.

The Sixth and Final Ward was the place of those who suffered from mental disorders. It was a motley assortment of people of random ages and symptoms. Most of the people there had to be under constant care from volunteers from the previous wards.

As the governor led them out of the last ward, the cavernous dwellings opened to the most beautiful forest they'd ever seen. He handed them each two refilled containers of water.

"This is as far as I can take you. You must cross the forest, but beware its layers. There are many dangers. Many strange peoples use the safety of its seclusion to hide from the powers that be. They are suspicious of everything and will defend themselves at all cost. Treat them kindly and you should make it through. Show yourselves a threat and you'll be devoured."

Hayden was still dumbfounded by what he'd seen.

"Governor, where are the physicians? Who cares for your people?"

The governor sadly shook his head. "We are here for each other. No physicians will venture into the dregs for the likes of us. We're the rejected lot, remember?"

"But how do you live?" He asked, obviously concerned.

"One day at a time. We live until we die, Sir Hayden. It's all we have known."

"But I saw no families here. No wives nursing, children playing, babies cooing. The laughter of adolescence is missing. How can you have joy without the affections of family?"

"We are all family. God has joined us so."

"I don't understand-"

"We care for each other. Love each other. Help each other. Protect each other. It's all we've got."

"How do you continue as a society, if there's no familial interaction? How do you grow with no children? Where's your legacy?"

"We can't have children. It's an impossibility."

"But why? That's absurd."

"Babylonian law."

"The law forbids you to have children," Hayden was shocked.

"The law extends further. It propagates its teaching on us, making it an impossibility."

"But how?"

"The Forced Sterilization Act. All handicapped, whether of mental or physical limitation, shall be made eunuchs, whether voluntarily or involuntarily, by order of the High Court of Babylon."

"That's inhumane. How can your Province continue to exist?"

"We will continue to exist because the world's discarded pour into our Wards faster than we can create space for them, and definitely faster than we are dying. In a couple of years, we'll be looking to expand."

"And there are no humanitarian efforts to aid in this process? Where are the people who line up to help your cause?"

The governor laughed. "Humanitarian efforts? C'mon, Sir Hayden. You must know the cycle of life. The poor get poorer. There is no one. Our kind are easy to forget."

"Then perhaps you should remind them."

"Remind the world what exactly? That just because we have handicaps doesn't mean we aren't human. That just because we have various illnesses, that doesn't mean we're suffering intellectually. Those aren't messages the world is interested in hearing."

"But they are messages the world needs to hear."

"I'd prefer that we just live our days out in peace. You do understand that I hope. Maybe one day someone will come along who will change all this. For now, we choose to exist and die together, and as quietly as possible."

Hayden's expression was obvious. The governor warmly chuckled.

"Don't be so sad. It radiates. I can feel your empathy. However, we don't want the world to feel sorry for us because of our burdens. We want to be respected for what we are, what we have to offer, what we can do. The same as any man."

"I understand, and I do not mourn because of your burdens, Governor. I mourn because of this world's insensitivity. Where is God in this?"

The governor ignored the question. He approached M'ya, walking straight toward her. He stopped only a few feet away.

"My lady, your beauty extends beyond your attractive exterior. Stay close to him. He's a man of honor."

He stepped further in and whispered in her ear. She grinned at his words. He spoke for a few seconds and then separated from her.

"Elder. You are marked. I wish I could tell you differently, but the sun will soon set for the final time. Live well 'til then. Eternity awaits."

Fear streaked across his face. "Can I not turn back the hands of fate? How will it come? What-"

"The reaper comes for us all, old one. We must embrace it with integrity. There is no death, only the changing of worlds. Live in this one like you want to be known in the next."

"But I don't want to die. I'm not ready. I have a family."

"No one is ever truly ready to leave."

"But how?"

"I cannot see the how. I do not know the why. Only that it's time."

He turned toward Darius. "A champion's heart beats within you. Use it for good. It would be easy for you to turn inward and allow the bitterness of your past to control your destiny. You must not."

He moved on before Darius could reply. Amarsin coolly stared back at him, wondering how the man could see so clearly with no eyes. The man shook his head a few times before speaking. Finally, he started.

"Amarsin, son of Shamash, your course has been altered. You've been drowning in the sea of your own arrogance, but this journey will thrust a new light into your soul. You don't want it, but change is coming."

Amarsin felt chills run over him as the man spoke. He'd never felt anything like it before. He wanted to challenge his words or reply with some well thought out wisecrack. However, nothing would come. He couldn't force himself to speak.

The governor tapped him on the shoulder. "It's okay, son. What you feel right now is something deeper than your Babylonian gods. Stay close to, Sir Hayden. He'll introduce you to the true way."

He turned to Hayden. "You aren't here by accident. You have lessons to learn. Learn them well… And Sir Hayden… Whatever you do… Don't let go… You have to hold on… You must hold on…"

Chapter Eighteen

"You have to hold on… You must hold on…"

Beeeeeeeeeeeeeeeeeeeeeeeeeeeeeeepppppp!!!!

The nurse frantically exposed his chest. She glanced at the monitor. It was glowing a deathly green. The once fluctuating line had now fallen flat. The once quiet and broken beep sounds had sharply turned into one monotonous and angry tone. A second nurse rushed into the room. She saw the first nurse with the familiar pads of the defibrillator in her hands.

"Clear!"

He rocked upward as volts of electricity surged through his body. He fell back onto the bed. The green line started to rise again. The steady beat began its relentless routine once more. The first nurse breathed a sigh of relief. This one had been close. Hayden Smith had almost died.

Dr. Harrison Poole barged into the room. "Is he stable?"

"Yes, Dr. Poole. He's stable for now."

The doctor checked his vitals and scribbled a few notes into his chart. He motioned for the nurse.

"Is this flutter in his brain activity real? I've never seen it like this before."

"I don't know, sir. If so, his brain was responsive for only a few seconds. I've been on the floor for the past twenty-five years, and I've never seen this before either."

He leaned in more closely. "God, please keep your hands on Mr. Smith here. He's in desperate need of you. If you don't intervene on his behalf soon, I'm going to be forced to pull the plug on him. I don't want to have to do that. Please, if not for him, for me. I'm not asking for much God, only a miracle."

"What? Did you say something, Doctor Poole?" The nurse asked from the doorway.

"Oh, no. Sorry. Talking to myself."

He started to walk away but stopped abruptly and leaned in again. "You have to fight, Hayden. Life is valuable. You have to fight."

Chapter Nineteen

Detective Torben Mayes knocked on the small wooden door. He got no response, so after a few seconds he banged again. He had just given up and was walking down the steps when he heard an agitated gravelly sound from the other side.

"I'm coming. Hold your horses. I don't move so well as I used to."

He turned back around and waited. The deadbolt clicked. He watched the knob turn, and was smiling as the elderly gentleman stepped halfway out onto the porch. The man pushed his wire-rimmed bifocals down on his nose.

"What are you banging on my door for in the middle of the night? I ought ta have answered with a gun."

"Sir, it's only eight o'clock. The sun just went down."

"I been sleeping a good three hours, son. I ain't as young

as I used to be."

"No, sir. Age is gonna get us all."

"Well it's already having its way with me. I tried fightin' it all those years, but it just kep' creepin' up on me. Finally I just laid down and surrendered. Grew too ole to keep on runnin'."

Torben grinned. "You look good to me, old timer."

"But not as spry as you, young whippersnapper. What can I do ya for?"

Torben reached into his inside jacket pocket and removed his billfold. He flipped it opened like he used to practice a million times. His badge was revealed.

"I'm Detective Torben Mayes. Metro division."

"Homicide detective. Right?"

"Yes, sir. How'd you know?" Torben asked with a surprised look on his face.

"I read the papers. Saw you in there a few times. You usually get whatcha goin' after, accordin' to dem papers."

"I haven't made it in there in a while. How is it that you remember me?"

"Oh. I may be old but my memory still works fine. I ain't suffering from dat Old Heimers disease just yet."

"Alzheimer's?"

"You know the one I mean. But it don't matter because I ain't got it. My memory works just fine. I never forget a face. Ever."

"Good, perhaps you can help me. I'm investigating something that you may have witnessed."

"Oh, no. No. No. I done stayed alive this long because I minded my own business. Ere-body dat comes around knows they can trust me. I ain't heard nuthin'. I ain't seen nuthin'. And I definitely ain't said nuthin'."

"Sir, I could really use your help on this one. I'm investigating an old case. It's been about a year ago."

"I ain't seen no murders take place around here in the past year."

"No. It's not a murder. It was an accident."

"Then why they done sent a homicide detective to my neighborhood."

"Honestly, sir, I'm off the record. No one sent me. They've sort of given up on the case. I'm having a hard time letting it go until I can examine the facts for myself."

"Well, detective, I would ask you to come in, but I'm afraid I really don' have nuthin' to say."

"Please help me. All I've got is the cross streets. All the other evidence has been lost. It happened almost exactly one year ago. It was at the cross streets right there in front of your home."

The man looked like he wanted to talk, but there was something holding him back. Torben put his hand on the elderly man's shoulder.

"What can I do to make you more comfortable, sir? You had to see something. You don't seem like the kind of man who would have ignored that. There would have been a terrible crash. The noise would have probably shaken the walls. Sirens would have engulfed the area within minutes and probably have lasted for at least an hour. Emergency personal would have scoured the streets. Flashing lights would have been bouncing off your walls through the windows."

The man shook his head and attempted to close the door. Detective Mayes stuck his foot into the jam.

"Please, sir. A man's family was killed. Please, help me bring the killer to justice. A man needs closure."

The man stared back, a hollow but firm expression across his face. "Perhaps you won't like what you find, Detective Mayes. Perhaps he won't like what he discovers either."

"What do you mean?"

"Trust me, son. Leave this one alone. It's not something you want to push. Too many people will be hurt."

"Who? The only man I know who would care is lying in the hospital in a coma."

The elderly male looked surprised.

"That's right," Torben continued, "he attempted suicide

last night. I'm hoping the truth will give him a reason to wake up."

"If what I remember from that night is true, and I know for certain that it is, he'd probably be better off just slipping away, son. Sometimes death is better than knowing."

"Knowing what?"

"The truth. Sometimes it's better to just not know."

Torben reached into his pocket again and pulled out a business card with his cell phone number printed on it. The man reluctantly took it. Torben moved more closely to him.

"If you remember anything. Please, anything at all. Please call me."

"Kid, why won't you just let this one go. It's for the best."

"Can't, old-timer. I feel a connection to him. I can't just let it go."

"No connection is worth losing your job. Be careful. There's some don't want the truth out."

"Who?"

"Can't say. Just some."

"Can't? Or won't?"

"Doesn't matter. Just walk away while you can. Please!"

Torben removed his foot from the doorway. "Remember to give me that call, sir. I'm sure you'll be persuaded in the next few days."

"Are you threatening me?" The man agitatedly asked.

"Not at all, sir. I just meant that you seem to be an honest man. Seems you'd want the truth to be heard."

He placed his hand up, thumb to his ear and pinkie to his mouth; the universal sign for *call me*. He didn't turn around to look back, and a couple of seconds later heard the dead bolt reconnect behind him. The finality of its metallic scrap rang true. This case was closed, and for all intents and purposes, it seemed to be locked away forever.

Chapter Twenty

Amarsin sat next to the gently flowing stream. Removing his shoes, he plunged his sore feet into the water. Its coolness seemed to ease the painful throbbing. Even if it were only temporary, it was better than nothing.

He propped himself up against a smooth rock firmly situated along the water's edge and rubbed his eyes, trying to relax from the stress of their journey. His head bobbed a couple of times, and then his heavy eyes closed.

It came to him then. He heard the hard flutter above the treetops. It sounded forceful, and seemed to be circling above him. He looked into the sky but couldn't make out the source due to the thick, leafy canopy overhead. He was afraid, not just because he couldn't locate the origin of the noise, but also because he'd never heard anything that sounded like it. It was brassy, but mellow. Ragged and harsh, yet eerily hushed. It was strong and bold, but cleverly concealed.

Swwwoooosssshhhh! Swwwoooossshhhhh!! Swwwooshh!

He pulled his feet from the water and hurriedly slipped on his shoes. The soreness that had bothered him only moments before didn't seem to matter now. The swelling around his ankles wasn't going to keep him from hastily moving back toward the camp.

He wouldn't consider them his friends. They were a nice enough lot, but they were too different. None of them measured up to him. He was a true Babylonian. Each of them had major weaknesses and unfortunate genetic flaws, but he was pure.

That's why he didn't trust them. It's why he couldn't bring himself to befriend a slave. He couldn't place his life in the hands of a half-breed Babylonian who embraced his role as a liberator of people suppressed by Babylonian injustices. He couldn't make himself care for a thief from the Dregs. As attractive as he found her, she was still a criminal, torn from a band of criminals.

However, friends or not, he only wanted to be standing back among them in this moment. Something was after him. He could feel it. As fast as he ran, he could still hear the harsh sound of fluttering wings behind him.

He was panting as he tried his best to run. He hadn't realized he had wandered so far away. Perhaps they had moved camp and hadn't told him. His heart beat mercilessly, as he tried to keep himself from full-blown panic.

"Hayden! M'ya!" He yelled at the top of his lungs, but no one answered him.

He felt the heat of his pursuer's breath on his neck. He heard the solid gasps of its inhalations over his own labored breathing.

"Slave! Darius! Old man! Help me!"

He slammed into the ground hard, rolling over to find that he'd tripped over a large root jutting from the dirt. He rolled fully onto his back and moved his hands and legs into a fetal position, attempting to block the oncoming attack. It didn't come.

Instead, it loomed over him. A large creature. Dragon-like. It's scaly back was easily five feet, pushing his total height to eight feet tall. The gaze of its steely eyes burned his skin. Its putrid breath repulsed him in every way. It was practically impossible to keep his stomach contents down. He gagged, partly from fear, but mostly from revulsion. He tried to crawl backward, but his weight kept him from moving.

The beast stepped forward on all fours until its first two legs were pinned against the side of his chest.

"M'ya! Darius! Hayden! Somebody! Please! I don't want to die."

The dragon's lips slightly parted. A gelatinous, bile-like secretion oozed down onto his shirt. The clear liquid created a trail of thin smoke, as it burned a hole through his shirt and started smoldering into his skin. He screamed through the pain, attempting to move his arms to put out the flames that were erupting.

The dragon looked upward. Its body shook, as a horrible sound erupted from its jowls. It was almost as if it were laughing at him. As it convulsed harder, a flame spewed from its mouth into the sky, illuminating the darkened area engulfing them.

He hadn't even noticed before this moment. It had been a beautiful and crisp sunny day. However, the creature had brought with it the façade of darkness. Amarsin recognized now how shadowy the world appeared around him.

Peripherally, he saw a sudden movement. He turned his head in that direction, struggling to focus through the blinding pain. A man was watching him. How could someone just stand there and watch? There was nothing more vile than watching a brother in a struggle and doing nothing to aid him.

What was more, the man carried the swagger of a Babylonian elitist. Amarsin was appalled. There was no doubt he was a Babylonian. Whoever this man was should know the creed. One of Babylonian blood would never allow the blood of another Babylonian to be spilled without just cause.

It was the way of things. One Babylonian could very well kill another, and all was right with the world. However, there was something different about an outsider doing it. To be killed by someone of lessor heritage was a disgrace. There was a special place in the afterlife reserved for those who had fallen to swords of weaker men.

That's why Amarsin couldn't understand. This man should be punished. He should be banished. It shouldn't be stood for. Why was he just sitting there?

The creature lowered its head toward Amarsin, gasping in air to take one final breath and ignite the atmosphere with its sulfuric spray. Amarsin screamed.

"Please, stranger! You have to help me! I don't want to die. I can't! Please!"

The stranger stood. He looked vaguely familiar. He walked nearer and stood over him. The dragon seemed not to notice. If it did, it didn't care. Through the tears in his eyes, Amarsin gasped at who was coming into view. His heart thumped wildly in his chest. He was staring into an image of himself.

"How? Who? Who… who are you?" His cries were short and loud, filled with fear and confusion.

The image only stared at him. Empty. Hollow. Soulless. Compassionless.

Finally, the image shook his head in disgust and slowly walked away. The dragon breathed in one final gulp of air, and spewed its blistering venom onto his face. The flames enveloped him, lapping at his flesh. He contorted in a painful death dance.

He could hear someone screaming through the haziness. "Amarsin, where are you? Amarsin, what's wrong? Amarsin!"

The voice. It was Hayden. Something touched him. It

violently shook him. He opened his eyes. Hayden stood over him, with a look of utter worry written over his face. M'ya appeared only a few feet behind them. Her concern was evident too.

He still felt the burning sensation on his chest. His breathing was heavy, but the fire on his clothing was gone. His shirt wasn't ripped or scorched like he remembered. He collected his thoughts, took another look around, and realized that it had all been a dream. His feet were still dangling in the lazily flowing river.

.   .   .

A few miles outside the forest, Abaddon Dearth sat cross-legged in an undisclosed tent. The clandestine meeting he'd arranged was only between he and the person currently before him. His private guard detail had been dispatched for the evening. He planned on meeting back up with them later. This was important business, and he preferred that no one know of his meetings with this sort of woman.

Her clothing was loose fitting, dangling from her body. She was young, and he supposed would have been pretty, except for the scars that marred her. She'd had one too many brushes with evil he assumed.

She was a woman of ill repute, but she was no prostitute. It was rumored that she once had served around the altars of Baal, but that had been years before. She'd since become the apprentice of Baal's highest priestess. The priestess had recently died mysteriously. Her body was recovered burned beyond recognition. This woman had been her only student;

so naturally, she'd been thrust into the glamorous position with ease.

She sat before him, poking a small stick in the midst of the large fire that burned in the center of the room. She removed a few ashes and made a symbol on her forehead. She then reached into a bag and removed a large snake, wrapping it around her neck. It slithered around her upper body, its tongue pursing back and forth in sickeningly rapid motions. Abaddon tried not to be noticeable, but he passionately hated snakes.

She opened a large box to the side, and pulled a cat from the vessel. The cat was large, no doubt wild. It's blood was hard to come by, and extremely expensive. The animal was alive, but it was docile. No doubt a potion from the apothecary had been given earlier, rendering the large animal harmless.

She placed the cat on a bulky stone situated near the fire. She then removed a curvy dagger from a scabbard on her side and buried it deep into the animal's fur. The cat didn't move, it only moaned, too hypnotized by the drug to respond.

She arched the knife upward, its sharp edge peeling through the animals skin. She reached inside and violently removed the heart. She watched it beat in her hands for a few seconds, before casually tossing it into the fire. The fire blazed brightly for a few seconds, and then returned to its normal glow.

She removed a small bowl and placed it under the

animal's chest cavity, catching the blood that was vigorously pooling there. After only a few seconds, the bowl was almost full. She removed it from the spilling blood and sat it down beside Abaddon. She picked the cat up and tossed the remainder of its body into the flames.

She picked up small bones from the corner of a small table and dropped them into the bowl. The snake straightened suddenly, tightening like a noose around her neck. She gasped, and then lightly brushed its back with her two-inch long black fingernail. It loosened its hold and continued its playful journey around her shoulders. She picked it up and grasped it tightly behind its head. It flashed its fangs at her, angry to be interrupted.

She removed a metal spoon-like instrument from the table and placed it under the serpent's fangs. As she pressed upward with delicate force, venom sprayed into the spoon. After she'd gotten the proper amount, she tossed the snake onto the floor in Abaddon's direction. It struck at him as it landed, barely missing his lower leg. Abaddon cursed and almost drew his sword. The serpent slithered away, blithely contorting its body through a small crack in the tent's hard floor.

Abaddon turned back toward her, his sword still half drawn.

"Make another disrespectful gesture like that again, and I'll forget whatever gods you might have on your side, girl."

She snorted, a soft breathy expulsion that wanted to resemble a laugh but didn't quite get there. He shook his head in disgust. This wasn't a game.

She ran her two-inch nail into the cup of blood. After stirring it, she poured the venom into the mixture as well. She stirred it again, and began an evil incantation. The bones rocked back and forth and rose to the top. A transparent image started to emerge from them. It rose from the bowl like a crimson bubble into the air. Abaddon stared hard into it. After a few moments the image became clearer. He could easily discern the face of Amarsin.

She smiled. "You said you wanted me to deal with him first."

"Yes! Deal with him!"

"Why may I ask, do you distract the bowels of Baal for such piggish filth? Is this hog so strong that you cannot overcome him without the fury of the gods?"

"I would destroy him if given the chance. However, those he travels with have thus avoided me. I want to find them. I want to kill them all. I know he travels to the Fortress. I must stop them from getting there."

"I sense an anger here. Hostility. He's not the one you really seek."

She stared at the bones in her bowl again. "You are searching for vengeance on another."

She stirred it again, by shaking the bloody contents around. "Ah, I see it now."

She grimaced, and then suddenly threw her arms into the

air as if holding something away from her.

"How could you involve me in this? This man is good. He will kill you. He will kill us all."

"I'm not here for a reading, you mindless, crazy witch. I'm here to get what I asked you for. That's why I paid you."

She reached into her money purse and took seven coins back from the bag. She tossed the coins at his feet.

"This is twice what you gave me. Take it and leave. Get out at once."

"What has got you so terrified, girl? You're the priestess of Baal. Nothing should rattle you."

"I see one coming. He will change all of this. He comes from the other side of the watery divide. Birthed in modest atmosphere. A radiant ambiance illuminates the darkened sky. Shepherds kneel. Kings tremble. And the world. The whole world changes at his first feeble cry."

You don't make sense, witch! Your ramblings are more babble than fearful. What do you think you see?"

"I don't think, captain. It's real. Time is broken. Laws rewritten. Battles fought. Humanity righted. Compassion reborn. Darkness obliterated. And… and the crooked places made straight."

"Woman… stop… your mutterings are-"

"Sin's supremacy unraveled. Judgment swallowed under a new order… grace… forgiveness."

"Stop it. You've gone mad. You're talking about an entirely different sort of chaos like that the world has never witnessed."

"It's coming. I see it. He will change the world."

"How? One man can't-"

"By challenging the darkness, disproving myths and legends of other gods by the power and authority he possesses, by turning time on its axis, by healing the affirmed, by casting spirits from vessels they've inhabited for years, by breaking the hold that evil has on the world, by giving men a choice to choose good again."

"One man can't do all that. It's impossible. And certainly not the man I'm after. He's wise that one, but he's not that important. Perhaps I should stop my search of revenge and seek this man of whom you speak. He'd be a most valuable asset, an honorable ally."

"He'll not forge alliances here. He's not of us… not earthly… He's establishing kingdoms and thrones of another world."

"You're out of your mind. The lunacy of which you speak is too foolish to be repeated. A man who builds here for things in another world; absurd."

Abaddon laughed. "And all of Babylon shall be overthrown by the charlatan actions of one man. That would be the day."

"Babylon will crumble. As will Rome. And the other

great Kingdoms already established. He'll amass a humble following that will possess such power the entire world will be influenced. Cultures will change. Civilizations will flourish. The great kingdoms will rise and fall, but this man's teachings will inspire a multicultural army that will endure forever."

"Babylon is no temporary fixture, witch."

"Dust. It turns to rubble. Your fathers built for the natural. They established legacies to span into the future. Their children and their children's children. The one coming will build for eternity. His empire shall never fail."

"How can I stop him?"

"You can't!"

"Destiny can be re-written. How can I stop it from occurring? There must be a way. Tell me and I will get it done."

"I see no way!"

She frantically swished the blood in the bowl harder in every direction, staring into it again.

"There is no way, but the one you seek carries an undeniable mark. The one who is coming has touched him. I don't know how. I cannot see it clearly. But perhaps if you can get him, you can force him to tell you everything. Perhaps he will know a way."

"Then I will keep him alive long enough to get what you need. We will seek the gods and make sure to destroy the seed of whatever this man is of which you speak."

"What's the fat man's role in this game you play?"

"They are moving south to make sure the fat man gets safely to the Fortress. He's the reason for their journey. If we eliminate him, the others will scatter, leaving each one of them vulnerable."

"I see. Strike the heart and the beast will fall."

Abaddon smiled. "Exactly… now pack a bag. You're coming with me. We've got to move quickly to stop the hands of fate."

Her eyes narrowed and her lips slightly parted. "I'll do my part Captain Abaddon Dearth, I'll soon kill the piglet."

She spilled the rest of the blood into the fire and burst the bubble with his appearance on it. As it burst, she screamed in another language, a language that sent chills down Abaddon's back. She turned and narrowed her eyes in his direction.

"It's set in motion. He'll be dead before the sun falls today. I'll travel with you to finish this, but you must know from the beginning, you don't own me."

"Agreed. We're two people working together for the same cause. Preservation of Babylonian heritage."

"You preserve your heritage all you'd like. I'm protecting something far more priceless."

"What's that, dark princess?"

"Death."

He shuttered. "Death?"

"Yes. It's the final realm. The reaper must come to us all."

"But why does it need protecting."

"Because the one coming plans on defeating it."

"Defeating death? That's preposterous."

"He plans to ensnare sin, capturing the very weapon of the underworld to use men's fleshly desires against them… He plans to take the victory of the grave… and to forever repeal the sting of death."

.   .   .

Amarsin groaned. He felt sick. Hayden tried to help him sit up, but Amarsin shoved him away.

"I can't. The earth is still spinning. I'm afraid I'll pass out."

"You need to sit up, Amarsin. We need to check you out. What happened?"

"I don't know. Everything was fine, and then I just got attacked by a dragon…"

"A dragon?" M'ya shuttered. "I thought those were only the things of legend, stories parent's told 'round campfires to keep the children close."

Hayden shook his head. "You're obviously hallucinating Amarsin. Did you eat anything strange that you thought was edible? Did something bite you perhaps?"

"No! And no! I'm telling you, I was sitting with my feet in the water, and just passed out. I must have been dreaming."

"That was some dream man. We were two hundred yards away, and you sounded like you were right on top of us. You should consider staying closer."

"I'm sorry. I didn't realize I'd walked so far. I just heard the water flowing and thought it would relax me. I'll be more careful."

Neither of them saw the snake slithering among the rocks. Its tongue flicked, hitting the large rock Amarsin had leaned against earlier. It inched forward. Finally, it coiled, its tail rocking in a manner indicating aggression. It sprang forward, shooting past Hayden and sinking its fangs into Amarsin's thigh.

Amarsin screamed, "Get it off. Get it off."

Hayden grabbed it by the tail and attempted to fling it among the rocks on the creek bed. However, it had latched on and wouldn't let go. Hayden's pull only caused a slight tear in Amarsin's skin, but it did nothing toward removing the viper's venomous strike.

"It burns. Please… get it off."

M'ya flicked her knife against the serpent's scaly flesh, right under the head. The body landed among the rocks and thrashed violently on their hard surfaces. She placed her dagger under the snake's mouth and pried upward with the blade, eventually forcing the fangs from Amarsin's skin. The two holes left behind were deep. Amarsin's skin was already turning dark blue and black around the wounds. His thigh had swollen to twice its normal size.

The two black men had been standing on the side observing what had taken place. The elder ran toward them now.

"Quick. We have to try and get the poison out. If we don't get some out now, he's going to die. That's the massasauga. There's no cure against its venom."

He made a slit in Amarsin's thigh with the blade and placed his mouth over the area. Amarsin passed out. The elder man sucked against Amarsin's skin with all his might, and then turned and spat the drainage from his mouth. He then frantically put his mouth back to the wound and sucked again. After a couple of minutes, he stopped and lay down next to Amarsin, exhausted. M'ya took a pouch of water from her shoulder.

"Here. Wash your mouth out. You don't need the venom staying around and getting in your system."

He took the water and swished it around in his mouth several times before spitting it onto the ground. He took another large swig and followed the same procedure. Finally, he took the container and walked down to the water's edge and refilled it. He walked back to M'ya and handed it to her. She smiled up at him.

"You're welcome… As much reason as you have to hate him, you might have just saved his life. Thank you!"

He smirked at her, "No man deserves to die by snake bite. Not even that of lowly pig boy."

They both laughed. Hayden moved toward them.

"We need to get him somewhere to rest, perhaps find him help. Surely the people indigenous to this area would know how to care for a common snake bite."

He motioned for Darius to come toward him. Darius came and stood. Hayden brushed his shoulder.

"You alright, man?"

Darius shrugged. "I'm alright. Just don't like snakes. That's all."

"Nor do I." Hayden looked at the wooded area surrounding them. "Does anyone know how to build something to drag behind the horses? We can carry him that way until we find help."

"I'll do it," Darius replied. "It'll only take about an hour. I used to be quite skilled with building things."

.   .   .

None of them were convinced that Amarsin would live much longer. His leg was continuing to swell. He was starting to sweat profusely. He occasionally mumbled incoherent words in his sleep, and his body involuntarily convulsed from the poison running through his system.

Darius had been trying to gather supplies to build something sturdy enough to carry Amarsin over rough terrain. It had been three hours, and he'd still had no luck.

M'ya moved more closely to Hayden. "We don't see too many of those snakes this far north. I don't understand how it was here, and why we didn't see it among the rocks."

"I don't know, M'ya, but if he dies, we're all as good as dead. Marcus Shamash seems to be a fair man, but he won't take too kindly to the fact that his blood died in a manner such as this."

"We're doing all we can, surely he'll understand that."

"I hope it doesn't come to that. If it does, we'll have the two most powerful men in Babylon competing to see who can kill us first."

She would have laughed, but the thought wasn't funny. A slight movement from the forest to their left suddenly interrupted her worry. Hayden leapt up, pulling the sword of Tiber from its scabbard. They were surprised, as the short man from earlier stepped among them. Hayden replaced the sword and stepped toward him.

"What are you doing here?"

The man moved to Hayden and extended his arm. Hayden leaned down and shook his hand. The man replied to Hayden's question.

"The Gov'nah wanted me to follow you all. He wants to make sure your group makes it safely through the forest. Although the forest is out of our Province, we do have a lot of… let's just say… influence in the region."

"So you've been following us?"

"Yes. I've been maintaining a safe distance, but-"

"Then why show yourself now?"

The short man turned to the trees and pointed to a certain spot, and then waved his hand toward their group. The tree line moved, and five men emerged, each dressed in animal skins and donning bows.

"These are some of the Huntsmen. They're a nomadic tribe that dwells close to this part of the forest. They are excellent hunters and more of the wild life experts of the region. If anyone knows how to help your friend here, it would be them."

Four of the men picked Amarsin up and started carrying him away. The fifth man looked toward Hayden.

"Follow us. You will be guest among us for a couple of days."

"Let us grab our gear and get the horses."

"We've already taken them," the man laughed. "If it's not too late, he should be through the worst part of it by then."

"How will you know if it's too late?"

The man chuckled again. "We'll know; if he dies."

Chapter Twenty-One

Amarsin was back on the ground. The dragon was standing over him again. He stared at the stranger in the distance. The stranger moved closer again. He looked into his own eyes again. The image stared back at him, and then shook its head in disgust and turned to walk away.

"Wait!" Amarsin pleaded, this time breaking the awkward silence he'd allowed to exist the first time this scenario had unfolded.

The stranger stopped, and turned back to face him. "I've nothing to do with you. Why do you stop me from taking my leave?"

"You can't leave a man here to die. It's not prudent. It would be most selfish of you."

"I am you, Amarsin. I can only live as I've learned."

Amarsin looked startled. "It's not too late to change. I'm learning that."

"You could never learn it fast enough, Amarsin. Do you know how vile you've been? I'm the essence that you've created, but he is the semblance of you soul."

Amarsin cringed as he followed the image's finger to view the hideous dragon.

Tears streaked down Amarsin's face. The image looked at him unsympathetically.

"Why do you weep? Tears are no ransom against death. They're only the portrayal of your greatest fear, losing yourself."

"No," Amarsin replied defiantly. "I do not cry for fear of losing my life."

"For pity then. You hope your tears will move me into aiding your escape from certain death."

"Yesterday, probably that would be true. Not today."

"Not for pity and not for fear, then for the recognition of what you are about to lose as this life passes from you."

"No. I cry for something you could never understand if you are nothing but what I once was."

"And what is that?"

"I cry for shame. I'm ashamed of what I've become. I've been no good to anyone, least of all myself. In my own arrogance, I've become an insult to the heritage of Babylon and a disgrace to the Shamash name. I shed tears for the legacy I've marred and the memories of heroic men that I've trampled on."

"And you expect me to believe you've changed so soon. You're all too intelligent, Amarsin Shamash. But I'm not buying your little act. You pretend to have turned honorable to convince the gods to let you live. But die you shall."

"Then I shall only hope to be granted one last request."

"What is that?"

"That I would be forgiven my actions of the past, that I may die with dignity and hold my head with honor as I enter the nether life."

"You? Honor? Dignity? Never… You can't buy those things, boy. You're as good as dead now. A leopard can't change its spots."

"No, but a spotted leopard can learn to live differently, although his spots are still painstakingly apparent… I do not profess to have changed, only to have taken a step in a new direction."

The image groaned. "You'll die soon enough, Amarsin. You'll come back to yourself sooner or later. You always do. You always do."

Amarsin sprang up in the bed. He was lying on a small mattress constructed of various leaves woven together in a linen covering. The small sheet that was covering him was completely drenched in sweat. He tried to sit up, and the world seemed to swim around him.

He batted his eyelids together several times, trying to focus on anything solid. Finally, his eyes locked on a figure sitting next to him. It was the small man he'd seen among the Wards.

"Dwarf," he quietly called. "Where are my friends?"

"Oh, so now they are your friends. Nothing like a near death experience to awaken the bowels of compassion within a man."

"Whatever it takes, I guess."

"Yes, Amarsin, whatever it takes."

Amarsin closed his eyes tightly, trying to shake off the cobwebs that clouded his mind.

"Where am I?"

"You and your… uh… friends are staying among some of my friends… a tribe of huntsmen. They are forest rangers who have a knack for survival."

"What happened to me?" He groggily asked.

"So, you don't remember?"

Amarsin thought hard. He made an apprehensive face. "I remember a dragon."

"A dragon," the dwarf laughed. "My, my. No, Amarsin, a snake bit you. Hardly a dragon I'd say. Although I'd imagine your stories would go much further around the campfires.

Perhaps even make you a little more popular among the ladies. Amarsin, the survivor of dragon attacks."

"Go ahead, short man. Make fun of my calamity."

He lifted his arm and scratched his head. "How long have I been out?"

"This is the tenth day, but don't worry. You're safe here, and your leader has come up with a wonderful plan. He and the others have been working to put it in motion. I'm so excited I think I shall embark on your journeys even beyond the trees. Might as well see what grand adventures await me beyond the boundaries I've always known."

The short man looked at Amarsin. "I guess although Sir Hayden is your leader, this expedition is funded by your family. I'd be remiss not to at least do your family the honor of asking permission to join you."

He nervously studied Amarsin, "I know you're Babylonian, and so I know your answer already. But, would you consider allowing me to follow you past the forest. I'll do as always and keep my distance."

Hayden entered the room in time to hear the little man's question. He was just about to reply, when Amarsin cleared the fog from his mind just enough to answer.

"I'd be delighted if you'd join us, little man, but not as you've requested."

"What do you mean, sir?"

"You cannot follow from a distance. You can only travel

with us, if you share our campfires and eat our meals."

The little man cracked a tentative smile. "What kind of joke are you playing on me?"

"None." Amarsin replied. "None at all."

He extended his hand. "What's your name, short one?"

"Leib. Descendent of the Sardans of Babylonian heritage."

He held his head low. "Of course, I was disavowed because of my short stature. The guardians found me and brought me to the Gov'nah. He gave me my name."

"And he named you well. Leib… the little lion."

Amarsin smiled. He saw Hayden for the first time standing in the corner. He still held Leib's arm firmly in his grasp.

"I, Amarsin Shamash, of Babylonian descent and with Babylonian royalty flowing through my veins, do grant you permanent reprieve…"

Chapter Twenty-Two

Torben stopped by the front office in the building and knocked. A man opened the door and quietly studied him. The man wore a black and gray pin-stripped suit. A white shirt was barely visible through the buttoned jacket, as he extended his hand.

"Reverend Kevin Michaels. How can I be of service to you, sir?"

"Reverend Michaels, are you the lead pastor here at the church?"

"I'm associate pastor, our lead pastor is overseas on a mission's trip. If you'd like, I could schedule you to come back when he returns. He'd be more than glad to meet you. We always love seeing new faces around here."

"That's okay. How long have you been a member at this

church?"

"Most of my life. My parents moved here when I was seven. My first week in the neighborhood and one of the church elders picked me up on the church van. I liked what they had going on in Sunday School, and I've been a member ever since."

"Wow! From the bus route to the associate position; you've sure come a long ways."

"God is good, sir… Is there anything I can do to help you?"

"Perhaps," Torben replied. "I'm investigating an old case."

He opened his wallet and revealed his badge. "I'm a homicide detective, metro division. I'm sort of reopening an old case that has lost all its leads. I was wondering if you or someone here could help me. Any information would be better than what I've got now."

"Sure. I'll try."

"I'm investigating the accident concerning the Smith family last year. Mr. Hayden Smith was a long-time member here according to his private journal. He and his family were also actively involved until the accident. Is that true?"

"Tragic story, detective. And from what I understand, Hayden… Bro. Smith is in the hospital, attempted suicide… I believe."

"That's right. Right now, I'm trying to start from the

beginning. I'm more interested in the details relating to the original case. Someone is closing it too quickly, covering the details, and I want to know what's being concealed."

The associate pastor cautiously shook his head. "There's not much I can tell you, detective. The Smiths were regulars. They loved God. They always contributed financially… They believed in what we were trying to do in the community."

"Was Mr. Smith ever in any trouble? Legal? Financial? Anything?"

"If he was, he kept it from us. I do the counseling for young couples here. If they had an issue, I was the one who would've known about it."

"And they never indicated anything?"

"Nothing. They seemed to be a happy couple."

"Their relationship was okay?"

The pastor shrugged. "There were no signs of serious marital trouble if that's what you mean. There was definitely no marital infidelity. The Smiths were both highly regarded."

"Were? Mr. Smith is still alive."

"Yes. He is. However, he's no longer the man we used to know. I'm afraid he has had a real difficult time dealing with the loss of his wife and children. Who wouldn't? Right?"

"What do you mean by 'a difficult time'?"

"Well, he hasn't come around. He's been extremely negative toward God and the church. He sort of closed everyone out. After the funeral, he didn't want to have anything to do with God. Somehow, he believed that it was God's fault. If not God's fault, then God should have prevented it. God should have protected them."

"And how do you explain that one, pastor?"

"I can't. There's no explanation sometimes for the pathway God chooses. At times, it's merely life. Time and chance happeneth to us all. It rains on the just and the unjust alike, I'm afraid."

"So, your best explanation is that sometimes there is no explanation?"

"Detective, despite how many American Christians feel, God is sovereign. We have no real concept of that. We only understand democracy, voting, freedom of choice, and freedom of expression. We don't like to be told what we do. We don't like to not get our way. However, God is still a sovereign king. He reigns and rules over all the earth. He does what He chooses, quite simply because He can."

"And we are just supposed to live blindly and like the choices that he makes?"

"Absolutely not! We are merely to walk by faith. Faith serves no purpose where one's feelings and motives aren't questioned. Only when one doesn't fully understand God, can true faith be demonstrated. At times, I cannot comprehend; I cannot believe what is happening; I may not agree or even like what's unfolding around me, but I can trust. I can always trust."

"And Hayden Smith has had trouble with that? He's had trouble trusting?"

"No more than the rest of us. Although, I do remember the few months before the accident, there was something not quite right about things. I never could put my finger on it, but something was a little off."

"Please, Pastor Michaels, think hard for me."

"I'm sorry, I've tried. That's all I can remember."

"Okay. That's okay. If you remember anything else, please contact me," he said, as he extended his business card toward him.

"Yes, sir. I certainly will."

Detective Mayes was almost to the door when Pastor Michaels called him to turn around.

"Yes, Reverend."

"I'm not sure, detective, but perhaps there are other questions you could be asking that would be more beneficial."

"Okay," Torben replied. "Such as?"

"You're trying to find the information that's being hidden from you. Perhaps the better question is why don't they want that information out. What are they protecting? Maybe if you find out *why,* it will lead you to *what.*"

Chapter Twenty-Three

Abaddon Dearth overlooked the meadow, waiting for the appointment to show. After a few minutes of silent anticipation, he stood up and started walking down the hill. The traitor had promised to be there.

Abaddon was just to the center of the field when he heard someone call to him.

"I didn't think you were going to come."

He whirled around. The scheduled appointee had appeared out of nowhere. He swiftly moved toward his visitor.

"You don't lurk in the shadows for me. I'm a Captain of the Babylonian Host. I wait for no man. You wait for me. Are we clear?"

"Yet, here you are, obviously frustrated because you did not see me sooner. A person doesn't live so long out here without learning how to go unnoticed."

"So, it's you who has been wiping the tracks away? You've made it most difficult to find you."

"Well, it would've been that much easier, Captain Dearth, if you'd not so coldly murdered your tracker."

Abaddon was furious. "I can kill you where you stand. What gives you the audacity to speak to me like a child?"

"You need me."

"You think it's that simple?"

"I know it is. Your animosity runs too deeply. You'd do anything to kill them, and I seem to be your best chance at getting you close enough."

"You've brought me the information that I asked for?"

"Indeed I have. You've made the proper arrangements that I have requested?"

"If your information is beneficial, you will be rewarded most expensively."

"I have no need of your wealth, Captain Dearth. I assure you, I have no request other than that you spare my life."

"Such a low price you ask. I shall not allow you to be given so meager a reward. You'll be openly blessed, paraded in front of others. They will learn that it pays to be a friend to the King's Guard."

"Whatever you insist sir. I'll not turn away the King's hand. I'll gladly and humbly accept whatever blessing he would wish to bestow."

"Does Amarsin Shamash yet live?"

"He does. He's expected to pull through. The locals have made sure of it."

Abaddon was angry. "What is their path?"

"We've decided to ride the river?"

"What? Don't you know the perils there? Pirates, savages, and wild animals to name a few. The terrain is merciless. The currents are strong. They won't survive."

"Then your job should be easy."

"How so?"

"You could pay the pirates to do your bidding. You could supply the savages with food in exchange for their loyal service in capturing the ones you seek. In both cases, you'd only ask for them to spare my life. Do with the others as they will."

"And if that doesn't work?"

"The elements will inflict their pain on our band I'm sure. I don't think we could come through such a treacherous journey unscathed. It's a grand opportunity for you. If they disappear in the torrential river's flow, they won't be missed. Others will only blame our group, for its haughty stupidity in believing we could master the elements. The word will spread that we have angered the gods and have been dealt with accordingly… As a last resort, Captain Dearth, you could be waiting outside the entrance of the Fortress. No one will be suspecting you right outside the gates. Defenses will be down. You could step from your concealed position, and have your men kill us all. Myself withstanding, of course."

"Are you sure Sir Hayden doesn't suspect you? You're far too evil to not be noticed."

"He'd never suspect me. I appear harmless. I'm weaker. I've gotten very close to him."

"How close?"

"Close enough. Trust me. He shant suspect me, and if need be, when the time comes, I'll shove the dagger in his heart myself."

Abaddon tossed his visitor a couple of coins. "Leave him to me. Do with the others whatever you desire, but Hayden Smith must die only by my hands."

Chapter Twenty-Four

Hayden quickly sat up in the bed. His heart was pounding. His chest heaved; feeling like it was about to explode. Sweat had beaded around his forehead and was trickling down his checks. His shirt was also moist from the sweat he'd produced. He felt the air in the room now. It was frigid. He exhaled sharply, a puff of thin smoke drifted into the cold room. His body wasn't reacting to the temperature. Something else had created this physiological response.

All of a sudden it came back to him. Not completely or with much clarity. Almost as if there were a hodge-podge of broken memories, randomly scattered through his brain. Like a puzzle he knew he needed to solve, but one that didn't have all the pieces. None of it made sense.

However, he had awakened with the dreadful feeling that he didn't belong here. Not just along the river, but with these people. He didn't belong in Babylon. He didn't belong in this time period. He didn't belong in this world.

It didn't make sense. Perhaps the pressure had finally caused his hardened exterior to crack. Maybe the tough guy persona he'd been trying to put on had finally wilted enough to reveal his true nature. Perhaps it was time for the others to know he was just as afraid as they were, maybe even more.

What he had seen terrified him. There had been a beautiful woman. Little children with them. They'd been in a small space traveling at a high rate of speed. He couldn't explain it, but the setting seemed surreal. Déjà vu. He'd been there before. He recognized them, although he couldn't remember who they were. Yet, it was real. Somehow, he was almost certain that he'd done it at some point in his life.

He'd looked at the beautiful woman and smiled. She'd taken his hand. Something was wrong. He didn't look right. Was he sick? What was the matter with him?

The horrible sound had frightened him. A crash, deafening explosion. Glass had shattered and exploded around them. The fast moving box they were in had turned circles, throwing the children in different directions. He'd landed upside down and tried to look around.

The woman. Bloody. Hanging limp from the seat. Unconscious. He'd looked for the children. One was lying across the seat. The other two were missing. He'd tried to break free. Tried to get to them, to reach them. To help them. He'd wanted them to live. He couldn't move. Why couldn't he move?

That's when he had awakened. The others around him

were startled.

"Hayden, are you ok?" M'ya moved next to him.

Leib stood up from the cot he'd been trying to sleep on. "What would cause a grown man to wail like a whipped wolf's cub? You scared us all, ya did, Sir Hayden."

Hayden scowled. "I don't know. Doesn't make sense."

M'ya motioned for the others to move away. After a couple of seconds, she touched his shoulder.

"We've gotten close, you and I. Do you want to talk about it? You know you can trust me, Hayden."

"I know I can M'ya. I'd trust you with my life, but I don't want to talk about it."

"Why not? It must have been incredibly frightening. You look like you've seen a ghost."

He looked up at her. She felt anxious. His eyes revealed a sickening worry she'd never noticed on him before. Not at the trial in Babylon. Not when they'd strapped him to the chair over the endless void. Not when they'd been lying among the lepers. Not when Abaddon had come for them at Marcus Shamash's home. Hayden had been a stone. He was unshakable.

Until now! Something had him rattled. He wasn't himself. The calm and intrepid demeanor had been replaced with an apprehensive alertness.

"Hayden, what's gotten to you?"

He faced her, "I don't know M'ya. I don't. I saw things. Frightening things."

"When?"

"While I slept."

She removed her touch from his shoulder and lightly placed her hand on his. "It was only a dream, Hayden. Look, it wasn't real. We're here. We're okay."

He shook his head. "It doesn't make sense, but it wasn't here. It was somewhere else."

"Then it wasn't real. It's nothing to worry about."

"It felt real. Almost like another life. But my life."

She shrugged. "What did you see?"

"A disaster. Glass. Lots of flying glass. A woman next to me. Children behind me. Badly injured. Maybe dead. I don't know. I felt angry and afraid."

"Angry?"

He moved his eyes from hers. "Yes, I woke up angry. Unexplainably so. I felt nauseous for fear, but more importantly, I felt bitter."

"What was the object of your animosity?"

He moved his eyes back to hers and said it without hesitation. Strongly. Defiantly. She could feel the intensity searing through his words.

"Are you sure, Hayden? You're certain that's what you felt?"

"I don't know why, but I've felt it the last few days. It's come back. I hate him."

She moved her hand from his. "Hayden, one should never be at odds with God."

Chapter Twenty-Five

A couple of hours had passed. The memories were still alive in his mind. He'd walked away from the others and stood for hours near the rapidly flowing river. After several attempts, he'd given up. He couldn't remember beyond the details of the dream.

It was as if the dream was real. It wasn't merely figments of imagination strewn together by the brain's twisted abilities. It was more like his mind had conjured memories that he'd chosen to forget. He was being forced to witness atrocities he would've preferred to leave behind him. His subconscious was forcing him to relive the most horrible and unfathomable details of his life.

Yet, that wasn't possible. He didn't believe in reincarnation. It couldn't have been another life, although it felt otherworldly. There had to be an explanation, but as hard as he focused on finding it, it refused to come to him.

He looked into his bag and removed the writing utensil and parchment he'd found at the cabin a few days ago. He sat down and began to write.

I'm torn. Conflicted. I don't have answers. What I felt was real. What I witnessed in my sleep was too horrifying to be my own carnal imaginations.

The woman next to me was familiar. There was a bond there I don't know how I could have forgotten. A closeness. A trust. In the moment before hell entered, there was peace. The way she looked at me. It was perfect. The sort of life for which a man can only dream. The children seemed comfortable. No care in the world.

Then, it all disappeared. A tragic accident that I can't explain. The perfection. The peace. The love I felt. It was all ripped from my fingers. It was stolen from me. Yet, somehow I feel that this morning wasn't the first time. I'm remembering events that must have transpired earlier in life. I don't understand how that could be.

And God. My God. How could you who reign so highly have allowed such calamity? I feel nothing but a burning rage in my soul toward you. I would that I knew how it were feasible for me to feel such contempt.

You have always been my hope. My rock and fortress. My strong tower. How is it that you could have chosen to forsake me? How could you have allowed tragedy to arise from the life of one of your most noble servants?

I'd have given everything for you, and the world knew it. You knew it. You were the essence of my life. The air I breathed. How could you turn your back on me when I needed you most? How could you allow such misery?

I don't know why I feel it, but I know what I feel. What has transpired I cannot understand, but the separation is undeniable. There is no love for you left. I'm overwhelmed with fury. The contempt of my heart toward you blinds me to whatever truth may exist.

I know others would speak of blind faith. Perhaps those others have never felt the sting of losing everything. Yet, I don't know for sure what losses I myself have suffered. I only know the brokenness I undeniably feel. The hollowness that seeing these images has brought to my soul.

So, let those who piously sit on invisible thrones and wear invisible halos; let them indifferently discuss the magnitude of faith in one's journey. Perhaps they've never experienced true and heartrending loss. Or, perhaps they are merely better beings than I. Perhaps their hearts are made of a different mold, their character is born of gold tried in the fire, and their minds are set in steel. Of these men, I am most unworthy. I am afraid. I am angry. I am hurt. And I cannot find it in my heart to believe.

Hayden closed the small parchment and placed it back in his bag. He tossed the writing utensil into the river. He'd lost his desire to write. It rose to the top and floated away on the rapids. The current pulled it under only to release it again moments later further downriver. He stared at it until it was carried out of sight. Like everything else in his miserable life, it was inevitably taken from him.

A small voice startled him, causing him to remove his eyes from the fierceness of the river.

"Have we gotten everything figured out, Sir Hayden? We cannot afford to delay much longer. Amarsin is able to travel now. The boats are built, are they not?"

Hayden wiped his eyes before turning around. He cleared his throat.

"Yes, Leib. The boats are complete. We will leave at first light tomorrow. Why don't you get with Darius and make sure each vessel is well stocked."

"Is everything okay, sir? You sound… uh… a bit distracted this morning."

"I've never been better. We-"

"Sir Hayden, I know fear when I see it. This morning, you wailed from your sleep a most fearsome sound. Like the monstrous demons of hell were lapping at your heels. Wha-"

"Forget it, little man. It's not worth mentioning."

"Should I be concerned with getting on that boat tomorrow? I must tell you now; I know not how to swim. It's not a commodity most teach the underprivileged."

"My wail had nothing to do with the river, wee man. Besides, if something happens and you end up in the water, just put your feet down."

"Really? You of all people mock my stature."

"Or perhaps he just wants you to drown," Amarsin quipped as he walked up to them.

"Someone feels better," Hayden dryly commented.

"Much better. I can finally walk again without feeling faint."

Leib playfully punched Hayden in the thigh. "We're standing in the presence of greatness, Sir Hayden."

"Greatness?"

"Yes. We have among us Amarsin Shamash, Babylonian aid to the High Council, and slayer of dragons… or was it destroyer of serpents."

Hayden laughed. "I'm not sure that wee thing that bit him was more than a worm."

"Go ahead and poke your fun, but this isn't over yet. You must protect me… I… I was specifically targeted."

Leib groaned, "So now the dragons target you…"

"I'm serious. I've thought it over a million times the past few days. I was targeted. Hayden, you must remember. The serpent sprang right past you. You were the easiest target; the one who posed the greatest threat. Yet, the viper struck past you and sank its fangs into my thigh. It was seeking me out."

"And why would it do that?" Leib questioned.

"Someone wants me dead. Someone who can use the elements to do its bidding."

Leib shuttered, before trying to lighten the mood. "Amarsin, slayer of dragons, at odds with Baal."

Amarsin didn't smile. "Sir Hayden, I'm serious. I need you now more than ever. Please, get me to the Fortress."

Chapter Twenty-Six

Abaddon swore. He knocked over the canisters she had positioned on the table in her special tent.

"You said he'd be dead by the end of that day. It's been over a week, and he still lives."

"And you are mad at me. You wanted him dead a few weeks ago. Yet, you've gotten nowhere. At least I drew blood. I've gotten much closer than you ever did."

"Don't tempt me woman. I'm not in the mood. I'll kill you today, and I won't miss."

"You could, but many of Babylon's most feared and respected elite would be particularly upset about losing their second Seer in a few months. Especially now losing one so young and… let's just say… alluring."

"I don't care what might upset other elitist. You've over-promised and under-delivered on every level."

"Have I? Are you certain, Captain?"

"Amarsin Shamash yet lives. I wanted him dead. I wanted them scattered. I wanted them to not be moving toward the Fortress. Their journey was supposed to stop here. We could have surrounded and killed them all."

She slyly smiled. "How many men do you have in your command here, Captain?"

"Fifty."

"Well, it appears that I know more than you, Captain Dearth. To attempt to carry out your plan against them is insanity."

"I'm the military strategist, you're the sorceress. You worry about casting spells and creating potions. I'll worry about how my fifty men will fare against the likes of them."

"Fifty against six. Perhaps if it were that easy you could be thus enlightened. However, in your haste, you're missing a few key factors. But perhaps you're right, I would be better suited at developing concoctions to raise you from the dead once your life has been taken."

"I don't die that easy, wiccan."

"Life will slip from us all. It's but the misty shroud lining the ground in early mornings. There's only a step between man and death. To pretend otherwise is the most foolish and haughty thought of life."

"Do something then. Protect me. Pray to the gods. Create a barrier 'round about me. Don't you have that power? You are the high priestess of the most powerful god in the universe. Don't you control destiny?"

"I can't create or alter destiny. I can only foretell. I can warn. What a man does with what he's been given is his choice."

"Then what good are you, wench? I should just cast you to my men and let them have their way with you."

"They'd not touch me, sir. No one touches the one in whom Baal confides."

"Be honest, girl, does he speak to you?"

"I hear the subtle whisperings at times."

"I want to hear him."

"No. You don't. It melts the soul. He's not gentle. A piece of me gets taken every time I encounter him."

"He takes a piece of you?"

"I diminish. I feel sick and small, unimportant in his presence. He isn't loving or kind. He doesn't care about my feelings. I am his servant. I do his bidding. Most cannot fathom that lifestyle, least of all you, Abaddon Dearth, Captain of the King's Host."

"Give me gods that I can talk to. Gods that I can confide in. Gods who scold me when I'm wrong, but only because they care about my wellbeing. Give me gods who long for me the way I long for them. I would that the world would present those sort of gods."

"I told you, sir. One is coming-"

"I don't want to hear about one coming. I want it now."

"I'm afraid there are none, sir. The gods are vile, ruthless, and rarely answer when man speaks."

"Yet, we offer up our lives to them. We sacrifice our children. We surrender our livestock and the fruits of our labor. We fight battles to defend their honor, and for what? So they can mock us in our day of calamity. Where's the godly honor in that? Why are we raised to be honorable men, only to waste our lives away fulfilling the desires of less honorable beings?"

"Watch yourself, Dearth. Your madness has afflicted your thinking. You mustn't blaspheme the very gods that have empowered you. Although they have their faults, the gods of Babylon are the most powerful in the world. You know that."

"Then let me make it up to them. Kill the fat man. Scatter the rest. Let me hunt them down and kill them like dogs."

"Sir, you aren't thinking sensibly."

He took another swig of the strong drink he'd been chugging down since he'd started the conversation.

"Then make sense of it for me, girl," he said, as he placed his hand on the small of her back.

She shoved him away. "Those days are over, Abaddon Dearth. I serve only Baal. My body belongs to him. I cannot be taken by another man."

He stepped toward her, but then decided against it. "Why should I not attack them now, pray tell?"

"Because, you haven't factored in the wild men of the river. They would much rather side with the lowly remnants of a few than an official entourage from the king's army. Out there, you'd be fifty against five hundred. You still like those odds?"

"Fifty trained soldiers against five hundred beastly savages. I've faced worse and am still alive. I'm not worried."

"Then worry about this. One of them still holds the sword of Tiber. It's too powerful to battle the one who wields it. He has the favor of the gods."

"Even if they don't agree with his causes."

"The gods have sworn allegiance to it, regardless of what it stands for. Right now, I'm afraid the gods are on his side."

"How can I change that?"

"You must disarm him."

"But how? I can't get close enough."

"But you know one who can. They must bring it to you. If you hold the power of Tiber in your hands, you may attack whoever and whenever you like."

"I shall request it to be so."

"And if they cannot bring it to you, there's always another way."

"How?"

"No weapons are allowed into the Fortress. He'll be forced to remove the sword at the gate. If you and your men are waiting, he'll be an easy target. The sword only protects the one wielding it. He will have forfeited his right by willingly releasing it."

"I shall try to have it stolen, and if that doesn't work, I will be waiting."

He tossed his half empty bottle in her direction. "Enjoy the rest, princess, I have someone to meet. We leave in the morning."

Chapter Twenty-Seven

Torben Mayes sat at his desk. He was coming up empty. Every possible lead he tried to investigate had nothing to offer. The associate pastor at the church had given him sound advice, but hadn't provided insight into the case. The old man on the corner hadn't given him anything useful. Both should have been credible witnesses. They should have seen something, but neither seemed to hold key details. The place he should have been able to find the files held nothing either. Someone had stolen them, which was alarming, because that could only have been someone with police connections. Someone inside was trying to hamper the investigation.

A short, pudgy woman rounded the corner and moved next to him.

"Detective, the captain wants to see you immediately… He asked that you bring your gun."

Torben was already halfway standing. He sat back down, opened his bottom file drawer, and removed his Glock nine millimeter from its location. He stood and slipped the holster to his hip.

"Ladies first," he motioned with his hand.

She took the lead and walked him the short distance to the captain's office. This couldn't be good. The blinds were closed. In the short time he'd worked there, he'd never seen the blinds closed. She knocked twice and opened the door, peeking in.

"Captain, Detective Mayes."

"Sure, send him in."

Torben walked in and stood across from the captain's desk. The captain motioned for him to have a seat. He nervously sat down. The captain placed a folder on the table and closed it.

"Have I not been fair with you?"

"Yes, sir. More than fair."

"You know you're the youngest detective this department has ever had, and by a good margin too."

"Yes, sir. I'm aware."

"You're aware that I took a chance on you son, when every other precinct in this city passed over you, solely because of your age."

"Yes, sir. I was aware."

"And you're also aware that I fully expect you to follow orders. When I give you a directive, I expect you to do what I say, when I say it."

"Yes, sir."

"And when I say I don't want you to do something, I mean it just as firmly."

"Yes, sir. I can ex-"

"I don't want an explanation, Detective Mayes. I've spoken with two people this week who claim you've questioned them about Hayden Smith. Did that file get placed on your desk and I didn't know about it?"

"No, sir. I just thought-"

"You just thought. I didn't bring you in to this precinct to think. I hired you to react, to do what I say, to investigate the cases I give you. I hired you to follow orders."

"Yes, sir. Sorry, sir. I-"

"Sorry. Son, we're beyond sorry. Sorry is for five year olds who got caught with their hands in the cookie jar. Sorry isn't for detectives who are working important cases. Sorry isn't for grown men who I am supposed to be able to trust with sensitive details of other people's lives. Sorry isn't for professionals who don't have a margin of error. I don't have the luxury of sorry around here."

"But I didn't do anything on city time, sir. I-"

"I don't care whose dime you were on. You showed your

badge, and that made it city business. As your direct superior, I gave you an order not to push this case, and you chose to disobey my directive and pursue it on your own-"

"Sir, I'm sorry. I didn't see it that way. I-"

"Didn't see it that way. What kind of excuse is that? Do you think it would be wise for me to allow all my detectives to choose what cases they want to follow and which ones they want to ignore? I can't run my department like that."

The captain's face was flushed red. A large vein in his neck was popping out from the side of his face. His bald head was flushed a fiery red as well. His normal easy going demeanor had been replaced with an anger that Torben wished he'd not instigated.

"Sir, I can't undo the few questions I've asked, but I can promise that I won't do it again."

"It's too late for that. I'm being pressured from the top. Somebody upstairs doesn't want this case being made public. My hands are tied. I'm afraid you've left me no choice, Mayes."

His voice was raised so loudly it almost rattled the windows. "Give me your badge and your gun. You're suspended without pay."

"What? Sir... That's a bit extreme don't you think. It was harmless. I won't pursue it... Please, I've worked hard. I've proven myself. I've closed two cases since the attempted suicide I'm looking into. It hasn't affected my performance. You know that."

He screamed. "I know I can't trust you to follow orders. That's what I know. And it's a disgrace to wear a badge and not be trusted."

"You can trust me, sir."

"Don't make this harder than what it is, Detective. Gun. Badge. Now."

Torben removed his gun and pressed the lever to release the clip. The clip fell into his hand. He racked the top slide backward, showing the captain that the gun was now empty. He racked it back into place, holstered it, and roughly placed it on the captain's desk. He removed the badge insert from his wallet and placed it beside the gun.

"You're making a mistake, sir. I'm a good officer. I'm a good person."

"Agreed, Detective Mayes, but my hands are tied."

"You couldn't vouch for me? Sir, I need this job. I-"

His voice was still shaking the closed blinds on the windows. "I can't vouch for someone who can't follow my simple directives."

Torben shook his head affirmatively. "I'm afraid I understand, sir. Thank you for the opportunity. Sorry I let you down."

He turned to walk away. The captain lowered his voice considerably.

"Torben, you're my best detective. A superstar. But

you've pushed in the wrong direction. Someone is very upset about what you're trying to uncover. I warned you this would happen."

"I don't understand. I haven't even found anything. It's been harmless."

"Whoever is up there is afraid you'll uncover something… Look, at the time of the accident there were a lot of people who felt uncomfortable about the way things were handled. No one knew why, but things just didn't feel right about the whole situation."

"Like what?"

"For starters, only a handful of cops were allowed on scene."

"How many?"

"Three."

"Who were they?"

"That's where it gets strange. They've all moved on to much better things now. One is the mayor of this great city. Another is our very own police chief. The third is our very own Senator."

"Yeah. I'd say they've moved up in the world. From beat cops to prestigious positions."

"And they moved up fast… too fast. All were in their appointed positions within nine months after the accident."

Torben let out a quiet whistle. "That is fast…"

He thought for a few seconds. "What about emergency personnel? There had to be someone on sight."

"Good question. One I've often wondered myself, because whoever was on scene, they never made any of the official police reports."

Torben shook his head. "Why are you telling me all this, sir? I have no authority anymore."

The captain smiled. "Nor do I over you anymore, Mayes."

"Sir, are you telling me-"

"I'm not telling you anything… Look, I don't care for your Christian evangelistic endeavors around my precinct. I'm not a believer and don't know if I ever could be. I prefer to stick with science."

Torben tried to interject but was silenced by the captain's stern look of disapproval at being interrupted.

"However, there's more to this case than Christian philosophical differences. I don't like the fact that good people died and with no explanation why."

He nodded for Torben to leave and suddenly raised his voice loudly again, pretending to be angry. "Don't let the door hit you on the way out, detective."

Torben's face was drawn taut as he marched past the room of curious onlookers. Some were staring in disbelief; others displayed soft smiles of opportunity. A higher up had fallen, and someone would be asked to take his place.

Perhaps his loss could be their gain.

Stepping out into the sunlight, he smiled. The captain had just given him the green light. He was officially, unofficially on the case. Privately sanctioned and publicly reprimanded. This case was only going to get tougher.

Chapter Twenty-Eight

Torben stepped into the posh high-rise office. The elder man approached him from behind a large desk.

"Hello, Mr. Mayes, what can I help you with today?"

"We should be able to just cut the initial performances, don't you think, Senator Winnfield. I'm sure you know exactly who I am."

The Senator's smile faded. "I do. What brings you to my office today? I have a feeling I'm going to regret agreeing to meet you here... I thought you were waved off the Hayden Smith case."

"I was. I disobeyed. Then I got fired. So here I am, on my own, still digging for answers."

"Well, one's got to like your tenacity. I guess you're going to just keep coming."

"I don't know how to let go. It's what made me a good detective."

The Senator smiled again. "I like your attitude, son. You remind me of myself when I was a youngster. So I'm going to permit you a few questions."

"Thank you, sir."

"Don't thank me yet. I said you could ask. I didn't say I would answer them."

Torben chuckled. "Fair enough… For starters, what did you see the night of the accident?"

"Not much. When I arrived, the scene was pretty much cleaned up. The bodies were all gone."

"What did the second vehicle look like? Did you happen to get a license plate or partial plate number?"

"No. The vehicles had already been towed."

"So, you never saw the suspect's vehicle?"

"I'm afraid not."

"Did you hear or read anyone else's report? What it looked like?"

"I'm afraid not. Look, I was approached that night and told that everything I had heard or seen was to be erased from my memory. I was rewarded well. Those chances are only available once in a lifetime."

"So you took it?"

The Senator nodded. "I did, detective, and as you can see, whoever was watching over us kept his end of the bargain."

"Were there any EMTs on scene? Surely with that sort of accident, there had to be someone else there."

"No. As I stated, I got there late. Once I arrived, the entire scene had been cleaned."

"Then why were you rewarded? What big secret were you supposed to protect?"

"I'm not sure. Never was, but I wasn't about to ask any questions either. If they were gonna pay me to keep quiet about something I didn't know, I wasn't gonna tell 'em any different. Why would I do that?"

"Of course… And I'll bet the others with you will all state the same thing. No one knows anything."

The Senator smiled. It wasn't a warm smile. More of a "get off my back because you aren't getting anything" smile. He extended his arm in a farewell gesture. The two men clasped hands, the Senator gripping Torben's hard and turning it underneath his.

"I'm pretty sure no matter who you ask, the answers won't vary. There was nothing to see. Detect… Ex-detective Mayes. You have a good day now."

Torben stepped from the room fuming. He was tired of being given the run around. He wanted answers. He wanted to know who was keeping him at bay. Most of all, he wanted Hayden Smith to know his family's killer had been brought to justice. Every man should at least be allowed to die in peace.

Chapter Twenty-Nine

The two flat boats sat safely lodged for the evening against the far bank. Several logs had been expertly tied together to form the large floating device. They had pitched the top and the bottom side with a mud-like material to seal the boat from water. The main deck was ten feet by ten feet. The logs were all well chosen, each at least a foot-and-a-half to two feet wide. The structure was solid, built to withstand the rapids and rocks of the great river.

Leib walked to the second boat and shook a few hands of the barbarians who made up its crew. It was his routine every time they stopped for the evening. They'd agreed to accompany him down river, lessening the chance that other savages would attack their small group. It had been almost three weeks since the journey had started, and they'd had no trouble. Most evenings, they'd continued floating downriver through the night. According to the river people accompanying them, there were only around three to four days left on the journey. Once off the rafts, it was only a full days journey before arriving at the Fortress.

The river people were a rowdy and unforgiving lot, but they rarely attacked their own kind. They'd murder and rob unsuspecting travelers, but they lived longer because of private pacts they'd made among themselves. Leib had been instrumental in negotiating the treaties among the river tribes. It's why, for the most part, they weren't in real danger traveling with him as their guide. Leib's assertion that he had never traveled outside of the forest hadn't been true. He'd ventured up and down the river a few times in his day, and had made a positive influence along the way. Regardless his stature, Leib had learned to stand tall among others. His ingenuity and wisdom separated him from the group, and it wasn't unnoticed by Hayden.

Hayden approached him soon after the camp was settled.

"Leib," he asked curiously, "what are your plans after this journey is completed? Do you intend to travel back to the forest?"

"I haven't thought that far. Some say I will be the next Gov'nah of the Wards, but I have no real interest in ruling there. I feel my destiny is somewhere else, although I've never known where."

"Babylonian reprieve opens many doors for you, does it not?"

"Theoretically, I suppose so. However, you know as well as I, the Babylonian papyrus could never cement my fine standing among the elite. They'll never be able to see past my short stature."

"Probably true for most of them, but I've got faith that you could win a few over. Marcus Shamash for one. He'd be indebted to you for being a key piece in getting his grandson to the Fortress. He's a fair man. I think he'd be reasonable. All you need is a seat at the table, Leib, the rest will take care of itself. You're an intelligent enough man."

He shrugged, "And what of you Sir Hayden, man of mystery? Where will your journeys carry you next? Perhaps I shall just decide to intertwine our fates a while longer. I like traveling with a reasonable man of like passions."

"I don't know. I haven't thought that far ahead either I suppose. I've only focused on getting Amarsin to the Fortress. Once there, my promise to Sir Marcus will be complete. I suppose I'll try to discover more of this mysterious world I've found myself in."

"Please, explain."

"I can't, just suffice it to say that I'm on a quest for answers that I don't even know the questions to."

"That could be a quite confusing conundrum. Perhaps I may stay a while and help you find what you're searching for."

Both men laughed. Hayden tapped the top of his head. "I'd be more than glad for your continued company. You've proven most useful, and a favorable companion."

Hayden moved away from him and walked back to his spot on the large raft. He moved his bag over and stooped down to pick up his sword. It was gone. He frantically searched the entire area.

No sign of it.

He searched around the area that M'ya slept.

Nothing.

"Leib. Come here."

Leib sensed the urgency and immediately jumped back to the raft their group shared. Darius had just finished tying off the raft and noticed Hayden's almost panicked intonation as well.

"What's wrong?" Leib asked.

"The sword of Tiber. It's missing."

Darius' forehead tensed. "Missing. How do you misplace a three-foot blade of that power? There must be some mistake."

"You don't misplace it," Leib retorted. "It gets stolen."

Hayden couldn't hide his agitation. "There's no mistake. I left it here. My bag was tied around it. The sword is missing, but the bag is still here. Someone took the sword."

"That's a sword of legend. Do you know the supremacy in battle the one holding the sword will possess? It's lightning in a bottle."

"I know. I know. It was there this morning."

"Are you sure?"

Yes, Leib, I'm sure. I placed it there myself."

"Hayden, no one has been on our raft today except those in our group. If the sword has indeed been stolen, it's been stolen by someone we're sharing space with."

"Let's not jump to conclusions, little one. If we do that, we can't rule anyone out."

Leib cracked a smile. "Not true, Sir Hayden. You can rule me out. That sword is taller than I am and almost as heavy. I'd have been a comical sight attempting to make away with it."

"That you would have," Hayden agreed. "Darius, please assemble the others. Don't tell them what we're discussing. I don't want anyone else to know that sword is missing."

"Yes, sir. Although I bet it's Amarsin. There's no way he changed that quickly. He's a serpent, that one. You better watch him."

"I'd be imprudent not to. One must always learn to trust but verify. Doing one's due diligence will save him from plenty of trouble down the road. With that said though, Darius, please understand that everyone of us must be looked at as suspects."

He glanced down at Leib, "Even you, Leib. You could have easily paid off one of your river rats to steal it."

Leib looked offended. "Do what you must, Sir Hayden. I may be a lot of things, but a thief isn't one of them."

Darius nodded in Hayden's direction. "I'll be right back with them, and I won't say a word about what we've discussed.

Ten minutes later Darius returned with Amarsin and the old slave. "Here we are, sir. I couldn't find M'ya. You know she likes her private time every now and then."

"Okay," Hayden appeared hesitant. "I guess we'll start without her."

"Start what?" Amarsin asked.

Hayden didn't give an introduction. He went for it directly.

"The sword is missing."

"Wait. The sword, as in the sword of Tiber. The sword that my family has sworn to protect. You're talking about the sword that gives its possessor the power and assistance of the gods. That sword?"

"Yes, Amarsin. That sword. It was here among my things only a few hours ago. No one has been on this boat but our group. Now, it's gone."

"Who do you think took it?"

"I was hoping you all could help me with that. Did any of you see anything?"

The elder black man stepped forward. "Sir Hayden, is

this your way of trying to get one of us to confess. I can assure you, it was none of us that took the ill famed blade."

"And how can you be so certain, old one?"

Leib puffed his chest forward, attempting to appear taller. "If you know something then you must spill it at once. Every second wasted is one that the sword could fall into the wrong hands. We can't afford for that to happen."

The elder breathed deeply. "I know who took the sword."

Each man looked at the others, afraid of the accusation that was coming. None of them wanted it to be the man beside him. They each suspiciously cast an eye in each other's direction.

"Well, out with it," Leib demanded.

"She's not with us right now."

"What?" Hayden didn't want to believe it. "When did she take it? You can't be serious."

"I'm as serious as I've ever been, Sir Hayden. It's been about an hour ago. She reached into your stuff and made off with it. She didn't move about suspiciously neither. She seemed at peace. Not nervous at all. That's why I didn't say something sooner. I thought you were aware of it. She took it like she had no care in the world. That's why none of you all noticed her. She walked right out with it wrapped in her blanket. In broad daylight."

"Which way did she head? We must find her at once,"

Darius asked.

"She was moving south when she stepped into the trees, but I'm no tracker. I'm not sure where she moved from that point."

Hayden pointed at Darius. "Get your bow. You're coming with me. Leib, have your men stay here to protect you all against danger. Amarsin, you're staying close to me."

"No offense, but you don't possess the sword right now. Are you sure I'm safe out there?"

"If you'd rather stay with the old man, the midget, and the river rats, feel free."

Amarsin looked around and quickly made his choice. He picked up a short dagger from his belongings as he moved toward them. He was just about to join them on the bank of the river when she emerged from the trees.

Her hands were empty. She was whistling a tune that none of them recognized. Darius drew his bow back, an arrow laced and ready to fly. She stopped walking, closed her lips, and gasped at Hayden's irate expression.

She held her hands forward in disbelief. "What's wrong?"

Hayden reached her in three steps and grabbed her wrist with his right hand. He yanked her away from the others. He'd been denying his feelings for her and was extremely hurt by her betrayal.

"M'ya, I trusted you. How could you do this?"

She was confused. "Do what? I don't know what you mean?"

He was indignant. "M'ya, it's over. I know you took it."

M'ya appeared to be humored. "Hayden, I didn't take anything. Please. I don't know what you're talking about. What did I supposedly take?"

"M'ya, the charade won't work. Someone saw you take it. Now where'd you put it?"

"Hayden, nice try. You got me. Good one, guys. I almost fell for it. You almost had me believing you were really upset."

"I am upset, M'ya," Hayden replied, as his grip tightened on her wrist.

He pulled her further away from them. Amarsin took a couple of steps in their direction.

"Hayden, I don't mean to prejudge this situation, but you know how hard it is to rehab a thief. She was in trouble when you first met her for this very thing. I see no reason to believe her now. She was lying then when accused of stealing. You saw her with the goods yourself. You know she was guilty."

She pleaded, "You all are serious? By the gods, please. You know me. I wouldn't steal from you."

"M'ya, he's got a point," Hayden retorted. "You were stealing someone blind, but you denied every bit of it."

"That was to feed my family. That is different."

"And the lies, M'ya?"

"Hayden, you must understand, that was to save my life."

Leib countered, "And perhaps to possess the sword would save your family for generations to come."

"Perhaps not. I would never betray you. My family wanted to sell me into sex slavery to save my eldest brother's hide. That isn't love. A woman isn't valued in Babylonian society. But you… you all… you treat me like the true family I never had. I wouldn't jeopardize that."

"Wouldn't you?"

"No. Never."

"But you did. The moment you walked off this boat with the sword of Tiber."

"Hayden, please."

Amarsin shook his head in disgust. "Darius, shoot her and be done with it. She's only dead weight now."

She pleadingly looked into Hayden's eyes. Unexpectedly, she found no compassion there. Darius still held the arrow pointed in her direction. He looked at Hayden for his directive. Finally, Hayden motioned for him to put the bow down.

"Tie her up. Once we get down river, she'll stand before an impartial counsel and have a hearing. She'll suffer whatever penalty is passed by their ruling."

"Please, Hayden. Trust me. Anyone could have taken it."

"But not anyone did, M'ya. You did. There's a witness against you, and now my heart is broken for what I must do."

She cried. The hot tears streaked her cheeks. "Please. Let me explain."

Amarsin groaned. "First it was 'I didn't do it.' Then it was 'haha, it's all a joke you're trying to pull on me.' Now, it's 'let me explain.' Why are you lying, M'ya? Why not just tell us the truth?"

"Please… Hayden… Look at me… Please… Hear me out. Let me tell you the truth."

Hayden turned away from her. "Save it for your trial, thief."

He motioned toward Darius again. "Bind her hands behind her, and chain her to the raft."

Darius moved toward her. She tried to run, but three of the river people had encircled her. One grabbed her and shoved her in Darius' direction. She tried to resist him, but it was futile. In a couple of seconds her hands were restrained behind her back. She was a prisoner on the raft.

·   ·   ·

Several hours had passed since she'd been detained. She was tired from fighting against the restraints and tried with all her might to break free from the knot he'd left her in. She could feel the blood trickling down her hands. It hurt, but she allowed it to continue bleeding, actually squeezing her hands more tightly, hoping the blood would serve as lubricant to slip her hands through the knots.

After several failed attempts, she fell back against the small stake he had tied her too. Furiously jerking a couple of times before giving up for good, she closed her eyes and resigned herself to being convicted.

Hayden spoke from beside her. She was startled to hear from him. She whirled around.

"M'ya… Why'd you lie to me?"

"Will you listen to me, Hayden? Please."

"I don't think I should. You haven't really earned that right. Everything has been a lie hasn't it?"

"There's been no lies between us, Hayden. I care for you… deeply."

"Okay, M'ya. Of every scenario I expected, that wasn't it. I didn't foresee you stooping to such lows."

"What?"

"I didn't think you'd use my emotions against me. I never thought you'd use our relationship as your secret weapon."

"What relationship Hayden? There's been nothing between us." She disappointedly stated.

Hayden was hurt and angry. "I'm done listening. You've been lying to me the entire journey. M'ya, I believed in you. I was willing to die for you. In some ways, I loved you. And…

and this is how you reciprocate my feelings. By taking the sword, you've shoved a dagger in my heart and unmercilessly twisted it."

"No. It's not what it-"

"M'ya look me in the eyes… Look me in the eyes and tell me that you did not take the sword. Please, tell me I'm wrong. Tell me he didn't see you take it."

"Hayden… I'm… I'm sorry."

"Sorry?"

"I had to."

"M'ya… please."

"Hayden, I did take the sword…"

Chapter Thirty

Torben Mayes sat across the desk from Doctor Harrison Poole. The doctor wore a grim expression, opposite the warm look he'd had the first time they'd met. He looked tired, perhaps slightly sick. The stress seemed to be getting to him.

Torben leaned forward, "Doc, why'd you call me down here?"

Doctor Poole hesitated, "Detective, this is the part of the job that I hate. Makes me cringe."

"Yes, what's wrong?"

"Your person of interest had something happen to him last night. We observed a brief flutter in brain activity. However, it seems to have caused further damage. I've never seen anything like this."

"Further damage?"

"Yes, detective. Normally any brain activity would be considered a positive sign. In this case, he demonstrated a brief flutter, but since then, he's only regressed. He's shown no other positive indicators. He's given us the opposite."

Dr. Poole looked up from the desk. "Detective, I don't know how much longer he's going to hold on."

"He seems to be a fighter, doc. I'm sure he's gonna pull through if given enough time."

"The state has asked for a second opinion. I tried to fight it, but another doctor has stepped in. I'm afraid I have no choice. If he hasn't demonstrated drastic improvement by tomorrow evening, I've been ordered to pull the plug."

"Doc, you can't do that."

"I have to. Exigent circumstances. We desperately need the space, and he doesn't appear to be getting better."

"He hasn't had time. It's a traumatic brain injury for heaven's sake. You know he needs more than a couple of weeks."

"I agree with you, but he's shown no progress, Detective. He has no surviving family. He has no one who has willingly stepped in to care for him. He seems to have no friends to fight his cause. As far as the state is concerned, he wants to be dead anyway. We can't continue to drain funds on lost causes."

"Doc, I'll stand in for him."

"I'm afraid you can't. You must find a family member if you want to save him. He needs a family member to buy more time and a miracle from God to come back from this."

"If there's someone out there, I'll find 'em doc. I'll do my part. We've got to trust God to do His."

Chapter Thirty-One

The rain beat mercilessly on the sandy shore. They were one day closer to their destination. M'ya sat cross-legged in the center of the raft, still tied to the tall stake they'd bound her to.

The rain pelted her, stinging her face from its blinding force. None of the men had spoken to her since she'd told Hayden she'd taken the sword. She'd requested to talk to him several times throughout the day, but her attempts to communicate had fallen on deaf ears.

Hayden and the others had completed a thorough search of the area before they'd left. They'd even enlisted the river rats to help them. No one had turned up anything. The sword was still missing. So, here she sat… drenched, cold, and utterly alone.

Darius suddenly burst through the clearing a few feet

from the raft.

"Riders approaching from the west, sir. They're coming fast."

Hayden leapt to his feet. "Abaddon?"

"No, sir. Not him or his men. There aren't many of them. I counted about ten. They were clustered tightly, so it was impossible to tell for sure."

"They're coming for us?"

"It appears that way. There was something else… a ways behind them is a horse drawn carriage."

He moved more closely so only Hayden could hear. "It bears the mark of Marcus Shamash. It seems he's sent riders ahead to stop us, and he wants to meet us."

"Then let them come. We've no reason to fear him."

"Do you suppose he's gotten word that the sword is missing?"

Hayden turned toward Amarsin, eyeing him suspiciously. "Anything is possible with that one, Darius. I guess I should be prepared for that. All I can offer is that once I get Amarsin safely to the Fortress, I'll come back and find the famed blade."

"What would you have me do, sir?"

"Head back out. Keep an eye on them. Make sure things are as they appear. If I'm to be ready for a threat, I'd at least like to know it."

Darius nodded and ran back in the direction he'd just come from. Hayden turned to Leib and called him forward with a wave of his arm. Once he stood beside him, Hayden sat down on one knee.

"Leib, keep your men close please. Darius reports that we're about to have company. Ten riders, coming fast. If we need them, it would be good to know where they stand."

"They'll stand where I do, I assure you."

Hayden rose and patted him on the head. "Thank you, Leib. You're a good man."

.   .   .

Forty-five minutes later, Darius re-emerged. He placed his hands on his knees, half bending over like he was going to throw up. He gasped for air.

"Sorry… They're five minutes out. Twelve of them. Double formation. The carriage bringing up the rear is ten minutes behind."

Amarsin stood. "Who is coming?"

Hayden turned to him. "Amarsin, is there any reason Marcus would be coming here?"

"No… he'd never travel this far out."

"Are you sure?"

"Yes… I'm sure. Why?"

"Riders are approaching under his banner."

"Something isn't right then. I can assure you, it's not him coming. He's never left his territory before, under any circumstances."

Darius flanked to the side, still trying to catch his breath. His position was concealed by thick greenery. Leib motioned for his men on the other boat, and they separated themselves among the few trees to the left of the rafts. Two archers took their bows to hide close to Darius.

Hayden knelt down beside M'ya. "If trouble starts, I don't want you sitting defenseless. I owe you nothing, but I won't have you dying without being able to put up a fight."

He flicked a small blade and sliced through the ropes binding her. She pulled her arms from behind her back and fervently rubbed her wrists. He hadn't noticed the rope had been rubbing into the flesh, and she hadn't complained.

She looked at him. "Thank you."

"This isn't over, M'ya."

"What are you doing?" Amarsin wailed. "She'll get away and go back where she left the sword."

M'ya looked frail compared to the strong and independent woman of a couple of days ago. She winced, but not from the pain. She apologetically studied him.

"Hayden… Please don't worry. I give you my word, I won't run."

"And why should he accept the word of a thief?" Amarsin gruffly demanded.

"The same reason he trusts an overbearing Babylonian aristocrat."

The beating of horses running through the brush stopped their conversation before Amarsin could reply. A few seconds later, the horses slowed. They could hear them walking toward the camp.

"Who goes there?" Hayden yelled.

A voice spoke loud and clear from the thickest part of the wooded area. "I am Hunzuu. I've been sent at the request of Marcus Shamash."

"Show yourselves then."

"We come in peace. Tell your archers to go easy with their arrows. Tell the ten swordsmen to make light with their blades. My men have outflanked them."

Hayden quickly looked to the left. In the haze behind the river rats, he noticed several archers who had taken position behind them. Their arrows were notched, and their bows drawn taut.

"We've been out maneuvered. Leib, have your men stand down. Take their positions back on the raft."

"Sir, if you put them out in the open, they'll have no chance."

"Leib, we're dealing with professionals. If they wanted us dead, we'd be dead already."

Leib reluctantly agreed. He waddled to the closest river

man and whispered to him. The man made a distinct clicking sound with his tongue, and the rest of the river men joined him on the raft.

The man spoke again. "Good. Now your archers."

Darius hollered from the trees. "I'll take my chances from here, Hunzuu. I've heard of you. You're a Babylonian legend, a war hero from decades ago. You're a knowledgeable man. You must understand my position."

"That I do. Just know if you make a move that appears to put me in peril, my men will not hesitate to put you down."

"And if you or your men make a move toward Sir Hayden or Mr. Amarsin, I'll not hesitate to shoot you through."

"Then, it appears we're at an impasse."

"It appears so."

A horse moved forward through the trees and emerged directly in front of the first raft. Four more horses followed, two flanking the first on each side.

He rode tall and appeared strong. He was older than Hayden imagined, but there was no mistaking that he was a seasoned warrior. His experience was apparent in the way he carried himself.

Hayden moved toward him, standing at the end of the raft, but not stepping onto the solid ground. If the man wanted to kill him, he'd make it as difficult as possible.

"Why have you been sent to us?"

"I'm only an escort sir. Your real guest will be arriving shortly. If it would be pleasing to you, I will have my men assemble a large tent on the beach here. Give you a dry place to meet him, as well as some privacy."

"Sure." Hayden replied.

His men dismounted and within minutes had the tent standing before them. Hayden stepped off the raft toward Hunzuu.

"Of whom do you have the distinct honor of escorting?"

"Marcus Shamash felt compelled to escort this renowned man to you. He feels you have need of speaking with him. That's all I know."

"Who is he?"

The carriage came noisily through the small opening and stopped sideways in front of the tent. Hunzuu dismounted and opened the door to personally escort the man inside.

He was old. Hayden guessed at least ninety. He walked with a cane and moved slower than anyone Hayden had ever seen. Hunzuu helped him down the steps and into the tent. He nodded for Hayden to follow. Once they were in, Hunzuu turned and closed the flap behind them.

"I've been instructed that he is never to leave my sight. I shall sit in the corner. Just pretend I'm not here."

"Of course," Hayden replied. "Are you going to give me

a proper introduction?"

"I don't know his name."

Hayden appeared concerned, but Hunzuu finished before Hayden could speak.

"Sir Hayden Smith, meet a pillar of the civilized world. I present to you... the Timekeeper."

Chapter Thirty-Two

The elder man sat down on the floor, gently folding his legs before him.

"Please… sit… welcome to my humble abode."

Hayden respectfully sat, wondering if the man was confused. It was a tent that Hunzuu's men had just constructed. The elderly man slowly rocked back and forth on his bottom.

"I know what ye are thinking, young man. I do. However, I live in tents. Where ere I lay my head becomes my abode. I've no place to call my own. Timekeepers job is ne'er done. All work and no play. Work… work… work."

"I don't understand. Why would Mr. Shamash intertwine our paths?"

"He spoke with me briefly, he did. Feels ye are lost, he

does. Wants me to help ye find tha way. Has nothing to do with tha current charge of reaching the Fortress, it doesn't."

"Lost?"

"That's what I just tol' ye young man. He feels ye are lost, he does… So are ye?"

"Am I lost? I suppose not. I've got the best guides on the river helping me reach my goal. We are close. After weeks, we're only a few days from our destination."

"Then why suppose ye did he send me thus? What propose ye does he mean, that ye be lost."

"I don't know sir. Did he give you anything else to go on?"

"Nothing else did he say. Nothing at all. But people seek not the Timekeeper and pay not his price unless they be certain the Timekeeper will be most helpful."

"Well, a few weeks ago, I asked someone what year we were in, and they referred me to you. They said no one kept time anymore. Only the Timekeeper. Perhaps that's how you can help me."

"And just why ye be so inquisitive about time? Ye be young. Many years left ye have. If ye be living the right way."

"How many years?"

"Life expectancy be most low. Fifty be considered old. Almost doubled that I have. And ye, how many years alive ye been?"

"Feels like more, but I'm thirty-five."

"Most men know not their age. More peaceful not to keep track, since the expectancy be so low."

The old man studied him for a few seconds before quizzically speaking again. "How is it ye come to this place? It be apparent that ye not be from here."

"What? I'm of Babylonian heritage."

"No. That's not be my meaning. The Timekeeper I am. I dwell on all plains equally. Most comprehend not my life. View eternity I do. And ye not be from here. That can I see."

Hayden was momentarily confused. He remembered the images he'd first seen when he'd entered the inner city of Babylon. The skyscrapers, the city streets, and the technology that was beyond anything he'd encountered here.

"What? I don't-"

"Ye be from another dimension. Another world, I suppose."

"You're out of your mind. What your saying doesn't make sense."

"Oh… but it does, does it not. Have ye not seen images you can't explain? Flashes that frighten ye because they seem so real."

"Yes, but-"

"T'ink hard. What be tha oldest memory ye have? T'ink back."

Hayden paused. He looked concerned. He leaned toward the Timekeeper, not wanting Hunzuu to hear his answer.

He didn't want to answer. "I can't remember."

"Ye memory, work it does not?"

"It seems to work okay, sir. For the past few weeks anyway. It's hazy… Almost like a dream… I woke up one day in an isolated cabin. I don't know how I got there. I don't know where I'm from."

He paused, contemplating the images again. "I don't remember important details of my life. When the time is right, I remember certain teachings. I know Babylonian customs and rules, but don't know how. I guess I am quite lost, sir."

"Lost ye are. Indeed, ye story is rare, it is. All my days, I've not heard its like. Ye memory gone, and with no reason why?"

"I don't remember why."

"Did ye suffer no accident? Did ye suffer one of tha plagues. Plagues are known for unexpected, diminished mental acuity."

"My mental acuity is fine. I have complete function and memory from the time I woke up in the cabin. Nothing has been lost. I just have limited memory before that day, and what I do remember makes no sense. Sometimes a dream… Sometimes a nightmare."

The Timekeeper pulled a few scrolls from a large sack

the men had placed in the center of the room. He leafed through them, found the one he was looking for, and then opened it.

"Here. This might be ye answer."

"What is it?"

"What time ye come from, stranger?"

"What?"

"T'ink back, what year do ye last remember?"

"I told you, sir, I don't recall it fully. What year is this?"

"Why… It be the fourteenth year of Lucius Sharukken, of course."

"What date, wise one? I vaguely remember divisions, A.D. and B.C. What date is it in correlation?"

The Timekeeper smiled. "I see what others cannot. Peer into eternity I do. Beginning of time til end. It's a gift."

"So what is-"

"Ye truly be of another time, my friend. Do ye remember Christ, the Messiah?"

"Of course I know of Him."

The Timekeeper's eyes opened wide. "Pray tell then, what be His name?"

"Why do you quiz me with answers that any charlatan could give you? My knowledge of Him proves nothing."

"Ah, but it does. Tell me His name if ye be aware."

"His name is Jesus, old one."

The Timekeeper couldn't conceal His surprise. "How impossible is! Cannot be, it cannot."

"What? What's not possible?"

"It be not possible for ye to be here. Ye are truly from later days, a darker time. But a time when the light shineth more brightly because of the darkness."

"I don't understand, wise one, what are you telling me?"

"Ye cannot know His name. It be impossible for ye to know. I only know because the gift moves me beyond the curtains of time. Hangs by a thread it does, and glimpse beyond it at times I can."

"I cannot know His name? I just told you, sir. His name is Jesus. That fact has been long established. It's no mystery. The whole world knows."

"Perhaps where ye are from that be true. Not here."

"You're telling me that people here have never heard of the Messiah? People here don't know of his coming to the earth and shedding his blood for the redemption of sins? They aren't aware of His deep love and compassion for lost humanity?"

"It be not possible for them to know."

"Everyone should know. Why is it impossible?"

The Timekeeper placed his hand over Hayden's, as if bracing him for what was coming. "Because, Sir Hayden… Here, the Christ has not been born. Here the world still awaits His arrival."

"That's ridiculous. You're telling me that Jesus Christ, God robed in flesh, Savior and Redeemer of the World, you're telling me that He has yet to be born."

"The world yet eagerly awaits, it does."

"How is that-"

The Timekeeper held up his hand, placing a solitary finger over his lips. "Shhhh. It's an enigma, the B.C. enigma."

"I don't understand."

The Timekeeper was slightly agitated at Hayden's lack of understanding.

"Same time it is… Living in same time ye are. Nothing changed, Sir Hayden. Same as always for you it is. Only difference is the Christ has not come yet. Living in a Christ-less world, you are."

"This is the year 2013, but without Christ ever having been born?"

"More or less… Woke up in world without Christ, you did. Lessons learn, you must."

"What are you-"

He held up his finger again. Hayden backed off the question. Finally, after leafing through several more scroll titles, the Timekeeper opened another one.

"This must be it."

He opened it wide and read it quickly, moving his finger up and down the antique parchment. Finally, he rested his eyes on a fixed spot.

"Here it is. Do you know what a prophecy is, Sir Hayden?"

"Of course. It's a prediction of the future."

The Timekeeper laughed. "Well, that depends on who it be ere tha prophecy gives."

"I'm afraid I don't follow you."

"Ye be right for some. For some prophecy a guess it does be. But to others, prophecy be much more powerful. It be a glimpse. A sliver of perception into another time. To some, prophecy be tha truth of eternity illuminating tha shadowy ambiance of today."

"What are you trying to tell me, Timekeeper?"

"Tha prophecies, as foretold by tha ancient scrolls across tha sea, they be real. They be tha learning of stately men who ventured into tha soul of God. Saw things coming, real events transpiring before them, they did. Saw them as if they were merely witnessing present times. Then, their eyes were closed to the eternal window they'd been peering through. And their vision of tha future was lost, it was."

"What of the prophecies, old man?"

"Alpha and Omega. Prince of peace. Everlasting Father. First and Last. Beginning and Ending. This be tha foretelling of Christ the Messiah."

"Yes, that's it. All of those passages are recorded in the Bible."

"The Bible? I know not of what you speak?"

"The Bible… the writing that revolutionized the world, the best selling literature book of all time. Surely you must know it?"

The Timekeeper searched through more of his records. "Aha… here it is."

"You have a copy?"

The man compassionately looked at Hayden again. "Sir Hayden, I'm afraid tha book has yet to be written. Many of its authors have yet to place pen to parchment."

"That's not possible."

"Take a look at tha world 'round ye. Does it appear the kind that has been affected by tha likes of such a man?"

"What do you mean?"

"The light of the world. His presence drives back darkness. The world awaits Him. Do ye know why, Sir Hayden? Do ye know why the hungry world waits? Do ye know the importance of what He carries?"

"Yes. He has already brought it to my world."

"Yet, not to this one, Sir Hayden. Ye are here to learn things ye must carry once you cross back. Ye are here to regain faith once lost, to leave a piece of yourself in others, to give hope to them in their ongoing struggle to await His coming."

Hayden was crying and didn't know why. "He's already come Timekeeper. He changed the world. He-"

"What did he bring your world, Sir Hayden?"

"Spiritual awakening."

"Look deeper… What else see ye of Him?"

"I don't… I don't know… I see a sacred revolution, a religious stirring. He pointed a lost world toward the hope of salvation. He restored faith."

"Not here… Faith is lost… Men have turned to the other gods. For far too long, heaven has been silent. We await the coming of the Messiah. Some suspect he will come as a warrior king, ready to overthrow the systems of this world. They long for a lion, but heaven sends a meager lamb to do its bidding. How can a war be fought with a lamb? No one would follow that."

"He is enough, Timekeeper. The Lamb is more than enough."

"Yet, ye still don't see it do ye. Look harder. What do ye see? What else brought he to your people?"

"He brought deliverance from demonic oppression. He brought-"

"Stop, Sir Hayden. Ye only see what ye eyes have been trained ta see. Ye only speak of religious things. Yet, his blood was more powerful than just to change religious candor. His life meant more than merely restructuring lost factions of faith. Why can ye not see His worth?"

"It's what I've known, Timekeeper."

"It's not enough. Not nearly enough… He didn't only come to change religion. That would only affect a few, for just a handful are religious. He came to alter the earth, to shake every portion of it and its people, to leave no nook or cranny of human existence outside of His grasp. Ye must look harder."

"I don't know what you mean."

"Look harder… Stop whining and look harder."

"You keep telling me to look harder, but I don't know what I'm looking at. All I can see is what I've already seen. All I can see is what I know. Tell me what to look for."

"Ye are here for a purpose, you are, Hayden. Search our world and ye own. What do ye see?"

"I don't know what you're asking?"

Tears streaked down Hayden's face. The elder man put his arm around his shoulders. He leaned in more closely.

"It's okay, Sir Hayden. I be here to show ye tha way."

Hayden tried to smile but couldn't, "Thank you, sir."

"Do ye know tha only difference 'tween this world and

ye own?"

"No."

"In yours, He has already come, and in our own He has not."

"So… I'm here to view the difference?"

"Ye must learn it. Ye must see it. Ye must feel it. Your faith need be restored."

"What's the difference? I feel as much hate toward Him here as I did there. It's the only thing I could feel when I woke up in the cabin the first day. I tried to write my feelings down and instinctively I knew. I just somehow knew that I hated Him."

"Ye be at odds with your creator. That mustn't be. Perhaps ye are here to find why ye shouldn't be."

"Perhaps. But there's still little difference, Timekeeper."

The Timekeeper growled, "Because ye see what ye want."

The Timekeeper diligently peered into the scrolls for what seemed like hours. Finally, he spoke again.

"Look 'round ye boy. Where be tha technology of your day? Tha education? Tha hospitals and schools? Where be tha orphanages? Tha humanitarian efforts to help tha underprivileged?"

Hayden started to interject but the Timekeeper stopped him again. "Where be tha freedom and equality for all people, regardless of race or sex? Where be tha reformation of a government established for tha people?"

"I don't know. I didn't think about it. I-"

"Because of Him your world has changed. He birthed a movement that cannot be stopped. It incessantly grows, leaving all who oppose it in its wake."

"The Christian movement?"

"Technology was awakened by tha p'wer of His presence. He was the light that came and removed the darkness from the earth. That wasn't just a spiritual awakening. His coming opened avenues of human existence that had forever been dimmed by demonic oppression. Early on, Christians were the forerunners of industry. Education is offered to everyone in your world, but it started with Christians who longed to spread His word. Tha poor live longer and have a higher chance of survival because His followers started humanitarian efforts to spread His love 'round the globe. People are no longer divided and defined by unfair class systems. Ye build to make ye world better for every one. It's because He came."

"But how? One man couldn't be responsible for-"

The Timekeeper spoke more clearly, almost as if he'd rehearsed it to be abundantly clear.

"Remember His lessons, Hayden. The world had remained in status quo, in the complacent mire of ignorance since sin entered in. It had existed on a linear plain of understanding for centuries. This meager lamb challenged the world order by His teachings. He taught tolerance to prejudiced bigots and love to leaders filled with hate. He taught mercy when judgment was the order of tha law. He taught grace when doom was demanded for one's mistakes. He taught selflessness instead of living for one's own carnal indulgences. He demonstrated compassion to those tha rest of tha world scorned. He desired that people would reach tha poor and broken, and that tha rich man was no more important than tha pauper. He demonstrated tha value of a soul, denouncing tha erroneous belief that people's lives hold little value."

Hayden couldn't hold back his emotions any more. They broke like a dam that had been barely keeping the deluge at bay. His tears no longer gently fell, they poured onto the sandy floor of the tent.

"I've been so foolish. I see it now. He has changed everything."

The timekeeper stood up and feebly moved toward the tent flap. He stopped at the exit.

"He has changed ere thing, Sir Hayden. I think ye are here to learn that. Don't forget. Never forget."

Hayden nodded.

The Timekeeper slowly walked out again. "Take ye time, Sir Hayden. Ye have much to ponder."

Chapter Thirty-Three

Torben impatiently waited in the back booth of the Huddle House. It was four in the morning, but he couldn't think of a better time to meet. Any of the patrol officers who might know him would have long since taken their late shift break for coffee. Most of them would be off the streets and in the station to write their final reports and get ready for shift change. The door opened and an officer stepped through the door. Torben wasn't alarmed. It's why he was here.

He silently motioned for the man to come to him in the back corner. The man nervously sat down.

"I could get in a lot of trouble for this, Torb. You know that."

"I know you could, and I'll never ask you to do anything like this again. I just needed to look over it real quick. You can replace it in a few minutes. They'll never know you left the station."

"Please hurry, Torben. I could lose my job."

"Let's have it then," Torben excitedly wiggled his fingers.

The man took out the plastic bag. Torben looked at the seal, it had already been broken.

"Who checked this out before you?"

"No one, Torb. Records show I was the first."

"Did you report that the seal had been broken already?"

"Yes, the guy that checked me in told me not to worry about it. Someone had obviously looked at it and not logged it. No big deal."

"No big deal. If they want, whoever is behind this could blame you for tampering with evidence."

"I've got to get it back to the station," the officer replied, as he reached for the plastic bag.

Torben swatted his hand away. "Give me three minutes."

He opened the plastic bag and held Hayden Smith's journal. He leafed through the book, skimming the pages to see if there was anything he could use. Three-fourths of the book through, nothing stood out to him. He was about to give up when something caught his eye. He stopped suddenly.

"That's it."

"What?"

"There are pages missing. Two pages right here in the middle. Look, he numbered them, and there are two pages missing. Front and back. There was something there they didn't want anyone to find."

"So anything useful has already been removed? Bummer."

Torben placed the book back in its plastic container and handed it to the officer. "Be careful getting back in. Don't let anyone see you. I've got a bad feeling about this."

"You. I had a bad feeling the moment you talked to me. Consider my debt paid, Torb. This was a big one."

"Agreed," Torben laughed. "Be safe out there, brother. Someone doesn't want the facts of Hayden Smith's accident coming out."

The officer got up and walked away. The tiny bell on the door jingled as he stepped outside, the only indicator of someone's going or coming. Torben smiled. Life, it is so fleeting. The space of a jingle, and then we are gone.

Chapter Thirty-Four

Hayden made his way from the tent. He'd taken a few minutes to compose himself after Hunzuu and the Timekeeper had exited. The sunlight hit him hard in the face, almost blinding him. He brought his hand to the top of his head, directly over his eyes, shielding himself from the bright rays.

He searched the area for the Timekeeper, but the carriage had already pulled out. There was no sign of him.

Hunzuu approached from where the carriage had minutes ago stood. He extended his arm and grasped Hayden's in an honorable handshake.

"I'm not sure what I heard or saw in there, Sir Hayden. I'm not sure I want to know, but I'm a man of integrity. I'll make mention of it to no one."

"Thank you."

"There's something else. Something the Timekeeper wanted me to do for you. He said it wouldn't make sense why, but he asked you to trust him. He said you would understand later."

"What did he want?"

"There's a large village over the next hills, only about an hours ride from here. He wants you to abandon your camp tonight. Let your group remain here without you. He wants me to escort you to the city."

"What city? The river people didn't mention it."

"They wouldn't. They never travel there. It's only for a certain kind of people. The most devout."

"What's the city called?"

"The city of the Elite."

"Why would he want me to go there? It doesn't sound like a place I'd be too interested in."

"He seems to think it holds something for you. He's the Timekeeper. He knows more than he puts on. If for nothing else, go for respect. He's almost one hundred years old. He deserves it. I've only worked with him a few times in my days, but I've learned not to question him. He talks a little strange, but he usually knows what he's talking about."

"And you will guarantee I'll be back by morning."

"If you have seen whatever he wants you to see."

"And how will you know if I have or not?"

"I won't."

Hayden looked confused. Hunzuu warmly snickered. "You will."

Hayden and Hunzuu topped the hill overlooking the city. It was a beautiful sight to behold. Large stone dwellings stretched for what seemed like miles. A gentle flowing tributary from the river flowed through the middle of it. Small boats were floating along its path, carrying the people up and down stream as they needed. It was a tranquil sight.

Much different than the camp he'd left behind. He'd had M'ya tied to the stake again and left Darius in charge of the camp. Amarsin's expression had not been flattering, but he had handled the charge well enough. It had still been raining there, the sun only breaking through for brief moments.

Here, the sun was warmly lighting the entire valley. There wasn't the slightest hint of rain. It was breathtakingly beautiful.

"Let's go down at once," Hunzuu said, as he spurred his horse. "If I know anything about the Timekeeper, then I know they're already expecting you."

Hayden spurred his horse as well, each man riding fast until they reached the gate of the stone wall surrounding the city.

A guard called from a tower on top of the wall. "Who goes there?"

"I am Hunzuu. I've been sent here to escort a guest to dine with your magistrates."

"And do you have an official invitation?"

"No, but they should be informed of our arrival. We were sent by the Timekeeper."

"Ah, a friend of the city indeed, but I'm afraid without an official invitation, I shall not be able to let you through."

"Do you know who I am?" Hunzuu inquired.

"I don't rightly care who you are stranger. You don't have an invitation; you cannot pass."

The gate suddenly opened and three men stood in front of them. They were dressed in proper attire and seemed to be brimming with confidence. The one in the middle spoke first.

"You'll have to excuse our over-zealous guard. I'm afraid he follows the rules too strictly."

"No offense taken," Hunzuu replied. "I'd have one of my men killed if he didn't follow my rules. At least you know you can trust him."

"Hunzuu, your legend proceeds you. We're honored to host you in our city. Word has it that you've brought with you another special guest. One who carries the blessings of the Timekeeper... and the sword of Tiber I might add."

"A truly dangerous duo," Hunzuu conceded. "May we enter in peace?"

The men parted and turned to walk away. Hayden

moved to follow them. Hunzuu grabbed Hayden's horse by the reins.

"Look," he said, as he pointed toward the guard in the tower.

The guard was still positioned above them with his bow drawn, arrow laced and ready for launch. Hunzuu pulled Hayden backward and the guard slightly relaxed, lowering his bow a little, but keeping the arrow notched.

"It's a test, Hayden, and he's doing his job."

"A test? Why would they test us? They were just friendly."

"It wasn't an invitation. No one enters without being invited… and these people… they test everyone… only the worthy are allowed to enter… only those who can follow the rules they've been given."

Hunzuu looked up and called to the strangers walking away. "Excuse me sirs, but may we be invited willingly to join you inside your city gates. My friend and I will not continue further lest we be asked."

The man in the middle turned back to them. "Yes, you may follow us."

Hunzuu didn't smile. "Not without an invitation, sir. The Timekeeper requested for us to have a meeting. I'm not sure why, nor do I care. So, I'll ask once more for an invitation and if not given one, we shall both leave."

"Don't bother asking… Sir Hayden Smith and Warrior

Hunzuu, will you both please come into our city? The Trio are asking for your presence in our courts."

Hunzuu nudged his horse forward without looking upward again. Hayden nervously followed, eyeing the guard above with every step. His bow hung loosely at his side, as he pretended to no longer see them walking inside.

The three men led them through a maze of stone walls, finally stopping at a stone hut beside a large well.

Hunzuu whispered, "This is where they stay."

"How do you know?"

"Because it's the location nearest the water. The leaders are usually lazy. They don't want to have to walk far, and if they send servants to fetch it, they don't want to have to wait long."

Hayden laughed. "Save me from such folly."

"I would the gods save me from it as well. Tiz why I've stayed a soldier. I would rather die in battle fighting for a just cause, than die on my back, an old man calling on young girls to do my bidding."

"Spoken like a true warrior," Hayden replied.

The three men entered the stone home. A moment later the one who had spoken to them earlier returned.

"You must come in for tea. We would love to hear of your stories, Warrior Hunzuu."

"Some other time I'm afraid. I'm not the reason for this

meeting. The Timekeeper left me strict instructions that Sir Hayden is to see the city. He must see the Historian."

"Ah, the Historian. Good luck with that. If you can catch him sober, he might have something to say. If not, our history will certainly be clouded in mystery and comedic influence. The truth would probably not be as grand."

Hunzuu grinned, "We shall have to take our chances. Timekeeper's orders."

"Try the center wall then. He usually goes there to think... or drink... which ere is his flavor of the day."

"Just point me in the right direction."

The man pointed to the west. "About five stone throws, if you're a strong lad. Ten if you aren't."

Hunzuu motioned for Hayden to move, and they both nudged their horses forward in the right direction. Hayden looked over his shoulder after a few seconds. All three men had disappeared into the hut.

Thirty minutes later, Hunzuu pulled up and turned his horse toward Hayden.

"West, ten stone throws. We've traveled thirty. I see no middle wall. This maze he's sent us through has only gotten us lost. We're losing daylight."

"What happens after daylight?"

"You don't want to be out here alone after dark. Not even with the warrior Hunzuu escorting you."

"Why not? There seems nothing to be afraid of."

"That's the way of things, Sir Hayden. It appears serene and friendly when the light is burning brightly overhead. However, once the illumination has diminished and men may hide their hearts, it's another world all together."

"Let them come for us then. I'd hate to disappoint."

"Sir Hayden, I didn't become an old warrior by being a fool. I know when to fight and when to fight another day."

"I wouldn't have pegged you for a coward, Hunzuu. Your reputation doesn't suggest as such. I thought you were a fearless man, who spat in the face of death."

"All the fearless men have gone on to meet their maker. Those of us smart enough to be scared live long enough to become generals."

Something moved behind them. A stone fell from a place in the wall. Hunzuu drew his sword and moved his horse in front of Hayden. Someone spoke from behind the rocks.

"Spoken like a true soldier indeed."

An older man moved into their view. He staggered toward them. Finally, he stopped and placed his hand to his chin in deep thought.

"Perhaps he thought you culd throw fu'ther," the man laughed. "He didn' thank you'd throw like a girl."

Hunzuu angrily started toward him.

The man staggered backward, cheerfully taunting him. "Where's tha wisdom of tha aged warrior now. It gots lost a' forst offense."

Hunzuu dismounted and held his sword aggressively low as he marched forward. Hayden lunged from his horse and quickly intervened.

"Give me one reason why I shouldn't run him through and shut his old mouth forever."

"Because, Hunzuu, the Timekeeper forbids it. If you kill him, I can't follow my orders."

Hunzuu looked at the man incredulously. "You've got to be kidding me."

"No, we've found the Historian.

"Indeed you have young man," the Historian replied. "Imma afreed you are gonnnnaa haf to fagive my mild intox… intoxication."

Hunzuu slapped him hard across the face. The man staggered backward, appalled.

"I'll dare you strike tha face of tha hist… hist…hist."

"Historian," Hayden finished it for him.

"Yeah… that," he replied. "But since you came for tha po'puss of seeing me. I guess my obligation mandates that I make sho ya get what ya came foe."

"Please, sober up," Hunzuu replied. "You're of no use to anyone like this."

"Follow me up tha stairs. Jus' make sho I don' fall. Would be a most gruesome death."

"I ought to just throw you off myself."

Hayden exchanged harsh looks with Hunzuu. He finally looked toward the old man. "Lead the way, Historian. We won't let you fall."

The Historian led them up a long flight of stairs. Once at the top, it only turned a few feet, before turning again and moving upward to span the same long distance as the first time. Once at the top of that set of stairs, it veered again into the same process. After the third set, it opened into a large balcony overlooking the city.

Just across the balcony was a large wall. It was at least forty feet tall and stretched as far as Hayden could see.

"It's magnificent," he exclaimed. "A rare beauty."

The Historian appeared somewhat more sober from their walk. "It is a marvel. And this is why you are here, Sir Hayden."

"Why? I don't understand."

"Nor do I, but the Timekeeper wanted you to behold its radiance and study its splendor."

"It's a grand work of art. It must be one of the hidden wonders of the world, but what is there to study?"

"Its purpose, Sir Hayden. You must examine its purpose."

Hayden moved further out onto the balcony where he could view both sides of the wall. On one side, everything was perfect. He could view the people intimately from where he was perched. They marched about like robots, moving in unison. Everything was in perfect order. They had wealth, livestock, and slaves. They seemed blessed beyond measure.

On the other side of the divide, the people appeared totally different. They didn't have the advantages of those across the wall. They had to work harder for their living. They had no slaves, little wealth, and only enough livestock to serve their purpose. They weren't as solitary in their mannerisms. Their blessings weren't nearly as apparent as the others.

The Historian moved out on the balcony with him. "Which group will you belong to, Sir Hayden? If you had to make your choice."

"I don't have to make that choice. I'd rather just be where I am."

"But if that weren't possible, where would you choose? On what side of this divide would you dwell?"

Hayden looked at them again. "I don't know. I guess the first one."

"Why is that, Sir Hayden?"

"Because they have more. I'd want more for my family. I'd want to be able to take better care of them."

"Good intentions indeed, but look closer."

Hayden stared back into the first side of the wall. He saw it differently this time. They were just as blessed, but they weren't happy. They had many more possessions and riches, but their faces were empty and expressionless. They seemed to be afraid of something.

He turned to the second side of the wall. They were happy. Their possessions were still much fewer, but they'd learned the art of contentment. They weren't moving with the confidence of the elitist on the other side, but they weren't robotic either.

"What's the difference between them, Historian?"

"There was no difference at first, Sir Hayden. But the disparity grew because of their beliefs."

"The only difference between them is their beliefs?"

"Yes. The one side believes that God should bless all those who serve him. They feel that the believers are privy to personal favors at the hand of God. The elect are always bestowed good things, and they are never to be bothered with the worries of life. Tragedy never strikes God's truly elite followers, for He always protects them. Sickness, depression, hardness of life, and poverty are all signs that one has fallen out of favor due to lack of commitment on their part."

"They seem truly blessed, but they don't appear happy. Why the paradox?"

"Why indeed. That's the ageless question, and one you're meant to muse."

"Why the distinction of the groups? Why are they so divided over a few simple beliefs?"

"The elitist group soon naturally separated themselves because they thought they carried God's favor."

"But by removing themselves from the rest of the people, aren't they distancing themselves from any opportunity to demonstrate the love and compassion of the God they serve? How can they demonstrate his purpose if they have no opportunity but among themselves?"

"Good questions indeed, Sir Hayden, and ones I cannot answer. I only write history and keep account of what has transpired. I have no control over the outcome, and no knowledge of why things happen. That's why you were brought here, I suppose."

"I don't understand. Why does he want me to see this?"

"You'll figure it out, Sir Hayden, of that I'm sure. The Timekeeper doesn't make mistakes."

"And what of the other side? Are they truly happy, even though they are less blessed? Or, is it a façade, both sides pretending to be something they aren't, just so the other doesn't know how bad each hurts because of their own decisions?"

"Wealth and health aren't the only way to measure blessings. You see the temporal. The Historian must view the entire spectrum. Look harder, Sir Hayden."

"That's what the Timekeeper said as well. Why does

everyone keep telling me that?"

The Historian moved from the balcony and pointed toward the sky.

"The sun looms lower Hunzuu. You must get him from the city before the night falls. The true nature of the city is revealed when the bright light fades."

Hunzuu motioned for Hayden to follow him. "He's right. We must make haste. Only about thirty minutes of daylight left. And it took us at least that long to get here. We've still got to make that awful climb back down."

The Historian walked toward them and stopped when standing in the middle. He took them both by one hand and led them to the opposite side of the balcony. They looked over the steep ravine under them. A forty-foot drop would kill them all.

"Trust me," he said, as he led them right to the side.

Hunzuu pulled back. "You're out of your mind. I'll not follow a drunk to his death. It's suicide."

The Historian stepped off the ledge, pulling them both by the arm as he fell. A second later, they landed in a deep pool of icy water. Hayden immediately surfaced and swam the short distance to the side. Hunzuu was already on the shore, panting for breath. The Historian pulled himself over the edge a couple of seconds later.

Hunzuu was furious, "You could have killed us, drunkard."

"But I didn't, and I saved you precious minutes."

He whirled around and looked Hayden squarely in the eyes. "Let that be another lesson for you to remember, Sir Hayden. Be careful at the top, one misstep and the entire journey to power and position may come crumbling down. Once you're where you want to be, protect it. The wolf is always at the door."

Hayden nodded. The Historian briefly continued, "Remember them, Hayden Smith. Study them. Both sides of the divide. Learn it well. Don't forget… Now you two must go."

Hayden mounted his horse, as Hunzuu had already mounted his and was slowly making his way back where they'd come. Hayden turned to the Historian one more time.

"I can't say I fully understand, but hopefully one day I will."

"Soon you will, Sir Hayden, I believe in you. We believe in you."

Chapter Thirty-Five

"I believe in you. We believe in you."

Reverend Kevin Michaels leaned over Hayden's hospital bed. Dr. Poole stood against the doorway, waiting patiently for the minister to finish. He couldn't hear his words, but he felt their sincerity.

Reverend Michaels moved more closely to Hayden and whispered in his ear.

"I'm sorry we weren't there for you, Hayden. I should have reached more fervently. I took it for granted. I've learned a lot now. I know I didn't display the love of Christ that I teach."

He paused, wiping tears from his eyes. "I failed you, Hayden. I failed your family. I knew something was wrong. I could feel it. I guess I just didn't want to bother anyone.

Maybe I myself didn't want to be bothered. I don't know. I have no excuses."

He placed his head down on the rail for a moment, and then lifted it again to continue. "I put the full weight of responsibility for reconciliation on your back. I was the one who was supposed to be connected to God. I was the one who was supposed to be spiritual. I was the one who was supposed to fight to restore my brothers who are overtaken in a fall. Yet, too many times I find myself faltering in that. If a man is wrong, I've felt that he should make the journey back. But that's not God's way. It's man's way. God loved us enough to make a way back for us. He gave everything to make sure we knew he was there. He carried us when he had to… How far I find myself from the passion and likeness of Christ. You should have never had to walk alone… Hayden, I'm sorry."

Voices behind him made him turn around. Doctor Poole had moved from the doorway and was walking toward him. The associate pastor recognized Detective Torben Mayes beside him. He extended his hand as the two approached him.

"Detective Mayes, if my memory serves me correctly."

Torben nodded. "And Reverend Michaels. What brings you here to visit?"

"Failed responsibility," the minister stated, holding his head down in regret. "I wasn't there for him when he needed me most. I feel my lack of active compassion allowed him to persist down the wrong road. I'm fighting for him now."

"As are we all," Doctor Poole answered. He linked hands with them. "Where two or three agree, right?"

Torben nodded, and Reverend Michaels smiled. They bowed their heads and the room was filled with the gentle prayers of earnest men seeking a miracle. Somewhere in eternity, heaven shook, angels stirred, the throne room was filled with a sweet savor, and God stepped from His throne.

Chapter Thirty-Six

Hayden and Hunzuu brought their horses to a stop just before reaching the beach. Darius called out from the darkness.

"It's okay, Leib. Have your men stand down. It's Sir Hayden."

Hayden tiredly dismounted his horse and walked toward the raft. The rain had mercifully stopped. He noticed that they were all studying him inquisitively. He shook his head.

"Nothing happened. Waste of time. Let me get some sleep, and I'll explain in the morning."

He lay down on his pallet and, within minutes, was sleeping soundly. Hunzuu sat quietly away from the raft and alertly listened for anyone coming through the darkness. No one came. After a couple hours, he laid his head back and went to sleep as well.

No one stirred. After a few minutes, M'ya gently kicked her feet in Hayden's direction. On the third try, her foot made contact with his right arm. He awakened and was startled to find she was the one who had touched him. He quietly moved toward her.

"What do you want, thief?"

She whispered. "Just once, I want you to listen to me."

"Why, M'ya? You've admitted to stealing it. There was a witness who watched you."

"I was set-up, Hayden."

"Set-up… surely you don't expect me to buy that."

"Yes… I do… Because it's the truth."

"Okay, because it's so late and I'm so tired, I'm going to humor you. Explain."

"I was warned that someone was going to try to take the sword from you. But no one knew who was going to take it."

"Who told you that?"

"The elder slave. He encouraged me to keep it safe."

"He told you to steal it?"

"No... Not in those words. But he told me it was about to be taken, so I took it first, to try to protect you. Hayden, I swear to you. I did steal it, but I stole it to keep you safe. I can prove it."

"How?"

"Because the sword has never left the boat. That's why you couldn't find it in the woods."

"That's absurd. We searched every inch of this boat."

"Hayden, it's right where it was supposed to be. In your spot. If you will untie me, I'll show you."

"Do you think I'm a fool, M'ya?"

"I'm not trying to play games with you, Hayden. It's there. Please just trust me."

Reluctantly, he moved to the stake and sliced through the hard rope binding her. "Don't make me regret this."

She crawled with him back to his location on the raft. She pulled back his small blanket and revealed one of the logs he'd been lying on.

"When we were building this raft, I had them build this especially for me. The carpenter mentioned it to no one."

She pulled back a top layer of one of the logs, indicating a hollow place just large enough to fit the sword. Hayden removed it from the space and held it in his hands, moving his fingers over the blade. It felt good to hold it again.

"I will keep it strapped on my waist at all times now."

Sudden movement caught his attention. Four of the river men were quickly lurking on the raft. Four others were stealthily moving along the bank, making their way toward them. Hayden stepped up to pull the sword from its scabbard. He was knocked backward by one of the men, sending the sword clanging against the log floor.

The noise of M'ya screaming alerted everyone, but it was too late. Eight river savages were already on them with daggers drawn. Darius got off a shot with his bow, hitting one of the men in the chest. The man fell backward onto the shore.

Hunzuu drew his sword and ran onto the small raft with them. Blades dinged, as swords clanked against each other in a mad onslaught. In the confusion, the rope holding the raft was severed. The raft was quickly caught in the current and dragged into the middle of the raging river.

Hunzuu had already battled two of the men, knocking both from the boat. He turned on a third. Hayden fought with another one near the center. Amarsin and the elder stayed toward the edge of the raft, trying to stay out of harm's way. As the raft rocked on the waves, the men moved back toward the middle, fearful they'd fall off and be swept away.

The lightning flashed, as the rain once again opened up on the warring men below. The savages were making a desperate attempt to obtain the sword of Tiber. They'd been hoping M'ya would finally reveal its location. Once she did, they'd quickly made their move. Everyone was collateral damage. They didn't care who died or lived.

M'ya caught a glint of the lightning on the sword's steel

casing and lunged forward to secure it. She rolled over and helped herself up, clutching the sword tightly in her arms.

One of the men attacked her from behind. He grabbed her around the throat and pulled her toward the edge of the boat. Darius notched an arrow through the driving rain. He shook his head to knock the water from his eyes. There wasn't a shot; the man had positioned her as a human shield.

M'ya fought against him to no avail. She was being choked and losing strength fast. Hayden hadn't noticed from his spot in the center of the raft, still occupied with the talented swordsman. Hunzuu saw it too late. He couldn't make it to her, as another of the river men moved on him with a dagger in each hand.

M'ya was on her own. She struggled to remove the sword from its sheath. After a few seconds, the sword was completely uncased.

She was growing sick. The world was spinning around her. Lack of oxygen was making her faint. However, when the sword was freed from its encasing, she felt a renewed energy. She flipped the sword upward and shoved it around her side and into the river man's belly. He fell backwards from the raft, but tugged her by her hair as well.

The lightning flashed again, momentarily illuminating the boat. Hayden head butted the man who had gotten too close to him. The man fell to the ground unconscious. Hayden immediately searched for M'ya. Hearing her scream, he looked in time to see her falling from the raft, landing with the man in the driving water.

He ran to the place from which she'd fallen and frantically searched the water around them. It was flowing too fast and was much too dark.

The lightning made it possible to see every few seconds. Hayden didn't even notice that Hunzuu had finished off the last of the river men. He was focused on getting M'ya back to safety. Leib moved to the side of the raft with Hayden.

"There," he pointed downriver.

Darius joined him, and they all three looked in the direction he was pointing. M'ya was struggling to stay above water ninety feet away from them. She was wildly thrashing, but still clutching the sword. She was pulled under the water by the churning current.

It was too dark to see. The lightning flashed a second later, but they never saw her resurface. M'ya and the sword had disappeared. They looked in every direction but couldn't relocate her.

Darius anxiously searched for her. Finally, he stopped and looked toward Hayden. "It's no use Sir. The water is too strong. M'ya is lost for good. No one could survive that."

Leib shook his head in agreement. "M'ya and the sword are gone... They are gone."

Chapter Thirty-Seven

Torben sat in the lobby with Reverend Michaels.
Reverend Michaels was still obviously distraught over what
was transpiring a few rooms over. He kept his eyes averted
from human contact, preferring to stare into the carpet.

Finally, Torben interrupted, "I don't know exactly what
is happening with you, Reverend, but I doubt your
compassion could run so deeply for a man you barely knew. I
get the feeling there's a little guilt at play here. Please, talk to
me."

Reverend Michaels looked up from his spot on the floor
and looked at Torben for half a second before turning away.

"Guilt. Shame. Yes. I let him down. His family. I let
them down."

"How, Reverend? You may know something that could

help me here. Somehow, I feel you know something important that you're not saying."

"I don't know anything, detective. If I did, I wouldn't withhold it. Isn't there a charge against that sort of thing?"

"If I were operating in an official capacity, perhaps. But I lost my badge a few days ago. Someone didn't want this investigated. I didn't want to stop. I feel like he deserves peace before he dies."

Reverend Michaels looked up again. "You kept pushing even at the expense of your job?"

"Some things are more important than what we do, Reverend. More important than what I do is who I am. I can't compromise one for the other."

"Thank you, detective... for speaking clearly... I needed to hear that. I won't compromise who I am any more either."

He paused and looked directly into Torben's eyes. "I'm not sure if I know anything beneficial. I'm being honest about that. However, ask any questions that you like, and I'll answer the best I can. No more stalling or hiding."

"Thank you, sir... What was Hayden like, before all of this?"

Reverend Michaels warmly smiled, recalling details that were of a better time.

"He was affectionate. Great personality. He could make anyone laugh, and without trying. He was highly intelligent too. Witty. A small business owner. Great father. Appeared to be a wonderful husband. Consummate professional and family man. Engaged in the church."

"What happened? I mean what was he like in the few months leading up to the accident?"

"I don't know. Something changed. He seemed exceptionally stressed most of the time. His time in church decreased drastically, although his family still attended regularly. My wife and I discussed it with Sis. Smith. She said everything was fine, that he was just working extra hours for a new business venture. But we could tell she was worried. There was something she wasn't saying. We just didn't want to push, you know?"

"Sure... I understand... Did anything of note happen before the accident? I've tried to access his financial records to no avail. However, a friend with a credit company indicated to me that Hayden's credit rating had dropped extremely low. He filed-"

"Yes, Detective. They did file bankruptcy. Sis. Smith told us that the business venture had failed. They were losing much of what they'd accumulated. I think that started his downward spiral."

"Downward spiral?"

"Yes, Detective. Hayden started drinking. Nothing serious from what I could ascertain, but enough that it created red flags in his wife's mind. She also suspected him of gambling from time to time... Sorry, detective, how is this important. I hate drudging through a man's past."

"When you're searching for a needle in a haystack reverend, you must remove all the hay, one strand at a time, until the only thing left is the needle."

Reverend Michaels grinned and nodded. "Amen to that. I think I understand."

Torben nervously bit his lip before continuing. "And what of Mrs. Smith?"

"Well, she was the perfect wife and mother. Kids loved her. Her children were always well mannered for their age. Yet, not to the point of not having fun. They lived life, and you could tell they lived it fully. They were happy. The entire family was."

"Go on?"

"She was strong willed and independent. I guess that's what you get when you're raised in a politician's home."

"What? How did everyone miss that? She's the daughter of a politician?"

"Oh, people around here don't miss it. That fact is well known. No one talks about it because she preferred it so. She was like royalty. If I ever met a modern queen, it would have been her. Beautiful, regal, fair, and kind. Unassuming. She didn't want any special attention because of who she was. She liked to forget it and pretend she was like everyone else. Just a normal wife and mother who loved God."

Torben was obviously upset. "All the questions I've asked around the department. Everyone I've questioned. And no one mentioned this to me."

"Perhaps they feel as I do. It's unimportant. It's not connected, detective. It has no bearing on who she was."

"Maybe… but it could mean everything… Which parent was the politician?"

Reverend Michaels chuckled. "You really don't know, do you? It was her father. Sis. Smith's maiden name was Andrews."

"Is that supposed to ring a bell? I don't know of any Andrews in politics around here."

"Oh… not around here, detective. You must think more globally. Laurence Andrews."

Torben swallowed hard. "The vice-president of the United States. You're telling me that our current vice-president is Hayden Smith's father-in-law?"

"Yes. Last year he was a Senator and presidential candidate. He realized he was slipping in the polls, so he joined with the top Democratic nominee. Both of them together became extremely popular, and the rest is history."

"Thank you," Torben said, as he jumped from the couch they'd been sitting on. "I've got to go. You've been most helpful."

Chapter Thirty-Eight

Torben walked down the long hallway, escorted by a highly trained security detail. He had been through three security checkpoints already. His picture had been run through facial recognition. His fingerprints had been scanned. He'd answered questions concerning his background check. They'd contacted his previous supervisor from the police department. Finally, his credentials seemed to be in order.

"What's next?" He playfully asked once of the armed escorts, "a lie detector test?"

The man didn't smile. He looked up, barely making eye contact. "That's only if you failed the first questionnaire. You passed."

"Good thing. I don't have much more time to waste here."

"We aren't on your time, sir. Not at the white house."

Torben nodded. "Understood."

The flight over hadn't taken long to acquire. He'd been on the ground in D.C. within eight hours after deciding to make the trip. The vice-president had been kind enough to send an escort vehicle to pick him up. Torben wasn't foolish. The vice-president had to have been expecting him. Sooner or later, the past always catches up to you.

The guards stopped in front of a large doorway. The lead guard took his key card and flashed it in front of a door on the wall. The door clicked from the other side but still didn't open. A finger display lit up by the door handle. The man sat his index finger on the display. After a few seconds, the door loudly beeped, and then it popped open. The lead guard entered the doorway and motioned for Torben to follow him.

The vice-president sat behind a huge elliptical desk. His version of the oval office Torben assumed. Torben extended his hand.

"Vice-President Andrews, an honor to meet you, sir. I hate that it has to be under these circumstances. I know it has been a while, but I'm very sorry for your loss."

"Thank you, Mr. Mayes. I'm afraid I haven't got much time. Takes a lot of work to help run this country. We don't need people like you distracting us from our job with local news stories."

"Sorry, sir, but this local news story just happens to

revolve around your daughter and your son-in-law."

"My daughter is dead, Mr. Andrews. Why shouldn't her memory be honored in a peaceful way? That's all her mother and I ever wanted."

"I'm sorry, sir. You're right; she is dead. But I've come to discuss the living."

"There is no one that fits that description."

"Your son-in-law sir. He isn't dead yet."

"Well, he's dead to me."

"Sorry, sir."

"Stop apologizing and just state your business, Mr. Mayes. You didn't get dressed up, take a flight, put up with White House security, just to let me know you're sorry. You have an agenda. What is it?"

"You're son-in-law is fighting for his life right now. The doctor is going to have to pull the plug by the end of the day if I can't find a family member for him. He's only got a few hours to live, unless you stand up. All I need is a family member. The fact that you're the Vice-President will only convince them further to give him more time."

The Vice-President stood up. "I'm now sorry that you wasted your time coming down here for this. You should've called me, and I could've answered and saved you the trouble. I'm not interested in saving his life. He can die and burn in hell for all I care."

The Vice-President motioned for the guards. They stepped into the room. "Please escort Mr. Torben back outside, I've got nothing else to say to him."

Chapter Thirty-Nine

The raft made landfall, and Hayden immediately jumped onto the sandy beach. He ran to the tall weeds and bent over. He violently threw up into the grass.

"You alright?" Leib asked. "You look mighty sick."

"I'll be fine. Just get sick every time I think of her. Can't believe she's gone."

Darius moved close, but stayed a little further back than Leib. He compassionately looked at Hayden.

"She was important to you, was she not?"

"Extremely," Hayden replied, as he bent down to throw up again.

"Perhaps she is still alive," the old black man said. "Maybe she survived the struggle. She seemed to be a decent enough swimmer."

Leib shook his head. "There's no way. I know the river. I've seen it swell too high before, but not like last night. It was most boisterous. That was different. No one could have lived through that."

Hayden picked himself up. "We have to finish this. It's what she would have wanted. We have to keep going until Amarsin is safe at the Fortress."

Leib looked at him. "If you're okay to travel, we can make it by nightfall tomorrow. Right over the next ridge is a tiny merchant village. We can stop there for food and water. We also have enough capitol left to purchase fresh horses. All in all, we should make it right before dark."

"Then let's depart, the sooner I can rid myself of this great responsibility, the sooner I can be on my way."

Leib shook his head. "It's not that easy any more, Sir Hayden."

"Not that easy. Should be easy enough to get there, a day's ride."

"Yes… To get there is the easy part… Once we're at the city, the elders must accept us before we're allowed to stay. We aren't granted permanent safety until they've reviewed citizenship."

Darius groaned, "You mean there's a chance we've traveled all this way and we'll be rejected?"

Leib shook his head from side to side. "All of us will be

granted temporary solitude. However, due to recent overpopulation, only so many people are allowed permanent status. So, we will have to see which of us are granted permanence, if any."

He looked up into Hayden's eyes. "Hayden, I'm afraid your mission isn't complete until Amarsin is heard by the board. Once they meet him and approve him for permanent residence, he cannot be touched by anyone, including Abaddon Dearth."

"And then my job will be done." Hayden replied.

"It will just be starting," Hunzuu answered. "The Timekeeper said that The Fortress is your turning point, Sir Hayden, but it's not the end of your journey."

Hayden shook his head in denial. "My journey ends when I say."

"No, Sir Hayden, You still have lots to learn. Lots to learn. Your journey ends when you wake up."

"I just love when you tough men talk in metaphors. Sounds like one of the great poetic masterpieces," Leib retorted.

Hayden didn't smile. "Metaphorically or not, it is almost finished."

Hunzuu didn't look up. "You must understand, your journey doesn't end until you rise from your slumber. You must rise from your slumber."

Chapter Forty

Torben sat in the airport, dejectedly waiting for his flight. He needed to get back as soon as possible. He wanted to be there when Doctor Poole pulled the plug. He didn't know why. There was nothing appealing about watching a man die. However, somehow he had always felt connected. He at least owed Hayden Smith that much. He couldn't do what he had intended, so the least he could do was make sure he wasn't forced to die alone.

Torben nervously jumped, as the vibration of his cell startled him. He answered.

"Hello. Torben Mayes. Can I help you?"

"Detective Mayes?"

Torben struggled against the static to hear the feeble voice on the other end. She sounded broken. Distant. Almost old, but something more than the weakness of years was behind the voice. Pain. He could feel her pain through the airwaves.

"Yes. This is Detective Torben Mayes. Who am I speaking with?"

"Detective Mayes. 'Who' isn't important right now. What I need you to do is contact Dr. Sherman Shultz. Do it now. Please. I'm sending his contact information in a separate file. Don't leave D.C. without talking to the doctor."

"Who is this? Who-"

"Sh. I don't have time. Just promise me."

"I have a flight to catch. I-"

"Cancel it. You must speak with Dr. Shultz. Please."

Torben stood up and walked away from the terminal. He begrudgingly shook his head.

"I'll check it out. I promise. Please just tell me why-"

He listened for several seconds at the empty silence. He hung his phone up and looked back at the caller i.d. There was no number listed. It had come through as blocked. He dialed the number to his department. A perky receptionist answered.

"Is this who I think it is?"

Torben replied, "Still got my number saved I see. That's got to be a good sign."

"Of course. Of course. You know I ain't letting them get rid a you that quickly. My work husband gotta come back and take care a me."

He laughed. "Crazy as always, I see... Can you do me a favor? Off the record."

"Sure. Anything for you Torb."

"Run my phone records. I just got a call. I need to find out who it's from."

He heard her clicking in the system. After a few seconds she stopped. "That's strange."

"What is it?"

"It's been blocked. Then deleted. It was deleted as I was looking at it. Someone with higher connections than I've got just hacked the system. I'm afraid you aren't gonna find out who made that call."

"Thanks, girl. I owe you."

As he hung up the phone, his text message alert signaled its soft beep. He looked at the single message displayed. It was a contact for Dr. Sherman Shultz. He stared long into the number.

Chapter Forty-One

Two hours later, Torben sat in another hospital room. He looked into the hollow eyes of a man almost gone. Cancer had taken its toll and was about to claim his life. He hadn't expected this when he'd agreed to visit the mysterious Dr. Shultz.

Dr. Shultz was in and out of consciousness. In moments of clarity, he'd try to answer a few basic questions. At other times, he'd ramble incoherently, stringing multiple topics together that made no sense.

Dr. Shultz looked at him again. "Larry… is that you, son. I'm so glad you're here. I've missed you so much."

"No, Dr. Shultz. It's not Larry. I'm Detective Torben Mayes… Remember, I've come to ask you a few questions."

"Oh… Sorry… I remember. Ask me now. I'll try to

remember… If you see Larry, tell him to stop by and see his daddy."

"I'll do that Dr. Shultz. Now, can you help me with these questions?"

"Yes, sir. Go head and ask me."

Torben moved closer to him. "I have to ask you about Hayden Smith. His wife and children were killed in an automobile accident last year. Are you aware of that?"

"Yes. Do you know who I am?"

"No, sir. I'm afraid not. I was just told to call you."

"Who told you? Do ya know that?"

"No, sir. I tried to verify, but whoever called hung up on me."

"I know who called. They called me too. Said to expect to hear from you."

Dr. Shultz rocked backward in his bed again. "Larry. Is that you?"

Hayden tried to hide the frustration. "No, Dr. Shultz. It's Detective Mayes. Remember? I was asking you about Hayden Smith and his family. Someone told me to call you. You said you knew who it was."

"Oh, yes. I remember who called me. They said you were gonna contact me."

"Dr. Shultz. Who called me?"

"Mrs. Andrews… The Mrs. Vice-President."

"What? Why would Mrs. Andrews want me to talk to you, doctor?"

"Because I was her husband's personal physician for many years. I was there for him."

"So? What does that have to do with my case?"

"Only everything. Son, I've lived with guilt now going on a year. Cancer wrecked my body soon after that accident. Perhaps it's poetic justice. God getting back at me."

"For what?"

"The cover-up."

"You were there?"

"Yes. I was-"

"Wait," Torben exclaimed. "That's why no emergency personnel were needed? You were on scene? You were the physician on sight?"

"Yes. I tried to save them the best I could, but it was no use. And Senator Andrews… Vice President Andrews… he watched them die. He saw them with his own eyes. It destroyed him. His grandkids. His daughter."

"I can't imagine the horror, sir."

"No. You can't. Most awful."

"But I don't understand Dr. Shultz. What were you

covering up?"

"Everything, detective. We covered up everything."

"Like what? I don't understand."

"Larry… Is that you, Larry… It's so good of you to stop by and see your daddy."

Chapter forty-two

Dr. Poole reported to the two other doctors on the floor. "He still has shown no signs of brain activity, but I'm telling you, he just needs more time."

The other doctor aggressively pulled the chart from his hand. "You see what the orders are. If he isn't showing some sort of progress within the hour, you have to end this. If you can't, then I'll do it myself."

"You have no heart," Dr. Poole retorted, and then turned and walked away.

The small caravan of travelers topped the hill. They overlooked the large valley spread before them. There it was. The Fortress. Its walls were at least thirty feet tall. Their thickness seemed impenetrable. Towers were spread over the walls every one hundred and fifty feet. Two archers held their post in each tower. Unless there was another gate on the opposite walls, there appeared to only be one way in and out of the city. A line of armed soldiers held their post just outside the main gate, ready to swiftly defend any of its inhabitants if needed.

"That's it," Amarsin whooped. "We've made it."

The excitement was broken after only a moment.

Dust was rapidly stirring diagonal to them on the desert plain. The elder black man took out a looking glass. After studying the dust for a few seconds, he looked at Hayden.

"It's Abaddon Dearth. He's trying to beat us to the gate. He doesn't want to let you in."

Hayden slapped Amarsin's horse on the rear and yelled. The horse leapt forward, running for the city. He spurred his, and the rest of the group followed.

The horses raced toward the gate, every fiber in their being sensing the urgency of those on their backs. Nostrils flared, muscles tensed, and hooves rapidly rose and fell. Hayden looked across the valley. It was going to be close.

Ten minutes later, Amarsin made it to the first line of defense. The soldiers stood erect, their spears pointed outward toward him. Hunzuu made it to the group only a few seconds behind him. He looked to his right. A few hundred yards away, Abaddon Dearth came with about forty riders.

Hunzuu dismounted and moved toward the group. "I am Hunzuu. Babylonian general. We need immediate passage into the city please. This man is the family of Parliamentarian Marcus Shamash. He needs permanent citizenship."

A man emerged from the group of soldiers, just as Hayden and the rest of the riders pulled up. He was tough, no nonsense about him.

"I'm certain you're aware that the Fortress isn't under Babylonian rule and, matter-a-fact, doesn't appreciate Babylonian law? Who he is and who you are have no bearing here. Are we understood?"

"Yes, sir. I meant no offense. We're just sort of in a hurry."

He motioned over his shoulder where the other riders were coming. The man looked past him into the stirring dust in the distance.

"They're coming for you?"

"Yes," Hunzuu replied. "They would like my friend here dead. Along with the rest of us."

"And what crime has been committed?"

"The crime of resisting the Babylonian laws you so openly detest. He stood up against them for a stranger. He offended one of their leaders and had him publicly reprimanded. As you can imagine, that didn't go over well against one consumed with Babylonian pride."

The man nodded. "I see."

After a few thoughtful seconds, he offered, "Two of you may enter at once. Select your two."

Hayden looked at Amarsin. "Go. Now. Make your entrance. Darius, go with him. Get him the proper papers please."

Darius nodded, "Are you sure. I can stay and fight."

"No. I need you to make sure he gets there. You're the only one I really trust to do it. Get him his permanence."

Darius took Amarsin by the arm and started to run toward the gate. Hunzuu moved toward the leader.

"And what of the rest of us. You would leave us here to die?"

"No one will be dying without my approval."

As the gate opened, Amarsin and Darius were escorted inside. Another large line of soldiers marched into the field to stand with the others. Hayden guessed there were now at least a hundred soldiers on the ground. He looked up and noticed that several archers had moved to the top of the wall as well. At least thirty were lined up tightly, ready for action if needed.

Abaddon and his entourage pulled up a few seconds later. Abaddon gallantly rode his horse toward their small cluster.

"I am Captain of the Host, Abaddon Dearth. I demand to have these men turned over to me immediately. We wish to do this peaceably if possible."

The leader of the men from the Fortress muttered under his breath. "What is it with you Babylonians. You just think everyone should bow down and grovel at your feet like whipped pups."

Abaddon was appalled. "I have come respectfully. I'll dare you talk to a Babylonian captain in such a tone. I'll have you hanged."

The man looked behind him and waved his arm in a sweeping gesture. "I'd advise you to take a look around Captain. If need be, I have four hundred soldiers just inside the walls. I've already got you outnumbered here. I've got several of the best marksmen you've ever seen just itching for a chance to let an arrow fly. You should reconsider your position."

Abaddon slowly looked around. His anger was blinding his judgment, but the protector of the Fortress was right. There was no chance he'd survive such an encounter. He decided to resort to one of his unwritten rules. When you can't beat them, you lie to them.

"All I want is the group attempting to enter now. I have no quarrel with the rest of you and no hostile intentions toward the city. This has long been in good standing as the last city of refuge. Even us haughty Babylonians keep our pacts. A Babylonian commander never lies. If you turn them over to me at this time, I swear an oath that you will be rewarded personally with double your weight in gold. Your top staff will each be given a Babylonian virgin as a concubine. You can have ten. Your city will be in great standing with all of Babylon, and we will owe you a favor.

You will have gained the most powerful ally on the planet."

"Generous offers indeed… And just to make sure we are clear, this is an offer… correct?"

"Certainly, an offer backed by my oath to you."

"And as with any *offer,* I have the right to refuse?"

Abaddon couldn't conceal his anger. "Why wouldn't you want to accept an offer with that much reward? You'd be foolish."

"Captain Dearth, in my experience with Babylonian offers, there is a fine line between the offer and a threat. If I take the offer, I will be thus rewarded, but if I do not…"

"If you do not, you'll be sorely pun…"

Abaddon caught himself and stilled his anger. He couldn't lose this one because of his hostility. "If you do not, sir, you will be sorely disappointed that you failed to make the right choice. That is all."

The leader turned to consort with the men closest to him. Hayden quickly approached the circle of advisors.

"Sir, you can't really be considering this offer. We've traveled far to seek the safety of this city. We believed in you for help. It's what the city was founded for. It's your sworn duty to protect us. Even if the protection is temporary."

The leader turned to him. "Times have changed, Sir Hayden. You aren't under our protection until you are in our walls. Back up."

"Please. Don't do this."

"We have the future of our city to think of. If we cannot afford to keep this going for future generations, where will the troubled and guilty go? We have an obligation to think about the thousands of others who will flee here. What shall we do if we've nothing to offer them? We're the last hope. The only refuge left standing. We're guilty man's last chance at redemption."

Redemption. Guilty. Hayden's stomach started turning knots and he didn't know why. Something about those words shook him to the core. He staggered backward. Hunzuu caught him before he fell.

"You okay? Sir Hayden, what's wrong with you?"

.   .   .

Dr. Shultz was momentarily coherent again. Torben placed his hand on the man's shoulder. The tired old-timer looked into his eyes.

"I'm sorry. I'm trying, detective. I think the shame of that night has overwhelmed me. I'm dying son."

"Sir, what were you covering up? I don't understand."

"The cover-up didn't end that night, detective. It's been an ongoing event. It never stops. One lie builds onto the next. It doesn't go away."

"What happened?"

"Long story. I don't have time to give you the details. I'm

afraid I'm slipping away soon. I feel the life slowly fading from my body, boy… You know, after you've dealt with death so long, after you've seen it so many times in others, after you've stared it down too many times to count, you can literally feel it when it comes for you."

His eyes were slowly fading. "I feel it now. I feel it coming."

.   .   .

The man left his group of advisors and stepped forward between Abaddon and Hayden. "Perhaps we can facilitate some arrangement between both parties. Bring a peaceful conclusion to this matter. Both sides can compensate the other for whatever ills have been done. Surely nothing is beyond absolution. Forgive and forget. Let's move on. Both parties can come inside and celebrate."

"And both sides owe you a favor," Abaddon bellowed. "Your advisors lead you well, if we were interested in your own good. Howbeit, we could care less about what you get from this. I was only being nice because it seemed the easier path."

"What could be easier than peace, Captain Dearth? I'm offering a chance at peace."

"Yet, peace isn't what I'm after. I want vengeance. I demand justice."

"Vengeance is for the weak. It only blinds one's ambitions and renders them useless to the kingdom they serve. Bitterness and rage only enables you to see your own cause. Your kingdom focus is lost to the failing of your own heart."

"Yet, at times it can drive a man, as it drives me now."

"It drives you, sir, but it's no longer a matter of the Babylonian empire. It's become personal, and personal affairs and kingdom matters must be kept compartmentalized. You cannot live with offense in your heart if you truly live in honor of your kingdom. You cannot truly stand for the oath you swore to your king, if you have allowed the transgressions of others against you to rule your heart. For, if they rule your passions, your king cannot. There must be room for forgiveness. Every man can change if he thus chooses. Everyone has that power."

"Well spoken, but I'm afraid you've left me no choice. Witch," he yelled, as he turned to the men behind him.

The witch stepped forward with a long encased object in her hands. The leader of the Fortress appeared afraid. He recognized her, the High Priestess of Baal. She removed the object from its casing and presented it to Abaddon. He held it high above his head. Hayden recognized it immediately, the sword of Tiber.

"Let's see how well your lofty principles hold up against the wrath of the gods," Abaddon belted. "Just remember Fortress leader, you could have done this peacefully."

The witch whispered in Abaddon's ear, her words a most sibilant sound. He smiled evilly and looked toward Hayden.

"Perhaps there is still a way to save this city."

"What do you propose?" The city spokesman asked.

"The leader of this rebel rabble, and the fat man who travels with them."

"The fat man just received his papers of permanent residency," someone yelled from atop the wall.

Everyone looked upward to see Darius clinging to the papers and holding them up for everyone to see.

Darius grinned, "If he weren't so out of shape, he'd be up here holding them himself. Those last few stairs were a killer."

"Then undo the papers," Abaddon demanded. "There's nothing that can't be undone. Get rid of them."

Hunzuu stepped toward them. "Captain, you've gone mad. You know the universal code concerning the city of refuge. Once a person has been granted clemency and permanent residency, there's nothing can be done to them unless they leave the gates."

"Then have the tub of lard hand delivered, and I'll take care of it from there."

"You also know that the subject must leave the city willingly. He can never be forced."

"So, you try my hand again. I still hold the power. I don't care about the law."

He motioned for the witch again. She came forward again, leading a small horse behind her. He reached over the saddle and untied a large sack. It hit the sandy earth with a thud. Abaddon seized it and drug it closer to them. Standing ten yards away, he cut the end off of the sack.

The sunlight hit her eyes, startling her from the dazed demeanor. She put her hands up to defend herself from the bright object blinding her. Through the shadowy haze, she made out Abaddon and the witch standing over her. She looked around to find herself surrounded. Then she saw him, a few feet away. Standing with a shocked expression on his face.

"Hayden," she weakly called, "you're okay."

Abaddon yanked M'ya from the bag by her hair. Hayden started toward him, but Hunzuu grabbed his arm. Abaddon swiftly pulled a crooked dagger from the belt at his side and placed it against her throat.

"It seems I have the upper hand, Sir Hayden. You have a choice to make. You can get the fat man out here, and she will live. Or you can let him remain inside the gates, and she will die."

The witch removed an hourglass shaped item from a cloth wrapping. It was small. She flipped it upside down, and the sand starting slipping through to the other side.

Abaddon wickedly laughed. "It's only three minutes, Sir Hayden. Who is it going to be? Whichever one is standing before me when the final grain falls through. That person is going to die."

"I can't do anything, Abaddon. You know the law. I can't

undo his permanence. It's already been granted. The city of redemption has already granted him forgiveness. His past mistakes have been atoned for. He can't be punished for those missteps, even though personal to you."

"But he's still guilty, Sir Hayden. He still committed treason against Babylon. That fact remains."

"No. It doesn't. You know the law, Captain Dearth. It's been omitted from the books. His record is now as clean as the day he was born. By the law, he's clean and has essentially done nothing to you."

"Then, what am I to do with the effects of his crimes? They weren't taken from me. I still feel their sting when I think of him."

"No. You feel wounded pride, Abaddon. There's a vast difference between wounded pride and an actual crime. You were only injured by your own arrogance. It's no fault of his."

"Then your choice is made."

Abaddon looked at the sand passing through the hourglass. Half of it was on the bottom of the other side.

"Let's just skip the second half and get this over with. At least someone is gonna die."

Hayden held up his hand as Abaddon tilted the knife further against her throat, ready to thrust it.

"Wait!"

"Why, Hayden? You afraid you won't be able to live with

yourself. The choices you made have led you down this path. You're afraid you can't live with the guilt? You might have to take your own life? You couldn't stand knowing that someone else you cared deeply about died because of you?"

The tears swelled in his eyes. He struggled to keep his composure, but he had that overwhelming feeling again. He was nauseous and dizzy. The world began to spin around him. He leaned against Hunzuu to try to steady himself.

"That's it, isn't it, high and mighty, Sir Hayden? You're guilty knowing an innocent person is going to die because of a foolish choice you made. You can't live with the thought. The guilt already overwhelms you. It eats at you, until it destroys you from the inside like a maggot. You feel the weight of culpability pulling you down, making you like a common man. You can't hide from it. It's always there. Constant reminders sending tremors into your soul. You know she could have lived if you would have chosen better, and not selfishly made the decision on your own."

Hayden almost passed out, but Hunzuu held him tightly against his side, not allowing him to slip.

"Hayden, stay with me. What's wrong with you? It's almost done. Your mission is almost over. Amarsin is safe, let's figure out how to get her home too."

.　　.　　.

Torben wiped the heavy sweat from the man's brow. "Sir, please… Fight through this. Just a little longer. I need you to help me. Mrs. Andrews wanted you to help me. Sir, if you feel guilty because of what happened, you have to let me know. You must find peace in the fact that you can help set things right."

"I can't. It's too much. It went too far."

"What did, sir? What went too far?"

"Senator Andrews. He took it over-the-top."

"What happened, doctor. Please."

"The boy. Hayden. He used to spend a lot of time with his father-in-law. Then one night, he saw something he wasn't supposed to see. It would have messed up the Senator's chances at moving up."

"What did he see?"

"The affair."

"The affair? The Senator was having an affair?"

The sick doctor tried not to laugh. The stifled chuckle caused him to choke. He coughed a few times and leaned over to spit in the plastic tray at his bedside. Torben couldn't help but see the blood. Finally, he cleared his throat again.

"No. He would have never done that. He might have been a lot of things, but he loved Mrs. Andrews. I was with him often, and he never even so much as looked at someone else."

He coughed again, and his eyes momentarily rolled back. He slipped from coherence for a moment before coming back to.

"It's here for me, son. Can't stall it much longer. Death is knocking. I can hear it calling."

"What's the affair? What did Hayden see?"

"It's too much to explain. There's a file in my office. Not at my home. I have a private condo in New York I escape to sometimes. There were also files in Hayden's car the night of the accident. Those files are all together. I took them all. Find them. They're behind the Mona…"

He slipped away again, his eyes fully closing. Torben lightly tapped his face.

"Please. Dr. Shultz. Don't leave me like this. Please."

Dr. Shultz slowly came to. "Find the file. You have to find the file."

"I will, Dr. Shultz. Now what happened with Hayden?"

"The Senator blackmailed him. He played hardball with his own son-in-law."

"How?"

"Assets. He used his son-in-law's business against him. That's why the business tanked. If Hayden couldn't financially support his family, he'd have nowhere else to turn. The business had been going well. They'd just moved into a new home. After years of living like happy newly weds in a cheap trailer park, she'd finally been able to move into the house of her dreams. He couldn't take that away from her."

"So the Senator used his leverage to hurt their business?"

"He used his leverage to kill their business… And no one knew it but Hayden. He couldn't just tell his wife that they were going to lose everything because her own father wanted to control them. So, he played the game."

"But it affected him?"

"It greatly affected him. He lost a lot of weight. He started gambling and acting irresponsibly. Eventually, he started drinking. The night of the accident, he-"

The man started to fade again. He tightly closed his eyes and squeezed on Torben's hand. "Oh, it hurts. It's tugging at me. It's trying to pull me in."

"Please, sir. Don't let go just yet. You're almost done. I need this. You need this."

The man grimaced. "He'd finally had enough. The night of the accident, he called Mrs. Andrews and told her the truth. He couldn't work up the nerve to confront them alone, so he'd been drinking. She could hear it in his voice. He told her that he was done with it. He was packing his wife and kids up and coming to their house. She confronted him about the drinking, but he swore to her that he hadn't been drinking in weeks. He just needed something strong to knock the edge off. He promised her that his ramblings weren't just a drunkard's tale. He had proof. He'd been secretly keeping documents for the past few months showing what the Senator had done to them. That's the files I mentioned earlier. The plan was for Mrs. Andrews to watch the children while the couple talked it out with the Senator-"

"But he never made it there? They never made it to the

house."

"No, detective. They never made it. He was about twenty miles away when the accident happened. Forty-five minutes after his conversation with Mrs. Andrews."

.   .   .

Abaddon stared into Hayden's eyes. "What's it gonna be, Sir Hayden. Time's almost up."

Hayden staggered forward. "I can't," he screamed. "I can't live with the guilt. Don't let an innocent person die because of me. I can't live with myself."

.   .   .

Torben leaned closer to the man. His life was fading and his voice was extremely faint. Torben wanted to get a little more.

"So, the Senator hired someone to make sure his son-in-law never got to his wife with the proof? That was swift response time. The plan backfired that much? Hayden lived, and the entire family was killed instead."

"The Senator may have privately made a few phone calls, but I'm not aware of it."

"Then how'd it happen? Who was driving the other car that was never found? Who was the Senator protecting?"

"That was the cover-up, son. The Senator was protecting himself. An investigation into the accident would mean that people would look into how and why the accident occurred.

He didn't want that. He would stand to lose it all. People would ask questions that would lead them back to him."

"The Senator was driving the other car?"

"Detective, you aren't getting it. There was no other car. That was the cover-up. It ended the investigation before it started. There never was a second vehicle."

Chapter Forty-Three

Hayden regained his strength and moved forward again. "Look, Abaddon. I have another offer. There's another way."

"What is that, Sir Hayden? Because your time just ran out."

Hayden looked at the glass and saw the last grain slip through. He winced.

"Wait. I have a suitable solution."

"I'm waiting, but not much longer. There will be blood."

"Take me instead. I offer myself. Hayden Smith. Babylonian elitist. Take my life."

"You'd give me your life for hers? A Babylonian nobleman for a worthless, thieving harlot. What a waste of a good legacy."

"Legacy isn't made merely by the purity of blood flowing through my veins. Legacy is made in the moment. It's not only defined by a man's choices, but by why he makes them."

"Honor? That's your choice, but I find no honor in death."

"And I find no honor in living only for oneself."

Abaddon sheathed the crooked dagger. He held the sword of Tiber upward with one arm, getting ready to rip it across the exposed throat of M'ya.

"Then I shall happily kill you both."

"Hayden… The sword," Darius screamed from atop the wall, as he let an arrow fly. The arrow flew straight and caught Abaddon in his left bicep, causing him to drop the blade at his feet. M'ya fell from his grasp as well, and hurriedly crawled away from him.

Abaddon stooped to retrieve the sword, but it was gone. Two feet away, Hayden stood over him with the blade in his hands.

The witch screamed an evil incantation toward the sky. It started to dim, the light of the afternoon quickly extinguished by whatever spell she was casting. Hayden tossed the sword to Hunzuu and dashed toward M'ya. He held her hand and gently yanked her from the ground. They quickly embraced before he pulled her back toward the group of soldiers near the wall.

The sky crashed with a deafening roar. Lightning flashed

in the distance. The heavens opened, and it began to pour.

Abaddon's men suddenly drew spears and formed a seemingly impenetrable line. Abaddon waved his injured arm forward, silently commanding them to advance. With their spears held high, they marched toward the wall.

The leader of the Fortress was frightened, but the moment wasn't too big for him. He motioned for the archers on the wall. They opened an onslaught on the advancing group below. The Babylonian armor was holding up well. The soldiers' open facemasks were the only point of entry for the arrows. Hitting such a small target from thirty feet overhead was no easy task. A few men fell, but for the most part the line kept advancing.

Hayden still held M'ya by the hand, as he ran toward the gate. He turned to see Hunzuu standing with the sword near the city's protectors. The elder black man was running toward him with a dagger that Hayden never knew he had.

M'ya had been right; the elder had been the traitor. Hayden started to yell to Hunzuu, but it was too late. The man was three feet behind him. He lifted the blade to sink it into Hunzuu's back. As he lunged for him, he was suddenly knocked backward. Hayden hadn't seen what had attacked the man, but he'd been stopped in his tracks.

Eyes wide, Hayden looked at M'ya. "Perhaps there is something to the legend of that sword."

She shook her head and pointed. "Look."

The elder black man rolled over. An arrow had been shot

halfway into his stomach. The arrow's velocity had knocked him backward. Hayden looked to the wall. Darius held his hand up in a victorious manner and smiled. His shot had not only saved M'ya earlier, he'd also now protected Hunzuu.

The sudden clash of weapons caused him to pull M'ya forward again. They were almost to the gate when he heard it start to open. It rose a few feet and then stopped, only to fall back to the ground.

"C'mon. C'mon. Let us in. You've got to let us in."

The gate started to slowly rise, but fell again only a few seconds later. They reached the gate only to have it slam in their face. Hayden turned back toward the battle. The city's protectors were fairing okay, but they weren't defeating the Babylonians. Their armor was too strong, and their spears were too long. They were marching through the protector's layers with relative ease.

Abaddon mounted his horse and kicked it in the ribs, pulling the reins toward the gate. Three of his men followed him.

The gate slowly began to lift again. He motioned. "Hurry, M'ya. There's enough of a space. Slip underneath it. Hurry. Before it closes again."

"No. I won't leave you."

"M'ya, now. You have to go now."

"No, Hayden. Live or die, my destiny has always been with you."

He pulled her near him in a warm embrace. "You're special, M'ya. You can't die here. Please, if you care about me, you'll go now."

The space widened just a crack. "Now, M'ya."

Tears fell as she separated herself from him and disappeared under the wall. The gate slipped and loudly crashed to the ground only a moment later.

Abaddon pulled his horse sideways in front of Hayden. "Looks like she didn't make it. That gates at least four feet thick. She'd have had to crawl fast to get through before it crushed her. Looks like your decision cost her life. How tragic."

Hunzuu retreated against the gate and stood shoulder to shoulder with Hayden. Abaddon shook his head in disgust.

"Two Babylonian noblemen, both going to die today. And for what? Pride? To save an awkward lad who couldn't be a true Babylonian if he tried. To protect a thief and free a slave. To help a handicapped troll. Is that what the chivalry of Babylon has been reduced to?"

The gate cracked again. This time it rose higher and higher. The cable on the upper end seemed to be holding. Within seconds, it was ten feet in the air. Abaddon launched his horse toward them. They both backed across the threshold, eyes still fixed on Abaddon and his men.

"No," he shrieked. "You cowards. Where is your sacred virtue? Come back across the threshold and fight like men."

"Another day perhaps, Captain Dearth. Another day."

Abaddon stepped toward them, but stopped when he noticed the four hundred soldiers quickly advancing. The Fortress warrior hadn't been bluffing. He also noticed from inside the walls, a few hundred more archers climbing the steps to get up the wall. He motioned for one of his men to sound the retreat. The drumbeat filled the air, and the Babylonian line moved backward, breaking their advance on the few guardsmen left pinned against the outer wall.

Abaddon furiously glared at Hayden for a few seconds before speaking. "You can't stay in there forever, Sir Hayden. I know your kind. You're too strong to hide among the rubble. You'll come out, and when you do, I'll be waiting for you. This isn't over."

"Til next time then. May God grant you peace and forgive your hostility towards your brothers."

Abaddon stormed away, leaving them standing just inside the Fortress walls. M'ya ran to Hayden's side and tightly embraced him. He smiled.

"You're making a habit of almost getting killed in front of me. You're going to have to be more careful."

She put her head against his chest. She needed him. It was the first time she'd felt safe in her life.

Chapter Forty-Four

Abaddon Dearth stood at the fork of the raging river. It was still storming overhead; part of whatever spells the beautiful witch had cast to aid them in battle. It had been a few hours since he'd dispatched her, promising to call on her again when Hayden or Amarsin decided to emerge from hiding.

Hatred raged within him. He could almost feel it burning his soul. It didn't matter what they thought about him or his Babylonian standing. He'd not let a day go by without reminding himself of his vendetta against their lot. He'd see them dead for this. All of them. Some sins just couldn't be forgiven.

He kicked his foot against one of the small pebbles that had fallen loose from the cobblestone walkway. It bounced a few times, before almost rocketing into the raging current a few feet from where he stood.

This was an ancient city. It had been one of Babylon's finest when he was a child. Yet, as Babylon had drawn inward, slowly becoming the most powerful kingdom on the earth, several of its more beautiful outposts had been lost. Babylon's technological and medical marvels were far past that of the rest of the world, but even technology couldn't aid in keeping some of the more historical places from being forgotten.

He remembered the place well. It was only a few hours hard ride from the Fortress. A little further south, it was set against the banks of the mighty river almost at the point that it joined the great sea. He remembered the stony path he used to run on as a child. He remembered his mother's smile. His father's rugged but tender mannerisms. The comfort of home. The many quarrels he'd had with his twelve siblings. That had been so long ago.

My, how the years had changed him. He looked at the site the old homestead had been on. He could almost see the image of the little boy running through the yard. His father was right behind him, pretending to be some monster. Finally, he caught him. They both laughed. Then, the man picked him up and threw him overhead, whirling him through the air like a bird. Those days had been most precious, but they were nothing more than a forbidden memory.

He looked at the image of the child in the yard. The tenderness and affection. The laughter. The pure joy. Now, he was nothing but hard steel and cold regret. Anger had driven him to the forefront of the Babylonian army, but it had calloused him to the point of poisoning every meaningful relationship he'd ever known.

Here he stood, on the grounds he'd once zealously played on as a child. Now, more like the emptiness of the place he'd once cherished, he stood alone.

He moved a little further down the path. They still stood as he remembered. The bronze statues he'd often played around as a boy. They stood opposite each other, the path moving between them. Each statue stood six feet tall, resembling a faceless Babylonian Guardsmen holding an ancient sword. The inscriptions at the base of each had always enamored him.

The one to the right translated as *Honor before family*. The second one translated as *Brotherhood before honor*. It had become a mantra. It's why he'd risen high above anyone else in the Babylonian Guard. It had become his life. It's also why he was only the shell of a decent man, and he knew it. He'd never admit it, but he knew that his life was unfulfilled.

He heard the stirring behind him and whirled to see who was there. Strangers approached from inside the wooded area. There were eight of them. Woodsmen. Highly armed.

"What do we have here?"

One of them whistled. "Looks like a Babylonian elitist."

"Indeed it does."

Abaddon wasn't shaken. He'd faced difficult circumstances before. He looked at the one who had spoken first.

"I wasn't always an elitist. I used to live here. I was raised right there where you stand. My mother used to fix our meals at about that very spot."

"Too bad she didn't starve ya then, stranga'. Cuz then I wouldn't have ta kill ya."

"And you still don't. We don't have to do this the hard way."

He wasn't sure where the sudden restraint was coming from. Perhaps memories of his childhood had brought with them a more mellow tone. He wasn't afraid, but he didn't want to fight either.

"The hard way is just the way we like it, stranger."

The man drew his sword and stepped forward. Abaddon thrust his own sword through the man's stomach. His blade was out that quickly. The other men paused for a moment, measuring him again. Their first calculations had been off, and it had cost a friend his life.

"Well, what are we waiting for? Let's finish this," one of them yelled, as they drew their weapons and rushed toward him.

Swords clanged. Bones were broken. Flesh was cut. Men fell. Abaddon faced the last of them. The man was a disgrace. He cowardly dropped his sword and ran.

Abaddon looked around at the others. No one was moving. He looked at his clothes. Blood. Lots of it. Much of it wasn't his, but he noticed something disturbing. A deep incision was running from the top of his left breast to the bottom of his stomach on the right side. He was bleeding badly.

He felt weak. He stumbled back down the path toward his horse. He'd try to ride to safety. Get someone to help him. He walked a few more feet, staggered again, and then lost his balance completely.

He landed on his back and stared up into the evening sky. The rain still pelted the cobblestones around him. He could hear the roaring of the river a few feet behind him. He turned to his right and felt life slipping from his grasp. The statues stood over him like angels come to take him home.

He stared longingly into their empty faces. He wasn't afraid of death. No true Babylonian should be. Gazing into the stony faces, he remembered the words of the Seer a few days before.

Beware the bronzed warrior by the cobblestone path. When the river overflows, you're life will be taken before the sands run out. Before the sands run out.

Abaddon Dearth closed his eyes and faded into eternity.

Chapter Forty-Five

Torben sat at the desk opposite the captain. They both stared in awkward silence. Finally, Torben broke it.

"I don't know what to do, sir. I followed the leads-"

"I know, son. I just don't like where they led you."

"I don't either, sir. I-"

"Going after the vice-president of the United States doesn't seem like a great career move, Detective Mayes. For any of us."

"You think we should just pretend it didn't happen."

"What he did was wrong, Torben. There's no doubt about that. But his actions didn't directly lead to his family's death. It appears that Hayden was drinking. He's ultimately responsible, as grisly as the other details are."

"But the cover-up. We just ignore it? He blackmailed his son-in-law, destroyed his own daughter's life to protect himself. That's not to mention the other officers involved. The first officer, Mayor Jenkins, recognized the victims and told the police department that it was code four. He called the Senator, and the Senator arrived shortly afterward with his personal doctor in tow. It was far enough out of the city that they were able to work the scene without further incident. They spent a year perfecting their scheme."

"It doesn't change the facts. It proves the vice-president is a crooked man, but he's a politician. Didn't we sort of know that already?"

Torben slightly grinned. "I suppose so."

"Let's just let this one go, kid. The vice-president will get what's coming soon enough."

"Yes, sir."

The captain opened his drawer and removed Torben's badge and gun, placing them on the desk.

"You'll be needing those again, detective. It's good to have you back."

"Good to be back," Torben said, but shoved the gun and badge back to him.

The captain looked confused. Torben stood up and walked toward the exit, stopping in the doorway.

"Don't worry, sir," he said, as he stepped into the hall. "I'll be back soon. I just need a little vacation."

Torben closed the door behind him. He felt bad. He hadn't told the captain everything. He'd left out the part about the files hidden in the doctor's unknown apartment. He hadn't mentioned anything about the "affair."

There were too many questions that didn't have answers, and for Torben Mayes, that was never acceptable. He opened the envelope in his hand and took out the one-way ticket to New York.

Chapter Forty-Six

Doctor Poole cautiously approached Hayden's side. He wasn't ready to do what must be done. The other doctors entered the room behind him.

"It's time, Dr. Poole."

Dr. Poole slowly made the long walk to the bedside. He silently and almost agitatedly muttered under his breath.

"God, I asked you for a miracle. You've given me nothing. Please don't let these faithless, scientific minded non-believers triumph over you. They know I've been holding out hope. They mock my faith. I could really use a favor."

"Stop stalling, Dr. Poole, and who are you talking to? Mr. Smith can't hear you."

Suddenly the monitor measuring Hayden's brainwaves

erupted with motion. The machine exploded with an urgent beeping. Dr. Poole leapt up and stared at it unbelievingly.

He muttered again, "You'll have to forgive me, God. You've answered and I stare in unbelief like Rhoda must have looked upon Peter."

He turned to the two doctors behind him. "I'm afraid I can't pull the plug just yet, gentleman. He made the deadline. By only seconds, but he made it."

"There's no reason for optimism, Dr. Poole. This patient had a recent flutter before. Remember? Even if he lives, chances are he will probably be a vegetable. At best, he'll be paralyzed forever. He wouldn't want to live like that."

"We don't have the right to make that decision."

"I'm afraid we do. The state ruled that because he has no family to make his decision for him, it's left up to us."

A tall, thin and very attractive woman entered the room behind them. She was no doubt in her fifties, but the years had been extremely kind to her. She pushed her glasses up her pert nose. She had a certain air about her, a quiet confidence that couldn't go unnoticed.

"I'm afraid Dr. Poole will no longer be needing your assistance, gentlemen. You can be dismissed."

"Who are you? You can't just dismiss us."

"I can, and I have. Mr. Hayden Smith will be receiving care from only Dr. Poole from now on."

"You don't have the authority to make that decision."

"I'm afraid I do. Mr. Hayden now has a family member willing to speak for him."

"We haven't heard anything about that."

"Well you have now."

"Who?"

"Me. I'm Mrs. Nancy Andrews, wife of the Vice-President of the United States, and Mr. Hayden Smith's mother-in-law."

Epilogue

Hayden stood with Hunzuu on the tall wall overlooking the city. From where they were positioned, they could see the city on one side, but if they moved to the other side, they had a mesmerizing view of the ocean. They watched the waves rolling in for several minutes. Neither man spoke, both taking in the incredible beauty of creation.

Finally, Hayden looked away from the endless water and toward Hunzuu.

"I understand it now, I think."

"What's that?"

"I understand why he had you bring me to that city, the one with different people on both sides of the wall."

"Yes. The one where you asked him what the difference was."

"Yes," Hayden laughed. "He told me it was only their beliefs. I didn't get it then, but I think I do now."

He looked back into the ocean. "It's the temporal verses the eternal, Hunzuu. One group lives bound by their own election. They possess freedom, but they aren't truly free... The other group lives free only because they've learned to embrace the hope of a more eternal reward. They sacrifice the present, learning patience and contentment, in order to gain a more profitable and lasting crown."

"That's a rather profound concept, Sir Hayden. Are you sure that's what he wanted you to see?"

"Yes. I am. He wanted me to understand that if our hope is in this life only, we will be most miserable. He wanted me to understand that the only way to overcome the guilt, pain, and resentment of today, is by believing in the promise of tomorrow. Today's tragedies only build in us the foundation for what God plans for our future. If we stay untried and shifty like the sand, we have no stability on which he can build the weightier matters of eternity."

Hayden looked at the city, and then he glanced back at the ocean. "It's all temporal, Hunzuu. This whole earth is slowly passing away. The only way to ensure our future and the future of our children is by embracing and valuing the essence of eternity."

"You're almost there, Sir Hayden. I think you've almost discovered what he wanted you to learn most."

Hayden looked at him again. "I know what he wants, Hunzuu. I'm ready for it. Pain, tragedy, hurt, and sickness;

they're all part of natural life. None of us are immune, and we are free because of it."

"Free? How so?"

"Free, because on the side where they expected God to protect them from every storm, there was no freedom there. They were all forcing themselves to live in accordance with God's desires because they were afraid if they didn't, he'd retaliate and destroy them. There's no love in that, and without love, there's no God in it either."

"So religion without love is empty?"

"Religion without love is lifeless. It's incomplete. We must learn to love… for where God is, always there is love."

"And what of the guilt and hatred you said you have been feeling?"

"Love lets all things go. The causes of those things are only momentary conditions of a temporal, messed up world."

"And you've done that, Sir Hayden? That easily, you let those things go? The guilt of your mistakes? The scars of your past? The bitterness toward God and the ones who've wronged you before? It's all forgiven?"

"Not at all, Hunzuu. I'm still human. I'm a temporal being, but I'm taking steps in an eternal direction. The journey isn't over for me yet, but this is a great beginning."

ℭoming soon

A family shattered. A kingdom on the brink of collapse. Only one hope.

The Sin Cloud

Jonathan R Walton

Coming January 2014

Ex-slave, Darius, discovers that his father, the King of Aksum across the great sea, has been murdered. He learns that the murderer is someone much closer than he could have imagined. This knowledge forces him to leave the safety of The Fortress on a mission for revenge. Hayden and the rest of the motley crew decide that they cannot leave their friend to such dangers alone. Being hunted by several elite assassins, the travelers uncover a conspiracy that will rock the very foundation of every thing they know about their world. They are also destined to meet the One child that will change each of them and all of humanity forever. With darkness overtaking the world, their only mission becomes protecting this Child against the cloud that has risen to defeat Him. The Sin Cloud is an unforgettable tale of forgiveness, love, and ultimate sacrifice.

Please learn more at www.jrwbooks.com.

For special promos please join my email list at www.jrwbooks.com/promos

THE FORTRESS

374